ILLUSIONS OF HAPPINESS

ILLUSIONS OF HAPPINESS

Elizabeth Lord

severn
House

This first world edition published 2013
in Great Britain and in the USA by
SEVERN HOUSE PUBLISHERS LTD of
19 Cedar Road, Sutton, Surrey, England, SM2 5DA.

British Library Cataloguing in Publication Data

Lord, Elizabeth, 1928-
  Illusions of happiness.
  1. England–Social life and customs–20th century–
  Fiction. 2. Love stories.
  I. Title
  823.9'14-dc23

ISBN-13: 978-0-7278-8257-8 (cased)
ISBN-13: 978-1-84751-473-8 (trade paper)

All Severn House titles are printed on acid-free paper.

Severn House Publishers support the Forest Stewardship Council [FSC], the
leading international forest certification organisation. All our titles that are printed
on Greenpeace-approved FSC-certified paper carry the FSC logo.

Typeset by Palimpsest Book Production Ltd.,
Falkirk, Stirlingshire, Scotland.
Printed and bound in Great Britain by
MPG Books Ltd., Bodmin, Cornwall.

One

Eight thirty – November's early morning sunlight beginning to peep above the tall houses on the far side of Holland Park, West London more open here, giving space to breathe. Hers was a lovely house, one of rows of similar high-class three-storied homes with attic and basement, steps down to the street, protective railings at the front and long narrow gardens at the rear.

Some three and a half years ago she'd bought this huge house out of a need to prove her independence. Instead she had found herself rattling around in it, refusing the comfort of staff apart from a daily woman who came in to cook and clean before returning home in the evening. Until recently she'd had plenty of friends but since October they had deserted her, or more likely she had driven them away, no longer able to face them.

The sun had begun to light up the room, reflecting off the big mirror on to the central chandelier, its crystals scattering a myriad of bright splashes around the walls of the huge reception room. She'd been up all night unable to sleep, and now she gazed up at the chandelier as she had done so many times before, except on this occasion not in admiration.

Madeleine Ingleton's gaze was thoughtful. This was where it would happen. It would be swift – over in seconds – and the heartache, the grinding sense of anguish, the lonely recriminations would be no more, a thing of the past.

No friends, her money already gone, she was now deeply in debt; soon the house too would be lost. Wasn't it well known that rats always desert a sinking ship? Well she was a sinking ship right enough, no denying that. In fact it had already sunk.

Madeleine found herself thinking back on her life as she

stood in the middle of the room where so many uproarious parties had been held: such wonderful parties, every room overflowing with joyous partygoers and hangers-on, most of them sozzled to the eyebrows on champagne or whatever else they could down, some making idiotic attempts to dance, seeing themselves as experts at the Black Bottom, the Charleston, Tango, One-Step or the Turkey Trot; the place stifling, filled with music and laughter and cigarette smoke.

A far cry from the quiet Buckinghamshire house she'd once known, where her parents had lived. Only her miserable sod of a father there now, rattling around in that mausoleum of a place, her mother dead these last thirteen years.

She couldn't recall the last time she'd laid eyes on him and as far as he was concerned, she could have been as dead as her mother. It didn't matter. Before long she'd probably join her to haunt the life out of him and serve him right, if he cared at all.

He'd always wanted a son to carry on the family name, but she had remained an only child. He therefore looked to her to marry well and have a son of her own who'd one day take up his grandfather's name of Wyndham at the same time as inheriting under his will.

He had even made it known that he'd added this into his will and as soon as she turned eighteen, an age when girls of good families were expected to think of finding a future husband of equally good background, he had pinned all his expectations on that wish.

Her mother had been in total agreement with her husband as women usually were prior to 1914. So why had she expected her to be otherwise? Even so it had hurt, left with no support or sympathy from either of them.

She was twenty when her mother died – tuberculosis, a disease that usually struck poorer families. She was now thirty-three but even had her mother been alive now, the hostility would still be there, neither parent ever forgiving her for what she'd done. To this day her father would still see her as having been the cause of her mother's death.

She could still recall that vile argument nearly fifteen years ago when they'd sprung the news of their plans for her future. Until then they'd looked on her as a model daughter, dutifully doing as she was told.

How wrong they were.

Two

She had enjoyed every minute of her two years at the Swiss finishing school for young ladies. Now Madeleine was home having just turned eighteen, her parents were already planning to attend her first social engagement of the London Season, her coming out ball, along with a host of other debutants in white ball gowns.

Each family looked to their daughter meeting some likely young suitor of equal good standing and, even better, heir to a vaster fortune, with a view to eventual marriage. But just in case, Madeleine's own parents already had their eye on one young man.

She and Hamilton Bramwell had already met at two or three social gatherings long before she'd gone to Switzerland so they weren't exactly strangers. With this in mind, Mummy and Father had approached his wealthy parents just prior to her return home, fully expecting her to be thrilled at renewing their acquaintance with a view to marriage.

It seemed they were taken with the idea, her father's standing being pretty high and the prospects of her bringing a fine dowry to the marriage, she being an only child, was most tempting. The drawback for her was that he wasn't the sort of husband she'd dreamed of while in Switzerland though of course she'd so far kept her thoughts to herself. Back then she and her friends had fantasized constantly about the man each would marry. Someone special; someone tall and strong and handsome, with smouldering eyes of whatever colour each preferred and gleaming blonde or glossy brown hair according to each girl's particular taste.

The drawback with Hamilton was that there was nothing, nor had there ever been anything, special about him from what she'd remembered, apart from merely being a quite agreeable young man with a gentle nature.

Now twenty-one, three years older than her, that

considered just right by both families, he was tall, slim, moderately good-looking but for a rather weak chin, somewhat washed-out blue eyes, and fair hair so fine it gave the impression of being in danger of wafting off his scalp at the least puff of wind. He certainly wasn't the man of her dreams back in Switzerland.

She too was tall and slender, but her hair though fair, was heavy and luxuriant and her eyes a vivid blue. In fact only a few days ago she'd been told by Freddie Dobson she was extremely pretty.

'Gosh, miss, you're far prettier than I imagined,' he'd said. 'If you'll forgive me for being a bit forward, I'd say extremely pretty,' which would have struck her as being very forward had it not been for his smile, so utterly appreciative that she had felt herself colour with pleasure rather than show pique or embarrassment.

She'd been home only two days and had been standing at the front door enjoying the warmth of late April's early morning sunshine, needing to calm herself after being faced by her mother's questions in the hall of all places, having only just come down from her bedroom. The last thing she'd wanted was to be interrogated on how things had gone between her and Hamilton after last night's sumptuous dinner organized for her homecoming with his parents as guests.

'All right, I suppose,' she'd answered in an offhanded almost negative manner, instantly putting her mother's back up.

'*All right*, you suppose?' her mother had burst out. '*All right*? Is that any kind of response to give us after the effort both our families have made on behalf of our daughter and their son?'

Her tone made Madeleine turn on her more than any nice girl should towards a parent, her own tone rising. 'Mother, I don't want anyone to make an *effort*! Yes, he's a nice person but he's not for me. At least I don't think so,' she ended trying to moderate her tone. Too late, her mother was already livid, her fair-skinned cheeks reddening.

'Then I think you should explain your feelings to your father and see what he has to say about it. He will not be pleased. He will not be pleased at all. What right have you, eighteen and still under our jurisdiction, to begin behaving so finicky when we're thinking only of your well-being, your future? Hamilton will make you an ideal husband,' she went on, her words gaining momentum from shock, disappointment and mounting vexation. 'He is kind and generous and gentle-natured. You might never find another prospective husband half as suitable as young Hamilton, look though you will, and—'

'But I *need* to look!' she'd cut in, not as any good daughter should to a parent, but she was angry too. 'This is nineteen fourteen, Mummy, not eighteen ninety-nine! I don't want to marry someone on whom my parents have already decided whether I like it or not. I like him, yes, but not enough to marry him. And anyway, how do I know he's what I want? I know you've mentioned him in your letters when I was away but last night was the first time we've met in two years, so don't you think you're somewhat jumping the gun, Mummy?'

'Jumping the gun? Jumping . . . What an uncouth expression for a well brought up young lady to use! Your father and I have . . . We have . . .'

'I don't want to talk about it just now,' she said, cutting through the stammering torrent of dismay. 'All I want at the moment is some fresh air – to think.' With that Madeleine swung away from her and let herself out.

To help control her rapid breathing, she stood for a moment watching their gardener preparing to mow the huge circular front lawn bordered by its line of trees on one side and the curving, wide gravel driveway on the other.

The rattle of milk churns took her attention. Glancing towards the sound she saw a young man, in a blue and white striped apron over trousers and a collarless shirt, the sleeves rolled up as he trundled a handcart bearing two huge milk churns along the gravel path towards the servants' entrance, as energetically as if they weighed nothing.

With growing interest she found herself taking in his appearance: the broad shoulders, the tanned skin of someone used to the outdoors, a shock of dark brown hair. It was a strong face, firm jaw, straight nose; she judged him to be around twenty-five.

Catching sight of her standing there looking his way, he gave a small, friendly nod, his gaze lingering for a moment before continuing on his way. In that moment, even from a distance of some fifteen feet she was aware of his dark brown eyes that seemed to her to smoulder, causing her young heart to quicken. So much so that on impulse and without thought of why or what had got into her, she followed him as he went out of sight around the far corner of the house.

Reaching the place where he'd disappeared she hovered, hopefully concealed, to watch him manoeuvre the awkward milk cart alongside the rear door to begin ladling out the thick creamy milk from a churn into the two large jugs that their cook, Mrs Plumley, had brought out to him.

As the woman retreated back inside he replaced the churn lid and deftly manhandled the milk cart around the way he'd come. The movement was faster than she had expected, too late to hurry back to the front of the house as he came abreast of her. Giving an impression of shocked surprise, seeing her there, he gave a dramatic execution of recovery as a broad grin widened his lips to reveal white even teeth.

'Good gosh, miss!' he burst out, 'you gave me quite a start!'

Not knowing how to combat the play of surprise she was on the point of apologizing when she heard him say, 'You're Madeleine Wyndham, aren't you?'

'Maddie,' she corrected impulsively. Warmed by his infectious grin, she forgot that she was talking to a mere tradesman. Mummy would have had a fit had she been here.

'I prefer Maddie,' she finished awkwardly. It was what her friends at finishing school had used despite the rules forbidding the shortening of names.

'I bet you're Madeleine to your parents though,' he chuckled, making her smile, in that moment feeling more drawn to him than she knew she should be.

There was a warm look about him, not just his smile but seeming to issue from him physically as if she could actually feel it. His arms about her would be warm. She had never had any man's arms around her, wondered how it must feel and suddenly she wanted them to be his.

'I guessed it was you,' he was saying, bringing her abruptly back from her thoughts, 'although I don't ever remember seeing you before.'

'I've just returned home after my two years education at a finishing school in Switzerland,' she answered, trying to sound composed although her heart still thudded from those earlier thoughts.

He gave a little snort of self-derision. 'Lucky you! Me, well, I was . . . *educated*, if you could call it that, a bit closer to home, local junior school here in Pilbridge. The three R's and that was that – left at twelve years old to work with me dad, tending the cows, milking 'em and learning the ropes. That was it, really.'

It sounded sad but his smile remained so wide and cheeky that she found herself smiling with him.

It was then he made the comment that he thought her pretty, adding, 'Hope you don't mind me saying, but when I heard this family's daughter was coming home from some finishing school abroad, in me mind's eye I saw some gawky girl all full of herself. But you don't seem like that and you're far prettier than anyone I've ever met, if you don't mind me saying.'

As she stood lost for a reply, he went on, 'And by the way, my name's Freddy Dobson. I work with me dad who has the dairy, the other side of the village. Dobson's Dairies, do you know it?'

No, she didn't. Most of her life had been spent away from home, her childhood in the care of a nanny until, as with most children of good families, she'd gone to boarding school; after that, college then finishing school. When home, recreation was visiting friends or they visiting her, any journeys would be in her father's Wolseley-Siddeley motor car he'd bought new in nineteen twelve, just before she'd gone off to Switzerland and which he still ran.

'It's not a large place, me dad's dairy,' Freddy was saying, jerking her thoughts back to him. 'It's at the rear of where we live. That's not all that large either, just a cottage, not like here where you live.'

Brookside, so named because the tiny River Pil flowing

beside it was indeed more a brook than a river, was the last in a sprinkling of rather nice houses this end of the village. The road went on to Beaconsfield some five miles further along with little in between. There used to be a couple of farms and one or two smallholdings on the other side of Pilbridge but she couldn't ever recall noticing a dairy. No doubt she would be obliged to pass it from now on, on her way to Gerrard's Green, four miles off in that direction where Hamilton Bramwell's parents lived in their big manor house.

But at the moment her thoughts were on the man in front of her, he now telling her that in between milking cows, cleaning out their stalls and delivering milk to the surrounding area, he was trying to educate himself by reading books in whatever spare time he had. Really she shouldn't have been standing talking with him at all. Were her parents to see her she would be severely instructed that young ladies did not converse with tradesmen on a social standing. To families such as hers, despite him and his father owning their own dairy, they were tradesmen and as such should keep their place.

'I usually deliver here on Monday, Wednesday and Friday,' he said, breaking into her thoughts – though why tell her this, she wondered. It was an unnecessary comment unless he was trying to make it obvious that he hoped to see her again on those days – in fact almost too obvious.

Even so a tiny thrill had rippled through her as she replied maybe a little too quickly, 'Then I'll probably look out for you,' trying to make her tone sound jocular to offset the strange excitement sweeping through her.

Today she hovered out front as she had these last two weeks other than both Wednesdays when rain had prevented her. It was Friday and he wouldn't be here again until Monday, two days without seeing him instead of just one.

Her excuse for lingering out here *in full view of everyone*, which was how her mother had described it, was that she wanted to enjoy the warmth of the early morning sun on her face. Even so her mother hadn't been at all pleased and said so.

'I'd rather you didn't, Madeleine. Much nicer to wait for the sun to move to the rear of the house when you can enjoy it in the privacy of your own garden. Standing in the front in full view like a common hawker . . .'

'The sun isn't so hot in the mornings, Mummy,' she'd cut in. 'And much fresher, and besides,' she couldn't help adding a little caustically, 'hawkers and tradesmen always go to the rear door.'

Her mother had reacted with a touch of pique. 'There is no need for sarcasm, my dear! I am merely suggesting that you display a little decorum if you must indulge in this odd habit you seem to have acquired recently. I cannot stop you, but please, do try not to let tradesmen notice you hovering there.'

Little did she know! It was precisely her intention to be noticed by one special tradesman; have him beckon her with a small tilt of the head as he went towards the servant's entrance, she following cautiously, coming to a stop just beyond the corner of the house, hopefully out of sight of prying eyes.

The milk delivered, Mrs Plumley gone back inside, as always he came up to Madeleine, pausing beside her and they'd pass the time of day. He'd ask how she did. She'd respond gladly, a little self-consciously to start with, telling him what she had been doing the days between seeing him, he in turn telling her what he'd been up to during that time. All the time her heart would beat heavily, excitement tingling through her veins at his closeness as she listened to his deep voice.

The days between not seeing him would drag, taken up by dreaming of him. But she didn't tell him that, nor how she counted the hours seeking anything that might speed up their agonizing, creeping progress; how she would linger over dressing far longer than was necessary, taking time to choose which morning dress to wear, which afternoon robe, which tea dress or evening gown, constantly changing her mind, to the scarcely concealed impatience of her mother's personal maid, Lily, who attended Madeleine too. But still the time seemed to creep.

Also she would prolong the time in having her hair done by the girl, first asking for her long tresses to be puffed out over her ears in the latest fashion, only to change her mind and have it taken down again and wound in a loose coil on the nape of her neck, ignoring Lily puffing and sighing.

Mealtimes also helped speed up the hours. Afterwards she'd go to her bedroom to write to friends or sort out her wardrobe, hobbies like painting and needlework and the like not being her idea of engaging pastimes, giving too much scope for dwelling on those days she didn't see Freddy. She would tell herself over and over how silly she was behaving but it didn't help.

Today she wore her beige-coloured tube dress with dark buttons all down the front that showed off her slimness. Her heart began to pound as she saw him come through the gates, guiding his milk cart along the smaller path that led to the rear of the house. In response to his signal and after a moment or two to make sure no one had seen the gesture, she followed as if idly sauntering.

It was exactly the same pattern as before – a few minutes' small talk, awkward pauses, she not quite knowing what to say as she silently pleaded for him to fill in for her. Then suddenly he bent his head towards her, his deep brown eyes searching hers.

The smile on his lips had faded, his expression grown serious. 'So, what are we going to do about these meetings of ours?' he asked in a low tone.

For a moment she was thrown. 'What do you mean?'

'I mean we can't keep on just meeting like this.'

He broke into a grin at the triteness of the remark. 'Just standing here chatting about the weather. Shouldn't we do more than that? I'd like to see more of you – somewhere else, more convenient. What d'you think?'

Caught unawares, she was stunned for an answer. Finally she heard herself saying: 'That might be nice,' in the tiniest of voices.

Before she knew what was happening, he had leaned towards her to plant an unexpected kiss on her mouth.

Startled, she flinched back, but even as he made to draw

away from her obviously feeling he'd overreached his position and expecting a frigid repulse, she lifted a hand. She saw him stiffen against the expected slap. Instead her fingers came about his neck, pulling his head down towards her again and, surprised by her own action, returned the kiss very briefly before stepping quickly back from him.

For a moment he looked at her. There was no smile on his face now as slowly he said, 'You'll meet me then, Maddie?'

'Yes,' she said somewhat breathlessly.

'Where?'

'I don't know.'

He thought for a second while she stood awkward, uncertain; aware that her body was quaking a little although no thought was in her head. Then he said almost matter-of-factly: 'There's a lane a few yards down the road, running alongside the Pil. Would you meet me there on Monday?'

Madeleine nodded, then burst out, 'I have to go!' suddenly aware of the jumble of thoughts now tumbling across her brain like tiny acrobatic figures.

Why had she done that, kissed him? Why had she agreed to see him? She was completely mad. All sorts of trouble could come of this. Yet she had said yes, and she knew she *wanted* to say yes, to see him, somewhere less obvious; she knew, and her insides were bubbling like a cauldron, her whole being shaking, trembling with excitement deep inside her – her first ever kiss from any man and it had felt wonderful.

Three

Even Hamilton had never kissed her, not truly kissed her. All the time in the company of others, dinner parties or social gatherings, they'd never been left alone together for a minute, both their families constantly hovering in their misguided attempts to encourage them into getting to know each other more.

Beyond the occasional peck on the cheek which she dutifully offered for the benefit of those around, that was as far as it had ever gone. Not that she wanted him to kiss her anyway. Compared with Freddy Dobson, he was an insipid shadow, certainly not the stuff of a promising husband.

The trouble was, neither was Freddy, a man who laboured for his living, forbidden to court her. At night, trying to sleep, she'd make up wild plans to run away with him, be married in secret, such schemes merely fantasy. Her dreams would be filled with people, she and Freddy kneeling hand in hand, taking their vows. It would be beautiful but the dream would then change. Her father storming down the aisle as the ring was about to be slipped on to her finger, a scuffle, she being dragged away, Freddy pleading, calling out for her – nearly always the same dream, she waking up in tears.

Losing him had become her constant fear. August soon, they'd been seeing each other for almost three months. At first it was in the little lane where they had arranged to meet after his work. That first time, hidden by bushes he'd taken her in his arms and kissed her, a lingering kiss making her body tingle, something she'd never known before. Lost in the pleasure of it she'd not realized that he'd been gently slipping the bodice buttons of her dress until she'd felt his hand inside her clothing.

Shocked she had made to push his hand away yet the urgent tingle had lingered as he murmured, 'Why would you come here to this secluded lane, Madeleine, if you were merely looking for a peck on the cheek?' speaking so soothingly that her fear had changed to a strange pleasure and she had once more lifted her face to his.

After three weeks meeting in the lane, she by then delighting in the pleasure of his tender petting of her, finding herself not wanting him to stop, he had found them a derelict old barn no one ever used. There he taught her about love.

So gently persuaded that first time she'd become frightened but was soon lost in the strange joy of him, that first tiny hurt soon vanished as the sensations he'd aroused took hold. She'd never known such a feeling existed, so strange that it had worried her it might even be harmful to her. But he'd soothed her fear, telling her it was quite natural.

'In fact it surprised me how quick it was for you,' he'd whispered as he held her close afterwards. 'Some girls would give anything to feel what you felt that quick.' Although it did dawn on her to wonder how he would know that, she was in love with him and so dismissed it.

Those first kisses in the lane had had her believing the tingle she'd felt each time was the most any girl felt. Now she eagerly sought it, knowing the culmination would be to be whirled away to some great spinning height, sighing and gasping, oblivious to everything but their uniting in a passion that made them one.

It was almost an agony to have to sit beside Hamilton at dinner, weekend after weekend. Dancing together at some function or other she was only too relieved to be held at arm's length as they moved. Very soon she would be attending her coming out ball, along with scores of other young debs, but it would be merely a formality, her father already having made up his mind that she would become Mrs Hamilton Bramwell by next year.

'You are beginning to appear far more at ease with young Hamilton these days, Madeleine,' her father remarked this Saturday afternoon as his chauffeur drove them towards Gerrard's Green.

'I admit, I very much approved of your reserve, as should become a young lady of good family towards her fiancé in those early stages, so long as it isn't taken too far. But I am very pleased, my dear, and so is your mother.'

'Yes indeed, dear, very much so,' her mother echoed, leaning over to plant a quick peck on her daughter's cheek only to move quickly back in her seat before her husband's frown at the small display of affection.

Madeleine said nothing, throwing her father a sidelong glance which he failed to notice.

On the Board of Directors of a grammar school outside Beaconsfield, Aldous Bardolph Wyndham was a stern and overpowering man as his name seemed to imply, named after his father who'd been an equally overpowering person.

She remembered him, not as children usually remember a grandfather, with love, affection and fond memories, but with awe and trepidation, a man who had seldom if ever smiled. And neither did her father, except to confer the odd appraisal upon a person, more usually her mother, Dorothy, who almost appeared to genuflect to any approval he might bestow on her.

But if he expected his daughter to do likewise, if he ever bothered to notice, Madeleine thought silently as they drove along, he was going to have to wait a long time, especially on the matter of Hamilton. She tried not to envisage the consequences of finally refusing him when he eventually did propose formally. As that prospect and its dread consequence began to creep over her, she forced it away as best she could, trying instead to concentrate on settling back in her seat between her parents. But it wasn't easy.

In her bedroom Madeleine sat by the window staring at the fields beyond, all bathed in the glorious sunshine of broad summer, but her mind wasn't on the glory of summer. It was almost the end of July and she still hadn't seen this month's period. She hadn't seen last month's either. Usually she was as regular as clockwork, always had been. Something was wrong. If it was what she now cringed at the thought of, what on earth was she going to do? She would speak to Freddy. He'd calm her fear. He would maybe even propose to her.

For some time she'd yearned for him to ask for her hand, well before this predicament had come upon her. Yet in a way she had dreaded him asking. What if he did, she could never approach her father for his consent knowing he would never give it, thus complicating any hope of them ever marrying.

To put off that awful refusal she had never made any approach to Freddy and perhaps he was of the opinion that she had no intention of being married to him; that she was merely out for a good time. If so how dreadfully wrong he was. She loved him with all her heart, wanted to spend the rest of her life with him. But now, what had been only a longing wish had suddenly become imperative; the consequences of not doing so suddenly become a nightmare. But most important, she needed to see Freddy and let him know what she feared regarding her condition.

Today was Wednesday the twenty-ninth of July. She would be seeing him this evening anyway. She would have to tell him today. In the barn he would take her in his arms, kiss her long and passionately and together they would sink down on to the small bit of carpet. There he would fondle her, she responding with sighs of joy and they would make love. But today they had more important things to consider. Making love could wait until after she told him.

In the barn she turned her face away from his kiss as they stood there; she needed to say what had to be said before they sank down on to the ground.

Her expression one of anguish, she poured out her plight to him in a rush. 'Freddy, I think I'm pregnant and I don't know what to do.'

Her voice fading away, she waited for him to speak, to tell her it would all be all right. But he'd gone very quiet, remaining silent for so long that her heart began to thump even more heavily than it had as they'd gone into the barn, his arm about her waist in all innocence of what she had to tell him. She found herself aching for him to say something now. When he did, his tone was even and very quiet.

'What d'you want me to say?'

'I just want to know what we are going to do,' she said, her voice quavering.

For a moment or two longer he stood looking at her, to her relief seeming in fact to be debating what they would do. Then he spoke again, softly, almost abstractly.

'We?'

Madeleine felt her body chill at that single word. What did he mean?

'You and me, us, what are we going to do, Freddy?' Her words began to pour from her in a frantic gush. 'My father will kill me when he finds out and he will in time, won't he? He'll never agree to us marrying. But I thought maybe if you and I run away together and get married before he finds out, he won't be able to do anything about it.'

For a moment he stood silently regarding her. His hands had dropped away from her waist. Then in low, measured tones he said, 'I don't know about me, but you're going to have to get rid of it before your father does get to see your condition, that's if you're what you say you are, because you can only be two months gone, three at the most.'

'It could be almost three.'

'Even so, there's still time to get rid of it. Then we can forget all about it and go on as we've been doing.'

'Get rid of it?' she echoed, bemused by his calm attitude, not really understanding.

He gave a half smile. 'You really have had a sheltered life, haven't you? I don't think you know much about life at all, do you? Now look,' he went on, growing serious. 'This is how it works. I take you to someone and you tell her what's happened and she does this small thing to you, down there.' He pointed to her lower body. 'It all comes away and you're back to normal. You'll have to pay her of course.'

'Pay her? Who is she?'

'The woman who does that sort of thing, but she don't like to be named and you mustn't tell anyone what you're up to because you and her could get into trouble with the law. Abortion's illegal.'

Madeleine stared at him, hardly comprehending what he

was saying. 'I don't understand,' she said. 'Abortion? What do you mean?'

She saw him give a long-suffering sigh. 'It means, my love, getting rid of the baby if you are in fact pregnant.'

She continued to stare at him. 'You mean it . . . it's . . . killed?' she stammered in sudden horror, her hand to her mouth.

'It's just a fetus, Maddie, at the moment hardly much bigger than, say a marble.'

'But alive. And to get rid of it . . . I couldn't do that! It's wicked, it's cruel! No, Freddy, I can't do that!'

'Well, you can't possibly have it, can you?' he reasoned.

'But—' She stopped, her heart racing. 'But if we're married, none of that will need to happen. We could—'

'Marry!' he broke in. 'Maddie, have I ever mentioned marriage?'

Madeleine stared at him. 'I thought . . . after us making love all this time, I thought . . .'

She saw him grimace. 'Maddie, darling, you thought wrong. Whatever gave you that idea?'

'But you love me!' Her voice was a tremulous wail.

'I do, but not in that way. Besides, you've got a fiancé. You told me about him. Well, if he wants to marry you, so let him. And make it quick before he finds out about your situation.'

'But I don't love him. I love you!'

He was beginning to look impatient, angry. 'Well, you'll just have to stop loving me. I'm not about to be saddled with a kid, nor have your father coming after me. Besides, I've got a fiancée too. Next spring we're going to be wed. So I'd have had to cut short our affair eventually.'

He looked at her as, almost in tears now, she began to back away from him. 'Surely you knew this couldn't go on forever. It would have had to come to an end sooner or later. You must've known that.'

Hearing him speaking so coldly, so calmly, she felt her legs suddenly lose all strength, giving way beneath her, and she sank to the floor, sobs beginning to rack her body. But instead of helping her to her feet, he gave an irascible sigh and stood over her curled form looking down at her.

'Look love, you're going to have to sort yourself out. I can't be doing with complications. I'm not losing my fiancée, that's for sure. And if you try to name me as the father, Maddie, I'll deny it. It could be anyone's.'

She stared up at him in shock. 'How can you say that?' she wailed, pleading. 'After all we've had together. I love you. I trusted you, Freddy! I let you make love to me and I thought you loved me enough to look after me.'

Her heart was beating so fast, pounding, her breathing rapid with terror of what lay in store for her now; unthinkable things, all so terrifying that she was being overwhelmed by them. She felt she was going to faint. Her clothing felt so tight about her body that it felt as though she were in a cage of iron. It made her want to tear off the constriction of clothing. Instead, all she could do was cry out, 'Help me . . .' her voice dying away to a faint breath.

The next thing she was in his arms, being held tightly.

'Maddie! Don't be so stupid!'

'I want to die.' It felt as if she were actually dying.

'Don't be silly, Maddie, pull yourself together,' he was saying, his voice sharp and urgent.

There was hope. He still loved her. He wouldn't let her go, wouldn't leave her. She let her body go limp against him as he held her. 'I'll love you always,' she sighed. 'Always.'

'Then you'll do what I suggest. Get rid of it.'

That brought her to her senses with a jolt. 'No! No!' she heard herself cry out. 'Just be with me, marry me, Oh, Freddy, I love you so much. We can still marry . . .'

'Oh, for God's sake!'

He let go of her so suddenly that she almost fell to the ground again but managed to keep her feet as he swung away from her. 'I've had enough of this,' he was saying. Now he turned back to her.

'Look, Maddie, I've told you, I'm promised to someone else. And I'm putting my cards on the table now. You can get rid of it or you can keep it, either way it doesn't matter. Maybe I wasn't as careful as I should have been but you never showed any wish for us to be anything else. Maybe I should have taken precautions but it wasn't all my fault, you practically ate me up when we made love and gave me no chance to be careful.'

She stood trembling, perplexed. What did he mean by precautions, being careful? But he wasn't done talking yet.

'But I promise you, Maddie, if you do have it and try to name me as the father, I'll deny it. No one knows about us, certainly not my fiancée. And if you do try to accuse me, she'll stand by me, because who'd ever imagine for a moment that some well brought up daughter of a distinguished man like your father – though I must say you've never behaved to me all that well brought up – having an affair with some tradesman like me, even to letting him have his pleasure with her.'

He stopped, breathing heavily from his furious speech. Through the many cracks in the broken planks of the barn the hot July sunshine pierced the gloom with shafts of dust-laden light. One shaft was lighting up those beautiful blue eyes she so adored but she hardly noticed them now.

'You've been making love to her all the time you've been with me?' she queried stupidly.

'Not making love,' he corrected, almost savagely. 'We're engaged. I've never touched her. She wouldn't have allowed me to, not until we marry. No decent girl would.'

'You mean I'm not decent?'

'I never said that. I thought you understood. You from a good family and me working class, where did you expect it to go?

'Anyway,' he went on after a pause during which she could find nothing to say, 'it's all over. If you need help finding an abortionist, I'll take you, secretly. If not, then that's it. Just don't start trying to pester me when I'm delivering milk to your family or I'll have to complain to them about it, all right?'

With that he moved towards her, brushing past her and out into the bright sunshine, walking off without a backward look.

As if turned to stone, Maddie watched him go. She wanted

to sink down again on to the barn floor, but now there was no one to help her up. Instead she backed slowly towards the far wall of the barn, letting herself lean heavily against it. And there she wept.

Four

Dwelling on one's own personal problems was expected to be put aside as trivial, the whole of Great Britain consumed by the need to show Kaiser Bill he couldn't walk into another country just as he pleased. Squabbles in Europe had been one thing, marching uninvited into a neutral country in order to invade France was quite another. With Great Britain ready to square up to Germany in defence of little Belgium, men were rushing in hordes to enlist and show the Bosch what British people were made of.

Madeleine's mind was as much taken up by the outbreak of war as anyone's but her own problems were hitting her hard. She'd not heard from Freddy for nearly a week. Instead his father was delivering the milk, so what excuse had his son given for not delivering it himself any more? He could be ill but more likely he felt it better for him not to show himself.

After the third non-appearance, she approached his father to ask why he no longer came. 'Didn't you know, miss, begging you pardon,' he said, partly with deference, partly with pride. 'My Freddy went off to enlist the day after war was declared.'

'Oh,' was all she could say, but was unable to prevent herself adding, 'What does his fiancée think about that?'

'Oh, she was all for it, miss,' was the reply. 'Hundred per cent behind him, she was, and so proud of him. If I was a younger man, I'd go meself.'

With that Madeleine stepped back letting the man get on with his job as, with a heart that felt like a lead weight inside her chest and a sick feeling in her stomach, she made her way back to the house. With all chance gone of persuading Freddy to change his mind about her, what was she going to do now?

'Are you not feeling well, my dear?' her mother asked as she went into the breakfast room. 'You look quite pale.'

'I just feel a little queasy this morning,' she answered as she glanced with distaste at the breakfast laid out on the sideboard.

'Then you'd be better eating something. Last night's dinner was a little rich. But a good breakfast will soon settle your stomach, dear.'

The last thing she wanted was to eat. Her mother continued, 'Come and sit down and I'll get you something. What would you like, egg, bacon or some ham, some kedgeree? Or perhaps a little porridge would be better?'

'Nothing, Mummy,' Madeleine said shortly.

'Toast then. A slice of plain toast? With a little marmalade.'

'I don't want anything, Mummy! Just a cup of tea.'

For an answer her mother came and put a hand on her daughter's brow. 'Your head does feel a little too warm. Perhaps we should call . . .'

Before she could finish, Madeleine leapt up and ran from the room, sickness welling up inside her. She just made the downstairs cloakroom, her stomach rebelling as she dropped on to her knees by the toilet to lean over the pan, heaving, bringing up, or so it felt, her whole insides.

Lying feebly against the cold porcelain she heard her mother tap on the toilet door, quietly calling, 'Are you all right, my dear. Can I help?'

'No, Mummy,' she answered weakly. 'Please, go away. I'm all right.'

'Have you been sick, darling?' her mother persisted.

'A little,' she made herself reply. 'You were right, Mummy. Dinner last night was rather rich. But I'm all right now.'

'Perhaps you overate. You must watch what you eat, Madeleine. We cannot have Hamilton seeing you putting on weight, can we? He is so proud of you and you are so beautifully slim.'

Beautifully slim. For Hamilton? The thought made her want to vomit again. 'Please go away, Mummy,' she begged desperately. 'I'm feeling a lot better now. Just leave me, please.'

Beautifully slim! What would he say, what would they all

say when she did begin putting on weight? And in one place only? Already her breasts had become slightly bigger than they had been. She had noticed that. And they tended to tingle as well, just a little. Was that a sign of pregnancy? She didn't know. Whatever it was it was strange and as she thought more about it, rather frightening.

Another paroxysm of retching caught her, now only bile, bitter, acid, stinging her throat. With it came tears flowing unheeded down her cheeks. Despite all effort to be quiet lest her mother hear, sobs broke from her. Any minute her mother would ask her what was wrong, demand to come in, then what? What excuse could she make? But from the other side of the door there was silence. Her mother had left.

Breathing a trembling sigh of relief, Madeleine let herself slip to the floor, her body curled like a fetus, and gave herself up to a welter of abject misery.

'I'm sorry, Father, I can't help what I feel.' Her response to his angry reaction to this evening as she cringed inwardly before his fearsome glare was heated and obstructive even though she knew it would never pay her to be so.

'I am not concerned by what you feel!' he blared back at her while her mother sat some distance away on the edge of one of the sitting room chairs, like a small girl awaiting her turn to be berated. Why did her mother have to be so meek before her own husband? Why could she not stand up for her own daughter?

But of course, she wouldn't. She was in truth of the same opinion as he. And even if she hadn't been she would have convinced herself that he was right. She always did. It was left to her, Madeleine, to stand up for herself, and this she was doing, too angry even to tremble before his glare.

'I'm sorry, Father,' she began.

Why did she never address him as anything but Father while her mother was always Mummy? It just didn't seem fit to call him anything other than that, certainly not Daddy, laughable had it not been so unthinkable.

'But I don't care for him in that way,' she ploughed on bravely. 'And I certainly can't love him.'

'What does that have to do with it?' he demanded. 'The first aim of marriage for a young lady is security and there is none more secure than Hamilton Bramwell, other than, as your mother says, a possible suitor with a title, except that the way you are behaving of late, putting on weight daily by your appearance, no one else will even look at you much less accept you.'

Her mother had melted just a little. 'You must admit, dear, lately you have been eating more than is good for you, despite all our cautioning . . .'

'Please do not interfere, Dorothy!' commanded her father, returning to his daughter. 'Possibly we've not allowed you to be alone together to talk privately of things you might feel a need to discuss. But you get on well together. Hamilton likes you immensely and you admit you like him.'

'As a friend, yes, not as a . . .'

'Enough of this!' he cut in almost savagely, making her jump a little. 'I have enough to worry about without being plagued by your foolish whims and fancies. We are at war. It has been arranged for young Hamilton to join his father's old regiment as a junior officer. During the Boer Wars his father attained the rank of colonel and Hamilton will be looked upon to follow suit. In time, my dear, you will become the wife of an officer of high rank equal to that of his father in his time and will enjoy all the fine prestige that carries.'

For the first time in many long months he smiled benignly at her. 'You will be proud of him, my dear. And grow ever fonder of him. So enough of this foolishness . . .' The smile vanished. 'I have decided to announce your engagement to Hamilton before the end of the month. It will no doubt be a military wedding as befits the times.'

Decision made, he strode away, leaving her as though rooted to the spot, staring after him. Her stomach felt odd, then a sudden spasm caught her, not painful but strange so that her head felt it was reeling, making her feel suddenly feeble. She felt herself sway. Her mother's voice, calling to her, seemed to be a long way off, her mother catching her as she began to slip to the floor, but she was unaware of it as blackness engulfed her.

Madeleine was lying in bed in her room. Her mother was bending over her. By the window the silhouette of her father's back was dark against the bright sunshine pouring into the room. Between the two stood a man, tall, thin, bespectacled, slightly balding; Murray, their family doctor. He looked grave.

Her gaze drifting back towards her mother, she saw that she had been weeping, her face anguished but not loving. Seeing her open her eyes fully, her mother straightened up and walked away, stiff backed. No one spoke and all Madeleine could say was, 'I'm sorry. I must have fainted.'

At the words her father whirled round to face her. 'Sorry! Is that all you have to say?' He came forward to stand over her like a dark monument.

'How dare you bring this appalling shame upon us?'

'I don't understand,' she quavered, still not quite back in the world. 'What have I done?'

A convulsive sob was torn from her mother at her words. Her father's reply to her question rumbled deep and sonorous in her ears.

'You know well enough. Doctor Murray has informed us of your condition. You disgust me. And I want nothing more to do with you. I wish never to set eyes on you again, do you understand what I am saying!'

From across the room, her mother broke in, her words tumbling out in a frantic torrent. 'How could you do this to us? I am so ashamed! How could you?'

Her voice melted into tears, Doctor Murray going to her aid. 'Try to calm yourself, my dear. Your daughter . . .'

'She is not my daughter!' she burst out, the words seeming instantly to freeze Madeleine's heart. 'I can't bear to look at her. I don't ever want to look at her again. What are we going to do?'

Madeleine felt sickness rising inside her, not from her condition but from what her mother had said.

'There is only one solution,' Doctor Murray was saying.

'She must marry her fiancée as soon as possible. She is only just above three months. If her fiancée hasn't yet realized her condition, you may use the excuse when the time comes that the child arrived earlier than expected. It happens quite often. But you should not delay. It is the only solution . . .'

'There is only one solution!' her father echoed forcibly. 'I have no intention of harbouring this disgusting *creature* that has the audacity to call herself my daughter under my roof. We know for a fact that her fiancé would never have . . .'

He pulled himself up sharply, leaving the rest unsaid. But Madeleine knew what he had been about to say. To say it would have lowered him in the eyes of all who knew and respected him, including their family doctor.

Instead he continued, 'But I thank you Doctor Murray, for coming here so quickly. You have been most helpful and I am grateful to you. But I expect you're probably needed elsewhere.'

As Doctor Murray took his leave, Madeleine got up from her bed and, going to the door of her room heard her mother say after they'd closed the front door on the doctor, 'She knows no one else other than Hamilton and I certainly cannot believe it is him.'

'Of course it's not him!' he answered irascibly.

'But who?'

'I'm not concerned who,' he growled. 'She has disgraced this family's good name. She is soiled, caring for nothing but her own disgusting desires and I'll not abide her living under this roof for one minute longer. I cannot even bear to look at her. I am sickened by her and I shall never forgive her, and neither shall you, Dorothy, at your peril!'

Madeleine wrenched open her door, ran out on to the landing, leaning over the balustrade. 'You can't mean that!' she cried out in panic. 'I never meant for this to happen to me.' She saw him look up at her, his expression, harsh and unloving, freezing her blood.

'That does not change anything. That you lowered yourself to let some filth have his way with you, be used for some stranger's appetite turns my stomach. My own daughter no more than a . . .' He stopped short of having to utter whatever immoral term he'd been about to use. Instead he drew himself upright, seeming to tower above his wife. 'I erred in calling you my daughter. I will correct that. You are no longer my daughter.'

'Who was it, Madeleine?' cried her mother but he cut her short.

'We do not wish to know. You will not ask that question again, Dorothy.'

Her mother fell silent but Madeleine found her own voice, descending the stairs at a run to face him. 'Father, I need to explain, I'm . . .'

Her words were sharply silenced by a stinging slap across her cheek. Never before had her father ever laid a hand on her. His voice and the sharp glare of his blue eyes had always been enough to chastise her.

'I don't want your explanations or your excuses or even to know who the father is. It is certainly not Hamilton. You've never been alone together. Had you been, it would not have crossed his mind to abuse his position.'

'What is he going to say when he is told?' came her mother's wail. 'The poor man.'

'Be quiet, Dorothy!' he barked, then turned back to Madeleine, his voice growing deep and calm.

'You will stay in your room. Your mother and I do not want to set eyes on you. Your meals will be sent up to you and you will not leave this house. Tomorrow I will arrange for you to be sent to an institution for unmarried mothers. We will not visit you and you will not contact Hamilton. Nor will you try to contact any of my wife's mother's family; not her sister nor her brother's family. If you attempt to contact any of mine, they will be told not to respond.'

Tears were already streaking down her cheeks. But having him refer to her mother as his wife rather than her mother tore a racking sob from her but he was indomitable.

'When the child is born it will be immediately given up for adoption. But you will not come back here, ever again. Your mother and I wish to have no more to do with you. When you leave that home you will find your own living and provide for yourself. I will put a small sum of money into an account for you. When that is exhausted, you will make your own way and never return to this house, nor come begging. It may be that you will marry this man whoever he is but your mother and I do not wish to see you or hear from you again, do you understand? Now please, return to your room. When the arrangements for you to leave are complete you will be taken out by the servants' door so that we do not have to look on you.'

Madeleine forced herself to speak through her weeping, her voice hoarse and cracked. 'You can't do this. You love me.'

'I am sorry,' he said slowly, almost as if her words had bewildered him. 'I do not know you.'

It sounded so terribly childish yet held a sting that went through her like a knife. In that second she had been cut out of his life as he turned from her to say something to his wife that they would take their nightcap together in the lounge before retiring to bed.

She watched them cross the hall, her mother trailing a little behind him. She saw him catch her arm as she was about to turn back to look at her, compelling the woman to continue walking towards the lounge door.

As they disappeared, the door closed with a click that sounded so utterly final that Madeleine wanted to fall to her knees where she stood. Instead she too turned away, her whole body a leaden weight under the burden she knew she had made for herself by her own folly, and she forced herself to mount the stairs to her room.

Five

How she had survived the trauma of leaving home she still couldn't believe. True, most of her life had been spent away from her family but the love of her parents had always gone with her. This time no love at all had departed with her.

That morning in late September, ordered to leave the house by the trade's entrance, there'd been no sign of her parents; no one to say goodbye to her or help her as she struggled with her weighty suitcase to the waiting taxicab. Only Mrs Plumley and Maud their kitchen maid, with no other reason to be elsewhere in the house, had been there to see her off; the other servants at their duties elsewhere – more by design than duty she suspected. So leaving had been lonely, heartbreaking.

There had been light rain as the taxicab pulled away down the drive; she watched her home disappearing in the early morning drizzle, but she was glad of that. A bright and sunny sky would have only made it feel worse, as if the weather itself had chosen to mock her.

Now she sat by the window of the small day room, ignoring the few other women sitting around as she recalled that day now almost six months back. In all that time she, like these other unmarried women in this place, had been conditioned to feel utterly shamed and unworthy of any genuine sympathy. Not that they were ill-treated or underfed, food was adequate if plain; but all were expected to do their share of work towards keeping the place in order, any excuses not to meeting with harsh frowns and little sympathy.

'You are not ill,' was the response to any complaint of feeling unwell. 'Pregnancy is not an illness and you have only yourself to blame for your condition!'

That hard-hearted approach, even though her father had paid for her to be there, had come as a shock. And to one who'd never done a day's work in her life: having to make her own bed, sweep, dust, made to work in the steamy laundry, carry damp and heavy linen baskets out to hang on clothes lines; to scrub pots and pans and tables, just as her own father's scullery maid had done, by the end of the day she was worn out, having to endure the misery of muscular pains all over her body.

It mattered not to those in charge that she was pregnant, that she'd been tenderly brought up. She was still an unmarried mother, disgraced, cast out by others to pull her weight alongside those less privileged than she. Like them she had allowed herself to be *used*, ignoring or ignorant of the consequences in an eagerness for a cheap thrill, looked upon with scorn and contempt, despite her family's high standing – maybe even more so. With her baby now due in three weeks, her loose white gown now bulging to a hugely distended stomach, she was still expected to work as hard as ever though maybe not lifting heavy washing baskets so much now.

In all this time not one person had ever come to see her, nor had she expected anyone. A letter to her parents had reaped no reply. Its purpose had been to tell her father how innocent of sexual matters she'd been.

She'd tried to explain that, brought up in ignorance other than those half understood, sketchy and preposterous and mostly erroneous bits of information exchanged at finishing school, yet imagined to be fact by sheltered young women, she'd had no idea she was getting herself into trouble; that if only she had been taught the facts of life, she would never have allowed to happen what had happened. But he'd probably refused to read her letters, no doubt forbidding her mother to do so too. As for Hamilton, all was silence. Not that she cared.

Her time drawing nearer she wondered more and more what would become of her once the baby was born and she was turned out.

It was an accepted rule here that the baby would be taken from the mother for adoption, usually by an orphanage. In most cases it appeared a girl was only too glad to be rid of it and go about her own life. To be saddled with a child with no known father was a disgrace in itself and no girl wanted fingers being pointed at her. An orphanage was the only answer.

After a few days recuperating, the mother would be turned out to earn her own living and be glad of it. A small amount of preparing for work would be carried out during her stay, usually as a housemaid somewhere.

The rule was that as soon as the baby was born it was whisked away from the mother before she had a chance to really look at it and thus form a bond. A representative from whatever orphanage it was destined for would be there to take it away. Should a baby arrive during the night, it was placed in the crèche until morning.

So it was that after two days of labour, Madeleine's baby arrived in the early hours. She now lay all alone, exhausted, grateful for the respite from those terrible pains at last, sure she would never forget those gruelling forty-eight hours of absolute suffering for as long as she lived.

She thought of the tiny unseen life that had in its own way rescued her from her agony at the very moment of its birth, how she had collapsed with relief, too worn out to even see the bundle in its wrappings being borne from the room. Now she lay, all alone in the darkened room, wondering what her baby had looked like. She'd not even been told if it was a boy or a girl.

Sleep had been fitful. She seemed to have been awake for hours. Through the tiny grill the sky seemed paler than it had been, so morning was probably not far off.

Lying on her back had now become uncomfortable. Needing to move, Madeleine eased herself to a more upright sitting position though still not a comfortable one. Carefully she inched her legs over the side of the hard bed, her bare soles recoiling as they touched the cold bare floor. She remained for a time perched on the edge of the bed, legs dangling, feet held clear of the chilly floor. Her stomach felt strangely soft and flabby after so long being tightly distended. It was many minutes before she could bring herself to move at all, but she wanted to get to her feet, to feel normal again, more like a human being.

Finally summoning enough strength to stand, surprised to find that she could, she held on to the bed rail for support, taking her time until her head ceased spinning and she felt steady enough to stand alone. All she wanted now was to get out of this room with its cloying taint of birth blood hanging in the air, if only to breathe in something fresher.

Now came a few hesitant somewhat wobbly steps taking her to the door. Carefully, quietly, she opened it. Not a soul in sight anywhere. Hardly a thought in her head, she moved out into the corridor, no longer worried about the chill on her bare feet from the lino there. At the moment she wasn't even sure where she really wanted to go but small hesitant steps were taking her in the direction of the crèche at the end of the corridor.

She came to a sudden standstill as a movement ahead made her give a smothered gasp: a nurse issuing from the crèche. Fortunately, the woman turned left without glancing in her direction and, too far off to have heard her intake of breath, turned right down a narrow corridor.

But it put an idea in Madeleine's head. If no one else was in that room it would be worth having a small peek at the baby she had given birth to. If the nurse came back in time to catch her, what could she do but tell her off?

She was about ready to drop by the time she'd reached the nursery. It was a tiny room. Going in she realized there was only one baby there, lying in a cot and so completely swaddled in a thick off-white shawl that only the little face was visible. But the sight of those tiny features, so pretty, so delicate, a little girl, gripped Madeleine's heart in a sudden welter of love.

'Ohhh . . .' Her sigh drew itself out in a profound surge of tenderness, her breath coming in small gasps as tears misted her eyes – her child, part of her own flesh and blood, hers, her daughter.

She bent forward and picked up the small bundle, held it against her. Through the shawl the warmth of that tiny body seeped into hers. Beneath the shawl the tiny hands moved, the little legs drew themselves up slightly then stretched, and she could feel the movement against her. The eyes managed to open, merely slits, but their colour that of some deep lake with sunshine glowing on it. They looked so directly at her that she bent her face to kiss the smooth little cheek. So soft, so warm, this baby, her baby—

'*What do you think you are doing, girl?*'

The shock of that voice made Madeleine swing round so abruptly that, still weak, she would have lost her balance had the nurse not sprung forward to catch and steady her.

'How did you get in here?' came the demand. Madeleine blinked.

'The door was open.'

A sudden aghast expression flitting across the woman's face made her realize that the nursery should have been locked when unattended, the nurse already aware that she had forgotten to do so. Now she was in trouble.

'You shouldn't be in here, girl!' she hissed, panic in her tone. 'I'll take the baby. You get back to your room.' Hardly waiting for it to be handed over she practically snatched it away. 'Now, go! GO!'

As she made her way back to the delivery room with its lingering taint of stale blood, Madeleine's arms felt strangely empty. It was almost as if they ached and in that short while she realized that she'd become one with her child – something no unmarried mother was allowed to do prior to the baby being taken for adoption. *Bad for the mother.* This way, in a short while the mother would forget all about the baby and get on with her life. So went the belief. But in these few short moments of holding it close to her she *had* become one with her baby and that brief experience would stay with her for the rest of her life.

Today, a week after having given birth, she was now out on her own, alone in a cold, hostile world, the home for unmarried mothers having done their job. Yet still that sense of emptiness persisted. And questions too: where was her child now? Who were the people who'd taken it away? Would they be kind to her or had they in mind to make her work hard for her keep as she grew up?

Turning from that devastating thought, she prayed they would love her. But brought up as their child, she'd never know her own mother. That one thing kept drumming in her head – she would never see her again.

Madeleine stifled a dry sob at the thought, clearing her throat against it as she emerged from Paddington railway station on to a street filled with all the noise and racket of London. After the peace of village life and the quietness of the nursing home, the rattle of taxicabs, the red enormity of buses and the stink of motor exhaust was a shock. She had almost forgotten the last time she was taken to London, as a seven-year-old child. That would have been in 1903, when most vehicles were horse-drawn.

Suitcase in one hand, a leather handbag in the other, in that handbag the recommended address of somewhere to stay, she made her way through the chilly April wind beyond the station towards a line of taxicabs – best to spend out on a taxi fare rather than some unfamiliar bus route or to risk venturing on to the underground.

She did have a little money with her, sent to the nursing home by her father until she could get to the bank where he'd at least opened a tiny account for her. But she felt no reason to be grateful. It was no more than any father should do for his daughter and had been such a small amount as to be an insult, not even accompanied by any note. Also, he had stopped the generous allowance she had always enjoyed, making it clear that she would have to somehow earn her own living from now on. The message couldn't have been clearer and her hatred for him began to mount as she fearfully approached one of the taxicabs.

She had begun to feel utterly out of her depth here. Assailed by an odorous smell of cooking coming from a nearby restaurant, she hurried past the raucous, tinny noise being played by an organ grinder at the kerbside, feeling herself under the gaze of a couple of uniformed soldiers who seemed in her imagination to be eyeing her as they passed – she was glad to escape into the taxi.

Aware of the restriction of her hobble skirt about her ankles after the loose clothing she had worn in the nursing home, she suddenly became aware of how out of date that skirt appeared against the bell-shaped hems of several women who had passed her; a drastic new fashion had exploded in these last eight or nine months since the outbreak of war.

Even her hat, a high toque, the fashion of a few months ago, now looked stupid against the harder crowned, larger brimmed creations she saw around her. Fresh from finishing school and suffering that home for unmarried mothers, she'd had no cause to follow fashion.

Telling the taxicab driver the address she had been given, she sat in the seclusion of the rear seat and once more gave herself up to her thoughts. Never to see her baby ever again left her in danger of breaking down afresh, giving way to a spasm of dry, hollow sobs, giving no comfort, no relief.

Recovering with an effort she took a deep breath, resolving to cast these thoughts out. But she knew without question that time and time again she would find herself repeating this agony, maybe a day later, maybe several days, but it would never go. There now came a silent resolve – she would spend the rest of her life if necessary looking for her child. She'd start by making enquiries, though how and where to begin she had no idea.

She must first get settled in the rooms where she was to live, the blessing of practicalities beginning to take over from grieving, for it felt like grief.

The journey seemed to take ages, the taxi wending its way through endless streets, at first fine and wide, lined with huge shops, but slowly they grew narrower, more seedy, the shops smaller, the kerbs lined at times with market stalls, the houses becoming mere tenements. Finally the vehicle drew up outside some two-storey tenements in a street behind Cheapside.

'This is it, miss!' called the taxi driver. 'Right, that'll be a shilling an' sixpence!'

With no idea of how cheap or expensive that was, she got out and handed over a two shilling piece, hovering, expecting change. Instead he glanced down at it with a grin, spat on it appreciatively and popped it into his pocket with a 'thanks very much, miss!'

Madeleine realized then, as the taxi moved off, that her expected change of sixpence had instead been seen as a tip for his service.

Six

As with every day since coming here a week ago, Madeleine's gaze moved despondently around her one room: a single sagging bed, bare table, two chairs, a cupboard, a double gas ring, a curtain across an alcove hiding her clothes, a window overlooking a yard bordered by similar tenements.

On the landing smelling of cooked cabbage was a stained sink and cold water tap, next to it a bathroom and toilet. One glimpse of the bowl was enough to make her heave as she tried to avoid contact with its wooden seat which all the so far unknown tenants had used before her.

An ancient gas boiler gave a dribble of hot water taking ages to fill the bath, and only just warm when filled, the bath sporting a wealth of yellowish stains. There was always the public baths which by law had to be spotlessly clean. She could go there, armed with towel and soap as often as possible so long as she had money for the entrance fee.

Her father had arranged a niggardly allowance sufficient to prevent her actually starving, its message clear enough – if she needed more, she'd have to find work. So what might have made him appear human enough to give at least some thought to the welfare of his only child, instead spoke in clear terms that he wanted nothing more to do with her; that her welfare no longer mattered to him, almost as if she no longer existed in his eyes.

Left more bitter than ever, she'd written a carefully worded plea to her mother the moment she arrived here hoping to melt her heart enough to talk to her father on her behalf. That had been over a week ago, still no reply. There'd never be one now. How had she managed to make such a mess of her life? Her sight misted over as she stared across at the other tenements of Moorgate's dingy back streets a stone's throw from St Paul's as thoughts of last night's dream stole back into her mind. She had had the same dream three times since coming here; so brief and so poignant: she'd be holding her baby close, nursing her, kissing her, such a lovely dream, but just as she started to croon to her, her own voice would wake her and she'd find herself alone in this still dark room, her arms empty, her pillow damp with tears she hadn't dreamed she'd shed, making her get up and walk back and forth in an effort to push the memory from her mind.

Now she pushed it away again, forcing herself to think of something more realistic. She was going to have to make her own life, though how, she had no idea. Never having been alone before, never having to shift for herself, knowing only a life of luxury, she was only now learning how to cook for herself, buy food and prepare it, make a cup of tea, even to wash her own clothes. But to survive she was having to learn.

A kettle and a small brown teapot had been provided. In the cupboard drawer were a couple of spoons, a few odd knives and forks, an old carving knife and a bread knife. There was a saucepan for boiling vegetables and a greasy frying pan for meat, fish, eggs, bacon, sausages or whatever else the tenant thought to cook. Had there been an oven she wouldn't have known how to use it. There were a few plates of odd sizes, chipped and of doubtful origin. With a little of her meagre allowance she'd have to buy decent ones from a market stall, as well as a decent towel, face flannel, soap.

The kettle and saucepan doubled as containers to boil water for washing clothes and bed linen in the bathroom. What she'd found here when she arrived had been so awful she'd drawn a little out of the precious pittance her father had put in the bank for her and had bought two pairs of sheets and pillow cases from the cheapest market stall she could find. At least she now had clean linen to sleep on.

This morning, seven thirty, after another uncomfortable night on the lumpy mattress and troubled yet again by the same dream, she was at the sink washing the old bed sheets as best she could in case they were ever needed.

She was so engrossed rinsing them that she wasn't aware

of someone emerging from a door down the passage until
a voice made her jump.

'Oh! You're using it – the sink!'

Swinging round towards the voice, her arms dripping wet,
she saw a girl of around twenty standing there. The girl's
lips parted in a grin. 'Sorry, did I give you a start?'

Madeleine tried to gather her jangled wits and smile back.
'You did rather.'

'Sorry,' the girl said again. 'I should've made more noise.
I was just coming to wash a couple of smalls, but I can wait.
Will you be long?'

'I'm nearly finished,' Madeleine said. 'I'll just wring these
things out.'

'There's a mangle downstairs in the back yard,' came the
advice. 'Bit chilly out there this time of year, and a washing
line too.'

'I know, I did happen to see it,' Madeleine said a little
stiffly. 'But I've not used the mangle yet.'

The girl's smile seemed to be a fixture on her face. 'I
don't hang me smalls out there,' she said brightly. 'Someone
might pinch 'em. I just stick 'em on the backs of chairs
round the fire in me room. When did you turn up?'

'I arrived here just over a week ago,' Madeleine supplied,
now feeling forced into some sort of politeness but the girl's
beam broadened still more.

'Don't you talk nice,' she remarked quite out of the blue.
Madeleine blinked.

'I beg your pardon.'

'I said, you talk ever so nice,' the girl repeated. 'Ever so
posh. What's the likes of you doing in rooms like these then?
I'd've thought someone that talks like you would've found
theirselves a decent hotel if they want to live in London.'

The girl's accent was very different from her own. Not
exactly coarse like the Cockney accent of their landlady;
more the way Freddy Dobson used to speak, untutored. The
thought of him brought an unexpected pang to her heart
and she turned quickly from it.

'How long you expect to be here?' the girl asked, breaking
into her thoughts.

Madeleine hurriedly gathered her wits back together. 'I'm not sure yet. I can ill afford anything else at the moment.'

An admission she'd not intended to make, but the girl interrupted any chance to correct herself.

'Can any of us!' she laughed. 'Well, as it looks as if we're going to be neighbours for a bit, my name's Dorothy – Dolly, Dolly Grant. I come from Kent originally, Holstead, but I left a couple of years ago – couldn't stand my family. Always arguing and rowing, so I walked out. What about your people then? And what's your name?'

Madeleine told her, shortening it to Maddie, managing to sidestep giving any information about her family. Dolly seemed not to notice but merely stared at her giving Maddie time to take her in. She was tall, nearly as tall as herself, but desperately thin. The cheap high-necked blouse and ankle-length tube-like skirt seemed to hang on her. Dark hair, abundant and done in a coil or bun seemed to swamp the elfin, not particularly pretty features.

'So what d'you do with yourself all day. Or in the evening?' asked Dolly.

'Nothing really.' Madeleine turned back to rinsing the bed sheet.

'You mean you've not been anywhere since you come here?' the voice behind her exploded. 'You can't go on like that, Maddie. Look . . .' Her hand came on Madeleine's shoulder, making her turn back to her.

'I've got to go off to work now. Part-time job for a window cleaning company, filling in for some chap who went off to war the day it broke out. But evenings I go out with some friends. Why don't you come? We doll ourselves up and go off up West, see the sights, though London's not as lit as it was now we got them German Zeppelins starting to come over. Dropped bombs in Norfolk y'know – killed some people. So the shops ain't lit like they used to be. But we usually meet a few soldiers, get them to take us to some decent club or pub and have a good time. You come along. You'll enjoy it.'

Madeleine nibbled at her lip. 'I don't know,' she said doubtfully.

Memories of Freddy Dobson made her cringe inside from any man. At home she'd never been out of an evening without her parents. The only time she had ever gone out on her own had been with him and only for a briefly snatched half an hour, telling them she'd taken a walk through the village to put a little colour in her cheeks. She'd always been on edge the whole time she was away, except when lost in his arms and look where that had landed her, paying dearly for deceiving her parents.

'You'll be all right with us,' Dolly was saying. 'We won't leave you on your own. They're a nice bunch of friends. Rather like yourself except they're still with their parents.' It seemed Dolly already guessed she wasn't living at home. 'Do come, Maddie. I'll make sure you come to no harm.'

What could she do but nod consent, hearing Dolly cry, 'Good!' as if she'd done her a great favour by accepting her invitation.

For the rest of the day Madeleine could think of nothing else but the evening when Dolly said she would call for her. Excitement pulsed through her veins such as she hadn't felt since those times when she'd anticipated meeting Freddy. It didn't matter that the very thought of that now made her feel sick and ashamed, knowing how she'd been led into believing all sorts of lies from his lips; what she was feeling now at being invited to join Dolly's little group of friends was akin to how she had felt then.

On a whim, when leaving home, she had taken a couple of her lovely dresses with her. At that time she'd never thought she would wear them again. Her purpose had been to sell them for what she could get, knowing she might need the money. Now she was glad she hadn't. This evening she would wear one of them.

It was the fourth time she'd taken the two from the curtained alcove where they'd been hanging on wooden pegs, to scrutinize each in turn. One was heavy silk, salmon pink, the other lighter weight pale blue silk or ninon. Neither had creased at all, looking as fresh as the day they'd been ordered for her from a Parisian couture house in London for when she would have 'come out'. Not too showy, quite modest in their way as expected of a young girl of only just eighteen, neither would look out of place tonight.

She finally chose the blue with its floating drapery about the upper arms, tasteful silver embroidery about the neck and narrow skirt. The black, glacé kid court shoes which she'd not worn since leaving home and the black velvet Juliet cap from last year which she still wore would go very well with the blue. A pity she had only the one coat, but on a chill February evening who would pause to pass judgement? For so long Madeleine had worn only plain, shapeless garments while awaiting the baby, but this material felt good to the touch as did the silk stockings that had lain so long unused until now.

The day was endless. With no interest in food as she waited, it was just as well there was little in the cupboard, half a small loaf – she'd have to buy another one soon – some margarine, a bit of cheese, some milk, a couple of eggs. She'd finally learned to make an omelette after several unsuccessful attempts, the ruined results of which she had bolted down in desperation at the time, all the while thinking of all those sumptuous meals she'd taken for granted at home.

Now at seven o'clock she waited on tenterhooks for Dolly's tap on her door. There came a moment of panic as she paced the room. Was she overdressed? If the others were casually attired she'd look silly. She'd dabbed her cheeks and nose with a little face powder in the box she'd taken with her to the home though with little use for it there. Regarding herself yet again in the tiny hand mirror she'd found on some second-hand stall, she stood biting at her lips to make them look pinker.

Manoeuvring the mirror carefully this way and that she surveyed herself, realizing that she looked quite pretty. While pregnant there had seldom been any wish to look at her reflection in any mirror, the face staring back drawn and blotchy, the once slim shape become gross, the breasts heavy, the stomach more bloated by the day. Now that was all suddenly gone, her slim figure back to normal, her blue eyes, once dull, seeming to glow. Her hair, lifeless during pregnancy, had regained its blonde sheen. She'd lost all interest in herself during that time. But now she was . . .

She almost jumped out of her skin as a sharp rap came on the door, hurrying to open it.

Dolly stood there in a nice but cheap-looking dress of pink crêpe de Chine, Madeleine experiencing a glow of relief that by comparison her own was of far finer quality. Neither did she feel out of place any more.

The girl gave an instant sigh of appreciation. 'My, you look a proper lady. That dress must've cost a fortune!'

'No,' Madeleine said quickly, almost apologetically, suddenly feeling bad for her moment of superiority though not for the sense of relief she'd felt.

'It's second-hand really,' she continued to lie, though it wasn't that much of a lie, having worn it before which might in truth make it second-hand.

'The only decent thing I have,' she went on, which *was* a lie. All the clothes she'd brought with her were of fine quality and expensive. She would have to take great care of them, make them last. She'd also take care of what she wore when with Dolly so as not emphasize their quality too much.

'Are you ready?' asked Dolly.

Madeleine nodded, hurriedly closing the door behind her.

Dolly's four friends, Bess, Millie, Florrie and Hilda, turned out to be chatty and sociable and instantly enfolded her in their midst, calling her Maddie which was nice and for a while she forgot that lurking, insidious weight in her chest each time thoughts came of the baby taken from her.

Gabbling and giggling, they introduced her to her first ever experience of the Underground, helping her on to a noisy, swaying train that had her on edge the whole time though they seemed not to notice the racket at all, merely lifting their voices above it.

Alighting at Tottenham Court Road, they wandered along Oxford Street gazing into half-darkened store windows and on to crowded Piccadilly to revel in being ogled at by young uniformed men most out looking for fun not knowing how long before they'd be sent to France and possibly the front line. Thus banter was exchanged eagerly, unashamedly, almost desperately.

Like Dolly they were from lesser backgrounds than hers, but had the advantage of still living with their families. London was their home. They wandered their city without fear whereas she had never before been let loose in London much less unchaperoned. But the war had changed a lot of things and tonight was an experience. Even so, they were expected to be home by eleven and would honour that. Though before then there was fun to be had.

Hovering by the vast incurving display windows of the huge Swan & Edgar store, itself darkened against Zeppelin raids, Florrie grabbed hold of Madeleine's arm.

'Now they look likely,' she hissed. 'Don't you think?'

Everyone's eyes discreetly followed her sidelong stare, careful not to look directly at the group of four uniformed men who had begun to slow their pace, having seen them. 'Don't look!' she breathed urgently, holding one hand up to her face as if to shield her words as the soldiers began to move casually across the Circus towards them as if by one accord.

'That's a pity. There's only four,' she continued to whisper as they drew nearer. 'Maybe they know some more friends.'

The girls spread themselves out as the young men reached them. Madeleine stood back, her eyes concentrated on the pavement, uncertain, loath to meet any of the male glances and appear forward. It had not been the way she'd been brought up.

Seeing her reaction, Dolly too moved back to stand with her. 'Are you all right, Maddie?' she asked. Madeleine half nodded half shook her head.

'I'm not accustomed to picking up men. We've not been introduced,' she hissed. But Dolly gave a low tinkering laugh.

'We're not picking them up, love. We're just passing the time of day – or night – with them.' She laughed at her own joke. 'No harm in that. If we stay in a crowd no harm will come of it. They may even buy us a drink. Lord knows, we can't afford much ourselves. Come on, love!'

But it was already too late. Standing back, they'd been

ignored as the young soldiers concentrated on the four who were happy to exchange banter for banter which was growing more enthusiastic by the moment.

'But we can't go off without our other two friends,' Hilda was saying. 'We can't leave 'em behind.'

'Then let 'em come along,' quipped one in a jolly tone, 'all the more the merrier, eh?' At which the girls giggled.

'By the way, I'm Joe,' he went on with a faintly East Anglian accent. 'This 'ere is Bob, an' Arthur an' Stan, OK? An' what's your names?'

While he was being told, Dolly and Madeleine included, the soldier named Stan gave Madeleine an appreciative glance only to quickly lower his glance as her wide-eyed, guarded stare met him, making him turn hastily back to the friendlier girls, leaving her aware that she had frozen him out with what must have appeared a haughty, stand-offish response.

Beautiful features or not, striking figure or not, he was a fighting man waiting to be sent to The Front and certainly not prepared to be spurned out of hand by someone who thought herself a cut above the rest. Madeleine could almost hear him saying the words to himself. 'Too stuck up for me!'

The trouble was, Dolly, hovering almost protectively beside her as they moved off together, was losing out too. Without her, Dolly might have been one of the lucky four. But Dolly had stayed with her and it made her feel wretched. She wasn't enjoying this evening half so much now as they tagged along in the wake of the now giggling, wisecracking eightsome.

Seven

They were wandering down Piccadilly towards Green Park so Dolly told her.

'That's where the Ritz Hotel is,' she said proudly as if she were giving a guided tour. 'Where all the rich lot stay or have high tea and banquets.'

Madeleine had a mad idea that they might be considering going into this grand place for something to drink. Moments later she realized what a silly thought that was. These ordinary young soldiers would never have that kind of money.

Instead, long before they reached there, Joe, who seemed to be the leader with the most to say, pulled up to gaze down a side street. 'That looks like a decent boozer, respectable-looking enough for you ladies if you don't mind going into a public house.'

Madeleine felt herself recoil inwardly. She had never been inside a public house in her life but Bess gave a little whoop. 'I know this place. Me and Florrie have been here before, with an escort of course – wouldn't dare go in alone! But it's got a snug, a saloon, and that's quite decent for women.'

'Come on, then,' cried Joe, steering them into the side street towards the place, Madeleine and Dolly compelled to follow.

Inside was quite pleasant, and quiet, only a few drinkers. The noisier crowd would turn out later from cheap theatres, cafes and restaurants.

They found a secluded corner of the saloon. Joe and Arthur, after collecting their orders, went to get them, port and lemon for the women, beer for themselves. Seeing the readiness with which they were willing to pay out for their female companions, Madeleine felt that they expected later to get some reward for their generosity and was glad that none of them had singled her out. Knowing this, she now felt slightly easier.

Through the open door of the saloon flowed the deep boom of men's voices but here it was much quieter. Sitting on a long bench by the far wall with Dolly one side, Hilda the other with Arthur's arm already about the girl's waist, next to them Millie being similarly mauled by Stan, she sipped her drink, glad that no one's arm was about her waist.

Conversation flowed easily back and forth, no one noticing that she sat quietly. Seated on a chair next to Florrie, Joe had been trying to kiss her cheek which she was resisting with much giggling and wriggling.

Suddenly she leapt up almost knocking Joe sideways off his chair. Having glanced through the open door between saloon and public bar as Joe tried again to get her attention with another slobbery kiss, she burst out, 'Oh, look! That chap in the bar, I know him!'

She leaned over the beer-stained table, calling out, 'Coo-ee . . . Alfie! Over here! In here!' making those in the saloon look round at her.

Moments later she was out of her seat, making for the open door, hobble skirt impeding her efforts to run.

Disappearing through the doorway, she could still be heard calling out: 'Alfie!' though more muffled now.

Moments later she'd returned, her arm through that of a young naval rating. Trailing behind them another young seaman, obviously a friend, was looking a little bewildered.

'Everyone,' she announced. 'This is Alfie. We met quite a while ago. When was it?' she asked, turning to him, 'Around Christmas, wasn't it? He was on leave. And I found out he lives in the next turning to me. We met just by accident and got talking and went out for the evening. I've not seen him since, have I, Alfie? Come and sit down. Your friend too. And you are . . .?'

'George, me name's George,' issued the faltering reply.

'Well, come and sit down then, George,' Florrie piped. 'Joe, move up, there's a love, and give him room.'

Begrudgingly, he moved to oblige, compelled to squeeze himself on to the bench, his body so close to Madeleine's that she found herself mentally cringing away from its imagined warmth.

'Ain't it wonderful though?' Florrie continued. 'Us short of a couple of nice chaps and along comes you two. Dolly and Maddie rather got left out so it's really fortunate finding you two. Maddie is Dolly's new friend and we only met her this evening but she's ever so nice, you'll like her.'

She stared across at Stan. 'Be a love, Stan, and find us another chair for Alfie here.'

The extra chair having been brought, Alfie promptly occupied it to instantly fall into reminiscent conversation with her, Dolly becoming occupied with the young sailor George, leaving the cocksure Joe to remain where he was beside Madeleine.

'Now, tell me about yourself,' he crooned. 'You've not said much so far but from what you 'ave said, I'd say you was somewhat on the posh side, well brought up like. Where d'you come from?'

Compelled to respond, she said faintly, 'I lived in Buckinghamshire.'

'Posh family then,' he said. 'Well brought up, eh.'

'Not exactly,' she began but broke off as his arm came about her, seeing him grin at her attempt to squirm out of the embrace.

'You said *lived*. Then if I've guessed rightly, you've left home, run off. And now you're free to do as you like, eh? I bet Mummy and Daddy would be horrified to see you now. Still, they're there and you're here and so am I. But don't worry. I'm not going to start anything, at least not here. I'll just tell you all about meself fer now and you can tell me all about yourself.'

Hemmed in on both sides, there was no room to stand up and walk off, and where would she go if she could? Stiff and tense she suffered his arm about her shoulders as he continued to tell her practically the whole of his life story: born in Norwich, one of eight children sleeping four to a bed in a tiny old house; hardly any schooling, had worked in a factory making jam, joined up to escape his humdrum job, seeing fighting as much more exciting, now hardly unable to wait to get into the thick of it.

'I bet you're edjication was somewhat more brighter than

mine,' he drawled. 'Boarding school fer young ladies, I don't doubt, no doubt finishing school to boot. You don't know how damned lucky you are, love. So tell me then, why'd you decide to leave home an' walk out on such a comfy life?'

He paused, awaiting her reply. Knowing she had to say something, she told him as best she could how she'd fallen in love with a tradesman's son to the disapproval of her family and consequently made to leave.

He listened sympathetically, every now and again nodding intently, so much so that without realizing it, too late she heard herself touch on her horrible experience of the refuge for unmarried mothers. To her dismay he picked up on it instantly.

'Oh, you've been a naughty girl then,' he broke in, his arm tightening around her. 'Well, who'd 'ave believe it, looking at you. Got you in the family way, did he? And left you in the lurch. No wonder you was turned out. Well, I'll tell you this, love, I'd look after you a damn sight better than he did.'

Alarmed, Maddie tried to pull away, but his grip tightened still more. 'I mean it, love. I'll look after you. I always do.' He gave a laugh. 'No out-of-wedlock nippers if I can help it.'

Realizing instantly what he meant she turned to ask Hilda to let her out so that she could escape, only to discover that Hilda and her other two friends had already got up from their seats, all three on the point of leaving with their respective partners, saying cheerio to everyone.

The clock on the wall showed ten forty-five. A quick kiss and a cuddle would be the order of the evening, perhaps even a little fumbling before they made off to be home by eleven.

She'd not even noticed that Florrie and her rediscovered sailor friend had already gone, only Dolly left, now in deep conversation with George.

Suddenly desperate, Madeleine leapt up. 'Dolly, I think I'd like to go home now.'

The girl turned to regard her in surprise. 'We don't have

to be back early, love. We ain't got people watching the clock, not like the others.'

'But I want to go!' From his seat Joe was regarding her with some amazement. Dolly began to look peeved.

'Well, *I'm* not yet ready to go. You go. Joe will see you home, safely, won't you, love?'

'I'll look after her OK an' that's a fact,' Joe said, a strange and eager ring to his tone. 'She'll be safe enough in my hands, as right as rain.'

He stood up, his arm coming about her waist. 'Get your coat, love, it's perishing out there, but I'll keep you warm orright.'

Hearing him, Dolly laughed. 'I bet he will an' all! I'll see you later, Maddie. Enjoy yourself. Be good.' With that she turned back to her Alfie, no doubt hoping to enjoy herself later too.

Such were the times, Madeleine realized as she stood uncertain how to escape. In the nine months since August and war breaking out bringing instant emancipation after all those years of suffragettes fighting for their rights, young women had come to feel they could do more or less as they pleased. Maybe such women had always done so, but now it was far more blatant.

Women like Dolly, taking over men's jobs, had come into their own after so long being cherished as sweet and delicate little dears to be protected, and now saw themselves no longer bound by male protection.

Perhaps she too had joined those ranks with Freddy Dobson, totally unaware of it at the time. But now she was aware, and frightened. Women might think themselves now on a par with men but when it came to a man taking advantage, their strength could never compare. What would she do if this Joe suddenly overpowered her in some dark place on her way home? The thought made her feel sick.

'Then I shall make my way home. *Alone!*' she told Dolly, yanking herself free of Joe's arm.

With Dolly staring after her, hearing her call, 'You can't, not alone!' she raced in panic now for the pegs on which she'd hung her coat by the door between saloon and public bar.

Yanking the coat off its hook, aware of Joe already making after her, she was halfway through the doorway when someone appeared to step out straight in front of her almost sending her staggering sideways.

'I do apologize, my dear!' the person exclaimed, his hands holding on to her shoulders to keep her steady. 'Are you hurt?'

As she shook her head, he smiled down at her. 'You came at me in such a rush.'

'I didn't see you,' she gasped, knowing that any second Joe would arrive at her side.

'So it seems,' the man went on in a noticeably educated voice, 'a young lady in a desperate hurry failing to look where she was going.'

She saw him look from her to Joe who had stopped short just a few feet away. 'Surely you were not intending to venture outside alone in the dark. You know, a young lady on her own at this time of night could easily fall prey to some unwanted company.' Again he glanced at the young man in uniform now standing very still.

'You really should have a reliable escort of some kind, at least to accompany you to your home or to whatever means of transport you intend to get you safely there. Do you live far outside London?'

Why he should assume that, she had no idea and without thinking gave the name of the road where she resided adding, 'It's between Cheapside and Bishopsgate,' glimpsing his brief look of surprise, though why he should be surprised, she didn't know.

'And were you going home there by omnibus or taxicab?' he asked evenly enough.

'I . . . I don't know,' she stammered, trying to collect her wits. 'I came here on the Underground with some friends but they've all left and I'm not sure of my way home. I've not lived in London for very long you see,' she explained and saw his face clear as he smiled down at her.

'Then if you would allow me to escort you for the sake of your safety? I am not a threat, my dear,' he continued as she made to draw back. 'I am a married man, or was . . . a widower now. I assure you I am quite harmless.'

He looked harmless and anything was better than randy-minded Joe. Madeleine nodded, almost grateful to find herself guided gently through the growing noise of the bar.

'My limousine is outside, a short distance along the road,' he said softly. 'That also is safe as my chauffeur will be with us.'

The last thing Madeleine noticed as the crowds in the bar closed in behind her was Joe standing like a surprised dummy in the centre of the saloon and she couldn't help feeling a moment of triumph that he would be left without any physical relief to his feelings this night.

Helped by her self-appointed escort into quite an imposing vehicle similar to her father's but bigger, she sat very still as he moved in beside her, to her relief keeping his distance.

For a while he remained silent as the motor gained speed. Finally he said: 'May I say that for someone who speaks as well as you, it seems a rather odd address to have. I hope you don't mind my saying but I rather thought it would have been some finer part of London. You appear to be a well brought up young lady and if you would pardon my rudeness, may I ask you what an obviously well brought up young lady is doing living in such a poor area?'

For a moment she felt herself rebel at his questioning but something about him had filled her with such a desire for a sympathetic ear, even from a stranger, that tears begin to prick her eyes.

Without any prompting she found herself telling him all about herself; how she, an innocent at eighteen had been rejected by her father for falling in love with someone he did not approve of, a humble tradesmen's son; how to her despair her mother had felt bound to support her husband in his harsh decision, how her young man had then let her down and forsaken her.

He sat listening so attentively, saying nothing that finally she touched on the true reason for her father's deep anger, of having being packed off to a place for unmarried mothers, the child taken away. At this point her resolve to merely state the facts as they were gave way. The next thing she knew she was crumpled in his arms sobbing her heart out.

'You poor child,' she heard him say through her weeping. 'What a dreadful tale. And you are all alone, my dear, with no one to turn to.'

Against his shoulder she nodded unable to speak for sobbing.

At the wheel, having been issued with directions as to her address, the chauffeur drove deaf to the emotion going on behind him, remote, his uniformed back stiff, his eyes on the road ahead. Like her father's own staff, he held no opinion of his own, would hear nothing, a mind centred on his duties and nothing else.

Madeleine had managed to recover her composure as far as possible, realizing how foolish she must seem collapsing into the arms of a complete stranger. She sat up, fishing feverishly into her handbag for a handkerchief to hastily dab her eyes.

'I'm so sorry,' she managed to mumble.

'There is no need to feel sorry, my dear,' he said very quietly. 'It is my guess that you have told no one of your true feelings for a long while and I feel myself privileged to have been the one you chose to tell. After all I am a stranger to you and perhaps that is a good reason for you to confide in me; no axe to grind, you might say.'

He was speaking brightly now. 'I'm afraid I haven't introduced myself. My name is Ingleton – James Aric Aylward Ingleton. My work is in the City. I deal in stocks and shares to put it simply. I have a place in Belgrave Square near Knightsbridge but I'm seldom there, my work being more in the City. I find Knightsbridge a lonely place these days. I prefer to work, my evenings mostly occupied by work although I do frequent the odd little public house where people are human. I loathe clubs.'

He was talking rapidly as if to cover some awkwardness. Suddenly he stopped, staring across to her in the darkness of the motor car. 'Forgive me, if I appear impertinent, and please tell me if you feel I am, but would it be in order for me to ask if I may take you to dinner one evening. After what has transpired I feel it uncaring if I merely leave you never to see you again.'

As Madeleine shot him a cautious look, he drew himself upright in his seat. 'Well, I see not,' he said simply.

Instantly Madeleine galvanized into action. 'No!' she burst out. 'I'd be quite happy to see you again. That would be really nice!'

A thought came to her. He had to be at least forty years older than she and far from her idea of a romantic image. But befriended by a man of obvious wealth, influence and prestige, such a man might help her find her child where alone she might never do so. *I'm not manipulating him*, came a small voice inside her. *But you are thinking of using him*, said a second voice. *But I don't care*, came the first voice, *I need all the help I can get and here is someone who might gladly give it.*

'It would be the only way I can think of to thank you for all your kindness,' she said in a deliberately meek tone.

She heard his breath escape him as if he had been holding it in.

'Then may I call for you tomorrow evening, take you to dinner, nothing too grand, somewhere pleasant?'

'I would like that,' she said simply as the motor car turned into the street where she was living, slowing to a stop at the tenement she indicated. She felt no shame about its shabby appearance. He already knew she had been well brought up, accustomed to money. If things went well she would know money again.

'I would like that very much indeed,' she repeated as an afterthought as he helped her alight from the vehicle to kiss her hand.

'Eight o'clock?' he asked.

Holding her excitement inside herself, Madeleine nodded, keeping her smile as calm and as sweet as she could. Yes, he could be very helpful.

Eight

She could hardly wait to tell Dolly about her encounter. She waited up but there was no sound of her returning unless she'd crept back in. Though now she strongly suspected she wouldn't be back until morning. Dolly struck her as that kind of girl though who was she to judge, she who'd so stupidly let one man take advantage of her leading to her own downfall? But never again would she be caught out. She was no floozie and vowed never to let any man touch her until he married her, no matter how much she was in love.

James Ingleton, however, had behaved impeccably and would, she was sure, carry on treating her with respect even though he had listened to her story. He hadn't blamed her but rather the man for taking advantage of a young girl's innocence. But if that reassurance did hide some secret hope for his own ends, he would be sent packing at the least suspicion of improper behaviour. That too she vowed.

All next day she found herself in a growing fever of pent up excitement at the thought of seeing him again. She'd have liked to have told Dolly but there was no sign of her all that day. Saturday was still a workday for Dolly, so maybe she'd already crept off to work, or she might have spent the night with that George and gone off to work from there. In a way Madeleine was a little relieved, Dolly maybe seeing it as being any old port in a storm thing.

That evening she chose her only other nice dress, the salmon pink, in which to meet James Ingleton. Struggling into it without the help of a maid, she finally managed with her supple arms to fasten the buttons at the back, thanking God there was no longer call for the restrictive stays of a couple of years ago having to be laced at the back to give a woman an hourglass figure. At least the war had brought freedom of dress, hems also giving some opportunity these days for pretty ankles to be on show as well as a more natural body shape. Her hair too had no need to be fought with and piled up any more. To be in fashion, she had taken the scissors to her own long tresses so that now her hair was free to curl gently about her ears.

In fact James had been surprised and approving, saying, 'My dear, your new hairstyle looks so utterly charming. It suits you very much.'

She'd felt so happy sitting with him in expensive theatre seats and afterwards a lovely supper in a good restaurant. And now, six weeks later, she hardly ever thought of him as being in his late fifties. Seated opposite her at some restaurant table, he looked at times so much younger despite greying hair which, thick still, had been dark judging by that still remaining in his moustache. Only a fraction taller than herself, although slightly robust and broad of face, he was very well preserved for one his age. On top of that he was a gentleman in every way. She always felt well looked after, felt utterly at ease with him, in some ways even drawn to him for all he'd never so much as kissed her or put an arm about her. The most was to take her elbow to help her in and out of his limousine, or up and down theatre stairs or those of whatever restaurant they visited. Bringing her home he would help her from his car, not waiting for his chauffeur to do so, would kiss her hand and always watch her go indoors before leaving, his brown eyes full of concern.

Every Friday and Saturday he would take her to dinner or a theatre and supper afterwards. Sundays, he'd show her London, perhaps a museum or other places of interest; if the weather was fine a stroll in one of London's parks. All the while she had been compelled to alternate between her few garments, wearing one of her two gowns for evening, and for day alternating between her three blouses and skirts. Often she despaired.

This Saturday evening while enjoying supper, after seeing *Pygmalion* at a small theatre he'd taken her to, he said: 'Forgive my asking, my dear, I hope you don't think me impertinent, but why do you insist on wearing the same two gowns of an evening?'

The question put her back up a little and without thinking she heard herself snap at him. 'Because these are all I have!'

Instantly she regretted her outburst as he looked chastened. 'I am so sorry, my dear,' he began, quickly adding, 'not for hearing that they are all you have but for embarrassing you with such a thoughtless question.'

Madeleine too became apologetic. 'I'm the one who should say sorry. I should not have snapped at you.'

He shook his head waving away her apology with a slight movement of his hand before returning to his meal, she to hers. The rest of the evening passed through intermittent silences, his remark and her reply having become a tiny barrier like a little ghost standing between them.

Her worst fears were confirmed when despite his tender kiss on her hand as they parted, he told her that he would be unable to see her on the Sunday as he had to go up to the Midlands for a few days. He didn't say why, nor did he speak of seeing her the following weekend; this worried her and she went to bed feeling wretched.

After a miserable, sleepless night, she spent the Sunday in her room staring out of the window at the row of tenements on the other side of the yard that separated hers from them. Those few words had obviously marked the end of her association with James. Something told her that some time next week a letter would arrive to say that he would not be seeing her this coming weekend, nor would he be able to see her for some time to come.

Sick and dejected, she knew that when she next saw Dolly she would have to confess that her relationship with James Ingleton had ended.

Dolly would be pleased. Whenever she spoke to her of James, Dolly had behaved quite distantly. Jealousy no doubt, a rich escort able to take her here wherever he, or she, liked. But then it hadn't mattered; she had James and life had been quite wonderful. Now of course, that was over.

No doubt when she was forced to tell Dolly, the girl would cheer up instantly, ask her to join her and her friends on Friday nights. Madeleine did not particularly fancy doing so but what else was there for her?

So far she had survived six weeks in this awful place with James's help. In his company she'd eaten well, had thus managed to save a little on the pitiful allowance her father had provided. Fretting about her lost baby had also diminished a little. Now without him it was all coming back, making her want to weep at any unguarded moment.

Without James life threatened once more to become a hand to mouth existence. To eat and pay her rent she was going to have to somehow find work and the thought appalled and terrified her. How did someone go about finding work and to what skill could she turn her hand? Absolutely nothing.

Monday crawled by. On Tuesday she caught Dolly coming out of her door on her way to work. Dressed in men's breeches, a linen coat reaching to her knees with patch pockets and tied in the middle with a belt, her hair hidden under a man's cap, she was so thin that she looked more like a young man than a girl – she, like many, was covering a man's job while he fought for his country.

'Seeing your swell bloke then this weekend?' Dolly asked, her tone touching on the sarcastic.

Madeleine fought to steel herself. 'I think it might be all off,' she said, trying to sound casual but it caused Dolly to pause, her expression changing to one of interest that looked almost eager though she was obviously trying to disguise it.

'Why, what's happened?'

'Nothing has happened,' Madeleine said lightly. 'I just thought it best not to let things get too serious. He is a bit old, you know.'

Dolly laughed, back to her old self with her neighbour. 'I wondered why someone like you who could've had her pick of blokes would've wanted an old chap like that.'

'He was nice, I suppose, that's all,' Madeleine answered blithely. Dolly gave a shrug.

'Well in that case might see you on Friday. Come out with us. Me and that George haven't seen each other since. He went back to his ship, wrote to me but only the once. A girl in every port they say! Still, it don't matter, had a couple of good times since. See you Friday if I don't see you before. Bye!'

Wednesday was spent alone, mostly lying on her bed moping, trying hard not to, but her mind turning over and over seeing again and again the baby that had been taken from her. Where was she now? A woman's voice, high-pitched and raucous, calling up from downstairs roused her.

'Miss . . . what's-yer-name, Wyndham, there's some bloke darn 'ere wants ter see yer!'

At the cry, Madeleine leapt up. A man! James? Please God let it be. A glance in the mirror showed her that she looked awful. Quickly she ran a comb through her now short hair, pinched her cheeks to make them look pink, bit her lips hard to give them more colour, then hurried downstairs, her landlady's voice still screeching impatiently up at her.

At the sight of her, the woman left the open door to retreat back into her downstairs parlour leaving James standing there beaming.

'I thought you might like this,' he said, holding towards her a large colourful bag bearing the name Harrods. 'A little present for you from me, which I hope you will accept, my dear, but I saw it and couldn't resist. I hoped you were at home. Couldn't wait until I saw you on Friday.'

He was talking fast, almost as if out of breath as he thrust the bag at her, compelling her to take it from him.

'Must be off!' he went on as if there wasn't a moment to spare. 'Need to be somewhere – business. Shall I see you on Friday, eight o'clock? I shall be here on the dot to pick you up,' he added as she nodded automatically. 'Please wear it. I plan to take you somewhere very special for the evening. And I also need to have a serious talk with you.'

He leaned forward, surprising her by planting a brief peck on her cheek before turning and hurrying back to the waiting motor car.

Madeleine stood half stunned at the open door as the vehicle moved off, one or two people staring at the unusual sight of such a grand motor having pulled up outside one of the tenements during the daytime.

Still feeling the kiss on her cheek, she closed the door

and went back upstairs, her heart pounding. He'd said he would see her on Friday. All that fretting! Moments later her heart had sunk. Was it only to say he didn't want to see her again, the gift a mere thank you present?

In her room she opened the bag. A tissue-wrapped parcel lay inside. Slowly she reached in, pulled it out, laying the bag aside to unwrap the flimsy package. Seconds later she gasped, holding up a beautiful evening gown, rich blue brocade with a raised pattern of silver thread throughout, sleeveless, a high waist, a décolletage not too low but, suitable for any evening occasion.

'I can't accept this!' she burst out to the four walls.

But to refuse it, he'd be so hurt. Yet to accept it, what sort of message might that convey? She dared not think.

The only thing she could do was to make it plain that acceptance didn't come with a willingness to participate in what was at this moment racing through her mind. He wanted her to wear it, had made a point of asking her to, so she had no choice but to do as he'd asked. She would of course thank him when they met on Friday but explain that it was not really proper for a young lady to accept presents from a man in this way. But on Friday he had another surprise for her.

As his limousine bore them towards the theatre in Covent Garden – she had once told him how much she enjoyed listening to orchestral concerts – he said suddenly, 'I've been thinking, my dear, the place at which you are currently living, I really do not feel it entirely suitable for a young lady of gentle upbringing. I have it in mind to find you somewhere far more suitable.'

In the darkness of the vehicle, she half smiled. 'It's a lovely idea, James, except that I can't afford anywhere else and . . .'

'You've no need to worry,' he broke in. 'I know your circumstances do not allow you any better accommodation but you have me now and I would be more than happy to take care of the rent for you.'

Madeleine caught her breath. On the point of crying out that she had no intention of being a kept woman, she curbed herself in time. Instead she said as steadily as she could, 'I don't think that would be quite the right thing to do.'

She could sense rather than see him staring at her in the darkness of the vehicle. 'Why on earth not, my dear?'

'Because . . . well, it's not right,' she stammered. 'It's as though . . .'

She floundered to a stop at a loss how to express what she was trying to say then began again. 'You've always been a complete gentleman toward me but if you began paying my rent for me it wouldn't take long for people to begin making something out of it and doubt your good intentions – tarnish your good name.'

She heard him draw a deep breath. 'That never crossed my mind but I understand what you mean.'

Was he being truthful? Madeleine's mind raced. Knowing she was what many people once termed a 'fallen woman' and even today those ideas hadn't changed, could he be harbouring some hope that she'd prove easy as time went on? If so he was in for a shock. She had fallen once through her own silly innocence. No longer innocent she certainly wasn't prepared to allow herself to fall even lower.

She became aware that he was speaking. 'There is another alternative my dear. I might write to your father and request that if only for charity's sake he might increase your allowance so that you may enjoy far more suitable accommodation.'

'No!' she exclaimed. 'My father is not your affair.'

She knew immediately that she'd hurt him as he leaned back into his seat. Almost apologetically she said, 'Oh, James, I didn't mean it to sound as it did. I meant . . .'

How could she explain what she meant? She fell silent but after a moment or two, he said quietly, 'If you feel that strongly about it, my dear, the only other solution would be not to reveal to anyone that I am financing better accommodation for you away from that awful area? I cannot bear to see you living where you are at present,' he added as he sensed her stiffen. 'Please, Madeleine, accept my suggestion. It would make me so happy.'

What could she say? She needed so dreadfully to get away from that awful place, from Dolly and her lifestyle, but to have him pay for her? Again came the thought, in time what reward would even the kindest man begin to look for? And would she feel obliged to yield to his requests out of gratitude?

'What would you expect of me in return?' The nagging question sprang into words before she could prevent them.

In the vehicle's dim interior she felt him turn slowly to look at her. 'Is that really what you think of me, Madeleine?'

'I'm sorry,' she blurted out. 'I don't know why I said it.'

'You thought it, my dear, or you wouldn't have said it.'

She could see herself in danger of losing him. 'It's just that I feel so vulnerable, living alone in London. I've never been on my own before.'

She sensed his tension melt away. 'My dear, you need not be alone.'

His voice had grown deep and gentle, almost fatherly. 'If you allow, I will always be here for you whenever and if ever you should need me. I will never ask anything of you if that is what you fear. I am as much in need of a friend as you. Since my wife passed away I have been very lonely. I have any number of business acquaintances, but they are purely that, acquaintances. I am wealthy and as such tend to attract hangers on, social climbers, but I do not enjoy social events all that much. I look forward to my home after an evening of it. The truth is that in the midst of company I am indeed lonely.'

He paused then continued. 'I need someone to be a friend, a true friend, who does not expect to gain from me. If you'll forgive me, my dear, I want to say that I deem you to be that person.'

She made no reply but on an impulse let her hand slowly reach out to him across the seat, a tiny pang of happiness flooding over her as she felt his fingers immediately curl around hers in a warm, firm grip.

After a while, he said, 'There is still the matter of the embarrassment of my financing better accommodation for you. I do understand, my dear,' he went on when she made no reply.

'Therefore, I feel some other arrangement would better suit you.'

The pause left her wondering what arrangement he was talking about but she could think of no way of asking.

'I know this may sound a little premature,' he was saying, 'and I will understand if you feel you need to refuse, but I feel it might be a solution to the problem if I asked . . .' He hesitated then plunged on. 'If I asked if you would consider marrying me?'

Madeleine was stunned, even wondering if she'd heard him correctly. She had known him for so little time. How could she even dream of marrying someone almost forty years older than her? Old enough to be her father, no, she could never do that. One day a young man would come along and they would marry and have babies . . .

That thought pulled her up sharply. She had a baby, one they had taken from her at the moment of its birth and for whom she'd catch herself pining at the least unforeseen moment; a baby she would do anything to trace and claim back.

Even now that empty ache came back into her breast and with it another thought. To ever be able to trace her, it would take a lot of money. Not in a million years would she ever be able to save up that sort of money. But James had money – had told her that he was a wealthy man. Nor had he frowned upon her when she'd told him that as a result of her own innocence she'd borne an illegitimate child. Now he was asking her to marry him. Were she to accept, there'd be enough money and more to trace her baby. But could she bring herself to marry an old man, for that?

He was kind, generous, of a pleasant nature, easy to get on with, she liked him, but she didn't love him. But what did that matter. He promised security, the chance of a good life. He hadn't said that he loved her merely that he needed companionship but was that sufficient for her to accept this offer of marriage? To get her baby back, yes, it was.

'It would be a solution,' she said quietly, answering his last question.

She felt him sit back in his seat. 'Then that will be arranged,' he said quietly. The rest of the journey passed in silence.

Nine

A sense of anticlimax stole over Madeleine as with an almost exaggerated show of disinterest Dolly glanced at the band of five large diamonds on the third finger of the hand that she'd held up for Dolly to see.

'My, that must've cost him a pretty penny! You certainly know how to land on your feet, but I suppose you know all about that. Connections, that sort of thing.'

The tone was almost spiteful, but what had she expected – genuine excitement, Dolly falling over herself with profuse congratulations? Even so, knowing the girl's hardly disguised attitude of envy ever since she'd told her about herself and James, Madeleine felt her own resentment rise, hearing her ratty echo, '*Connections?*' laying emphasis on the word.

Dolly shrugged. 'Well, people like you, brought up posh and all that, they always manage to fall on their feet, don't they?'

'I wouldn't know,' Madeleine said tartly, letting her hand with its gorgeous engagement ring drop to her side, looking now only to escape back to her own room. But if Dolly noticed the sting in her tone, she ploughed on without regard.

'If you want my opinion, yes, it's a nice ring. But I don't think I'd be all that overjoyed with some old man three times my age, even if he do have money. What on earth can you see in him? Though I suppose you know your own mind.'

Madeleine wanted to say that she hadn't asked for her opinion, but Dolly had more to say, studying her with a disbelieving gaze. 'Surely, you can't *love* him? You with your looks could easily find someone a blooming sight younger with just as much money as your old toff's probably got.'

Just in time Madeleine stopped herself blurting out in retaliation to this that there *was* no time to wait for any young man to come along; that marrying James was the only way of getting back her baby before she lost her forever. But that would have given her a wonderful opportunity to call her a gold digger, an opportunist. But wasn't that exactly what she was?

Hurriedly she turned away from that thought as to her relief Dolly moved off towards her room, saying over her shoulder as she went, 'Anyway, wish you luck. Don't suppose you'll be here for much longer now you've got yourself all nicely sorted out.'

The door closed behind her with almost exaggerated care, leaving Madeleine only too glad she hadn't let herself be motivated into blurting out her thoughts. She'd never told her about her baby, fearing to be looked down on. All she felt now was relief that she'd not be seeing her for much longer.

She'd finally accepted James's offer of a nicer place to live until they were married, now assured that his intentions were indeed honourable. She had a ring to prove it and the knowledge that they'd be married quietly, no fuss, just a small affair.

Sitting on the hard upright chair by the table, she glanced again at her ring. It had been so formal the way he'd proposed, quietly, in the dim interior of his limousine, no attempt to embrace her when almost as formally she had said yes in an almost sombre tone.

'Thank you, my dear,' he'd said, 'so long as you are very sure.'

When she told him that yes, she was very sure, he had reached into his coat pocket and withdrawn a dark blue velvet box.

Removing the ring, he had gently taken her left hand to slide it on to her finger, saying, 'I hope you realize, my dear, how very happy you have made me.'

Hardly ever did he call her Madeleine, always 'my dear'. But it was the sheer formality of his proposal that had shaken her as he added without any trace of emotion in his tone, 'How would you feel, my dear, to marriage three months from now? Shall we say August?'

In the dim interior she'd sensed him smiling. 'I think a quiet affair would be best if you are happy with that, a small formal reception, not too many guests, at my home which will then also be your home. Maybe your parents will agree to be present. How can they possibly refuse a decently wedded daughter, your father giving you away, as it should be? I think a brief honeymoon in the country. I would have taken you somewhere abroad, but that's hardly possible with the war. When it is over we may take good advantage of an extended cruise somewhere, what do you say, my dear?'

Somewhat stunned by the cut and dried way he'd apparently had everything already planned, she could only nod, half expecting him to lean over and kiss her on the mouth, maybe a lingering one to which she would have to respond. Instead he'd sighed contentedly and sat back, still holding her hand and thus they travelled to the theatre where he'd been taking her, he carefully handing her down from the limousine and guiding her up the steps to the theatre as if she were made of delicate porcelain.

That was last night, Saturday. Now she sat in her room knowing that come Thursday she'd be vacating these awful premises forever. She hadn't told Dolly, had no intention of telling her now, not after what she'd said. Nor had she told her she would be nineteen on Friday. James was giving her a birthday party next Saturday. It was to be at his home. And what a home!

Yesterday had been the first time she had ever seen it, practically surrounded by beautiful London parks, Hyde Park, Green Park, St James Park, every bit as fine as her old home in Oxfordshire, maybe even more so as he showed her around the many lower floor rooms, stopping short of showing her the upper rooms that were the bedrooms, to her relief.

When he'd brought her there after the theatre, on the way saying with a small smile, 'I hope you don't mind, my dear, I thought it would be far more suitable to have supper at home rather than a restaurant – after all it will be your home soon,' there had come a sharp sense of alarm that he might be thinking to cement their engagement.

There had also come a surge of distaste at the thought of having his hands exploring her body, wondering what she had got herself into, agreeing to marry a man three times her age. She had prepared herself to tell him very gently that she wasn't ready for that sort of thing before marriage, instantly recalling that she'd been ready enough with Freddy Dobson. But it had been different – he'd been young and she innocent. She was no longer an innocent, but refusing James might cause him to withdraw his proposal. Then where would she be? Without his money, his help, she'd never be able to trace her baby.

With that in mind she had steeled herself to endure his embraces but she need not have worried. He'd been a perfect gentleman the whole evening.

Waited upon by Merton his elderly butler and a rather plain-faced maid called Beattie, they'd sat at either end of a small, rectangular table, his cook Mrs Cole having supper already prepared almost as if he'd expected his proposal would be accepted. That too had raised the question of his proposal being anticipated, one she'd soon shrugged off as she put her mind to considering all the benefits this union could bring.

She'd intended to tell Dolly all about it. Now she was glad she hadn't. Dolly, in her present jealous mood, would have shrugged, maybe said something nasty. It didn't matter any more. She had a future now.

James had found her a nice little furnished two-roomed apartment not far from where he lived. 'I shall be able to see you more often,' he'd said cheerfully, but for her leaving this hole of a place felt far more important.

She could hardly wait for Thursday, to see the back of this place, and Dolly, and that common, rough-tongued landlady who was always yelling up the stairs to any tenant who had a caller. The next five days would seem endless. Of a sudden she felt desperately cooped up in this room, verging on claustrophobia. She needed to get out, find some fresh air even though the day was deeply overcast.

For much of May the weather had been wonderful but today hardly conducive to cheering her up after her encounter with Dolly. Little to cheer anyone up these days: the war expected to be over by last Christmas still dragging on, the fighting in France seeming to be going nowhere, the Huns now using a terrible weapon, gas. The outrage at the sinking of the Cunard liner *Lusitania* by torpedoes within sight of British shores with the loss of well over a thousand lives, not even military, but civilian men, women and children, had angry crowds descending on shops owned by Germans, people stoning their owners or covering them in paint, no matter that they'd been in this country half their lives. Madeleine had heard the ruckus only a few days ago, windows being broken in a nearby parade, shouts and screams, police called, trying to quell their fury. She had shut her window to keep out the sounds and prayed to soon leave this awful area.

Now her wish had been granted. By the end of the week she would be gazing around at a bright and beautiful little apartment. The thought of her coming marriage suddenly excited her as she snatched up her hat and coat and hurried down the stairs as quickly as her out of date hobble skirt allowed, knowing that soon all her clothes would be the latest of fashion.

On a whim she turned in the direction of the nearby post office. There she bought herself some notepaper and envelopes and a couple of penny stamps. Armed with these she turned back to where she lived, almost at a run, all thought of enjoying some fresh air swept from her mind.

Seated at her table she began to write the letter, having to resort to pencil, all she had to hand, ink and a pen a luxury she'd so far had no need to afford until now. But suddenly this letter was important and pencil would have to do. Maybe the letter was somewhat premature yet she wrote as if there was no time at all to spare, her usually cultured, careful handwriting becoming a scrawl in her haste, hardly allowing herself time to think lest an attack of misgiving made her change her mind.

In the over-furnished drawing room that still reflected the old Edwardian days of over a dozen years ago, Aldous

Wyndham had left the cheap-looking envelope to the very last in his usual pile of morning post. Most probably from someone begging monetary help of some sort, of which he received quite a few, being a man of some standing on a board of directors of a well known, well sought after Buckinghamshire grammar school.

Sighing at the likelihood of declining whatever the sender was begging from him, he slit open the envelope to scan the single sheet of thin notepaper prior to screwing it into a ball and throwing it into the wicker waste paper basket at his feet. But the moment he began to read, he froze.

Leaping to his feet, almost knocking over the waste paper basket, he hurried to the door, tore it open to bellow at the girl who was dusting the hall stand just a few feet away, 'Where is my wife?'

The maid started as if struck, collecting herself to mumble, 'I don't know, sir,' her head respectfully lowered.

'Then find her,' he commanded, at which the girl scuttled off, duster still in hand.

He was seated at his bureau when Dorothy finally came in, a little diffidently. Their maid had appeared harassed, leaving her to feel something must be terribly amiss, something she must have done was probably annoying him.

'Where were you?' he demanded, glancing up at her. The tone of his question made her catch her lower lip between her teeth.

'I was in the kitchen with Mrs Plumley, planning today's menu,' she offered. 'What was it you wanted, dear?'

'Look at this!' He held out the sheet of notepaper to her, his face now turned away from her, compelling her to come forward to receive it.

'Read it!' he snapped.

Quickly she began to read but only got as far as the first sentence. 'It's from Madeleine,' she gasped.

'I do not recognize the name,' he growled, still with his gaze on the surface of his bureau. 'Just read what it says . . . to yourself,' he added as she started to read aloud.

As bidden she took in the words in silence, reading quickly and as briefly as she could. Finally she looked up. He was staring out of the window from where he sat. 'It says she is getting married in August. She has asked us to be present.'

'Never!' he exploded, leaping up to go over to the window to gaze out.

'She asks if you would give her away,' Dorothy ventured timidly.

'I cannot give away what I do not have,' he returned, his back still to her.

'But she is our daughter, dear. We ought at least . . .'

Swinging round so viciously that he caused her to jump, he blared, 'Enough! We have no daughter, Dorothy! The author of this letter is nothing to do with us. You would be well advised to remember that fact.'

It sounded as though he were addressing his board of governors. His tone seemed to stab into her heart like a knife wound, so harsh did it sound and quite suddenly his anger made her feel bolder than she could ever remember.

'You may not like it, Aldous,' she heard herself say, 'but she is still my daughter. I bore her, fed her at my breast, tended her and cared for her. She is . . .'

'Enough!' he thundered, moments later drawing an impatient breath as she began to weep. 'I am not prepared to countenance her nor be present at the wedding of someone I do not know, whoever the man is. Nor will you, Dorothy. I am disappointed in you. I did expect you to be in total agreement, which is why I called you in here. But it seems your answer to everything is to dissolve into tears so there is no point saying any more. As to this letter I shall not even respond to it. And neither will you. Now you may go back to whatever you and Mrs Plumley were doing.'

With that he returned to his writing desk and sat down, continuing to ignore her presence until slowly she turned and went from the room.

Outside the door she stood sniffing back the tears. Finally she slowly straightened her back and lifted her chin, whispered softly, almost defiantly: 'But she is still my daughter.'

She began to make her way back along the hall, not to the kitchen but to the stairs leading up to her little parlour on the second floor where she would write her own letters to people she knew, one letter which at this moment she needed very much to write.

After only three months of preparation, neither she nor James hardly needing to lift a finger towards the day, his having arranged it all to be done for them, she had still felt that she was living in a dream world, that nothing was real. From that very evening when James had proposed to her, such as it was, and she had accepted, again such as it was, everything had felt as if it wasn't happening, the world itself seeming to have receded, as if she were floating through it.

The war too, even now, seemed to pass her by. And yet it held enough stark reality to make her feel otherwise – daily the newspaper headlines, the sight of maimed and blinded men on the streets, Lord knows how many thousands more languishing in hospitals all over the realm, the sight of drawn blinds in almost every other street – to make it all real, so horribly real.

Sometimes she thought of Hamilton Bramwell. She rather felt he still survived, conducting operations from some safe distance, a command post well removed from the front, maybe still safely entrenched in some HQ in England. Other times her thoughts wandered to Freddy Dobson, a common soldier no doubt fighting in the trenches. That was if he was still alive or had he been killed, shot in what they called No Man's Land or blown to pieces in some trench? If so had he been found or did he lay buried, unknown? Had he married his fiancée never uttering a word about his casual affair and a silly young girl he'd left pregnant with his baby? Did he and his wife have a child of their own, a child borne in wedlock? Another thought, if he'd been killed, his wife would now be a widow. Or maybe he'd been sent home maimed for life or blinded by chlorine gas, which the papers had reported to be like a sickly, greenish-yellow fog that drifted across open ground towards the still mainly unprotected Allied troops. Freddy's wife would be left to nurse him for the rest of their lives, that once handsome and vigorous young man who had turned her heart, stricken and scarred forever.

Part of Madeleine's reaction to that speculation was that such an end was exactly what he deserved, moments later to feel chastened and full of remorse at such a wicked thought. But it was no concern of hers any more. She had a new life now and it was wonderful. Whatever had befallen Freddy Dobson was way in the past.

Ten

Amazing how quickly summer had flown. Only two weeks to her wedding. Not that there'd been much for her to do, James having taken charge of almost everything.

It was to be a quiet affair, with few guests invited. 'Far better that way don't you think, my dear?' he'd said, and as she nodded, glad enough for it to be so, continued, 'Not as though I were marrying for the first time and I assumed you wouldn't care for anything ostentatious in light of the present situation between yourself and your family.'

Even though it had been said kindly with smiles intended to comfort, his words had bitten deep. But she knew what he meant. There'd been no reply from her parents to his invitation, not even to decline, making her half wish he hadn't included them at all.

There had been one reply; from her mother's sister Maud whom she hadn't seen in years but had hoped might accept but even that had been to decline with the excuse that a recent bout of ill health would prevent her attending. Whether true or not, Madeleine rather suspected she'd more than likely been influenced by her father.

No one on her side would be there so in a way it did come as a relief that it would be a simple wedding. Most were these days; hasty marriages, little to celebrate, young men dragged off to fight almost immediately upon being conscripted; the food shortage dictating meagre wedding breakfasts coupled with a natural reluctance to indulge in anything too showy while perhaps in almost every street more than one woman was grieving the loss of a husband to an enemy bullet or shell. So it was only right that her wedding should be-a quiet one.

No bridal gown for her. She'd be wearing a simple, two-piece tailor-made tweed costume with a white blouse of hand-embroidered voile, together costing all of six pounds eighteen shillings and sixpence, expensive but which he'd insisted paying for, together with a lovely double row of pearls. All she'd taken with her on leaving home for that place for unmarried mothers had been just a couple of pieces of jewellery, left to forever regret the other fine pieces left behind. Now there was no longer need to fret. James was here now. Provided she wasn't greedy he'd buy whatever jewellery took her fancy.

What she didn't fancy were the few days they were to spend at a small hotel at Buxton in Derbyshire after the wedding and the intimate part of it as his wife. She'd grown fond of him of course but their relationship had been purely platonic, he seeming to prefer it that way somewhat to her relief. Now faced with her prospective duty as a wife she was becoming increasingly concerned at the thought, even to wondering what she thought she was doing, getting wed to an older man like James.

Another uneasiness had been her parents' refusal to see her married, something one would have thought they'd be only too relieved to see happen. She'd hoped, maybe foolishly, to at least have had some reply to the letter she'd sent her mother months ago telling her of James's proposal, but there had been nothing. She found herself making excuses for her, aware that all post going through her father's butler who, being answerable to him, would have shown him the letter only to have it taken and torn up.

Now, ten days to the wedding, she had finally made up her mind to turn her back on them and concentrate on the lifestyle she now enjoyed, a nice little apartment, James spending out on her while still as gentlemanly as ever. The one thing that worried her was that he continually side-stepped any mention about her desire to trace the child taken from her.

'So much to think about just now,' he'd say. 'For the time being we should concentrate on the wedding, my dear.'

Said so gently that she could hardly badger him further, especially as just lately the stress of the coming wedding was beginning to show on his face worrying her that by the time the day arrived he might even fall ill, the whole thing then having to be cancelled. At times she even dreamt that he had collapsed and died, all her hopes dashed. It wasn't wise to push him until after the wedding.

The day was here. It had been arranged for James's younger brother Henry and his wife Lydia to be witnesses. Having arrived from Northampton, they were now here with her in her apartment waiting for the car to take all three to the registry office not far away.

Having met them only once before it was like having strangers about her. Her mother should have been here, fussing and fiddling. These two virtual strangers served only to heighten that absence. The thought made her eyes grow moist.

Only a bride would know how emotional this day could be, tears of overwhelming joy, but for her they were tears of longing for her mother and it was all she could do to hold them back.

Lydia was looking at her in mild consternation. 'I know, dear, it must be a little overwhelming for you but try not to spoil your face. It'll soon be over. Then you'll be as happy as any. James has been so lost since losing his first wife and you'll be a good companion to him. It is what he needs.'

That unfortunate little speech did nothing to help her but at least she managed to dry her eyes enough to smile at the woman as she suppressed the longing to have her mother here beside her.

The limousine had arrived. The chauffeur helped her into the vehicle together with a close friend of James in black morning suit as if going to a funeral who sat down stiffly beside her. It should have been her father giving her away, not this man, this stranger. Hastily she pushed that thought aside as well, relieved when they drew up outside the registry office.

It was then she saw her. The small, thin woman in a long skirted grey suit and a high beaver toque trimmed with tulle that practically hid her face. But Madeleine recognized her immediately.

'Mummy! Oh, Mummy!' Hardly believing what she was

seeing, Madeleine ran to her, leaving the other two standing. 'You came!'

She stopped in her tracks as her mother recoiled. Madeleine stood where she had paused, having to speak across the small distance between them. 'I never dreamt you would come. Where's my father?'

'He isn't coming.'

Madeleine smothered the pang that swept through her. She should have known. 'You travelled here alone?' It was hardly believable. Her mother never travelled anywhere without him.

Lydia and Henry were hovering, uncertain whether to go on inside or not. She ignored them. 'Does he know? Surely he didn't let you come all on your own?' She couldn't bring herself to say anything other than 'he'.

'Your father is in the City. Miles drove me to Beaconsfield Station and helped me buy my rail ticket and I had a taxicab bring me here.'

'How did you know where to find this place?'

'Your father's chauffeur made enquiries for me. Miles has been so very helpful but I cannot say anything to your father about it. He would be livid if he knew I'd come here, and Miles could be in such trouble.'

The words seemed to stress how bitter her father was towards her still. She knew now that for as long as he lived he would never forgive her. Yet the thought seemed to strengthen her. It was also a concern for her. Her mother had defied him. Should he find out, how would her mother fare? He'd never lifted a hand to her, but wouldn't have to. He was capable of making life hell by words alone which was the reason why, until now, her mother had always been the subservient little woman.

Madeleine experienced a passing thought quite out of keeping with the situation – what had her mother been like when they were first married? Strong-willed? No, maybe not, but feeling loved and returning that love with an easy will. Only with the passing of years would she have diminished to become what she was now. Yet here she was, brave and strong and defiant. Madeleine wanted to cuddle her close but her mother would have shrunk away from the embrace, she was sure.

'Would you introduce us, Madeleine?' Lydia's voice behind her made her jump. She gathered her wits.

'This is my mother,' she announced proudly.

Someone was running down the steps from the registry office, a young man, full of bounce and energy, his tone cheery but urgent as he called out:

'Sorry to interrupt but Uncle James is waiting. I'm Anthony by the way – his only nephew, his sister Eileen's son, who's a widow. Lost me father ages ago, killed in the Boer War. I was eleven, and when—'

'No more, Tony dear!' Lydia cut in. 'We must go in. Is your mother coming in with us?' she asked Madeleine, who turned anxiously towards her mother.

'Are you coming in, Mummy?' Her mother gave a small nod, and meekly allowed herself to be guided up the steps by the effusive Anthony.

It made her day for her, having her at the ceremony, brief though it was. But her mother left almost immediately it was over, not staying for the celebratory gathering.

'I don't know how long it will take me to get home and I must be home before your father or I shall have to tell lies or get poor Miles into trouble,' she said, already becoming tense at the thought. 'I told Cook, Mrs Plumley – she's still with us – that I was going to visit a friend in Beaconsfield. So I must make sure to be home and settled in time for your father.'

'Are you sure you'll be all right, Mummy?' Madeleine asked anxiously.

Her mother nodded. 'I shall be just fine.'

There was an unusual confidence in her voice. 'I shall telephone from the station for Miles to come and collect me.'

This was another surprise. Her mother had always been intimidated by the telephone. As she left she gave Madeleine a kiss on the cheek saying, 'Take care of yourself, Madeleine my dear, and be happy. I'm so very pleased for you. You will be fine from now on. And so shall I.'

With that she got into the taxicab James had found for her, waving as the vehicle drew away, leaving Madeleine weeping silently deep inside.

'I love you, Mummy,' she whispered as the taxi turned the corner out of sight. It was the last time she ever saw her mother.

She wrote during her short honeymoon in Derbyshire, saying that she hoped she was keeping well but she never received a reply. She guessed that her father would have probably intercepted it, opened it, read it and torn it up. Her mother would have been left never knowing she had written to her.

She was glad that she had purposely not mentioned their meeting, knowing her father of old, merely said she was happy being married, had plenty of money and didn't need handouts any more – this meant for her father's eyes – so there was no need to worry about her any more. She had not expected a response from him nor did she get one.

It was eighteen months later when she did hear – a letter arriving through his solicitor saying that her mother had been suffering from a galloping consumption for near on a year and had passed away early the previous week, her funeral having taken place two days ago. Such was her father's attitude towards her, his own daughter, that he'd not even told her of her mother's condition much less informing her of her death except through his solicitor, even worse deliberately keeping the date of the funeral from her.

The shock of hearing it in this way was like a fist hitting her between the eyes, grief like a dagger to the heart. James found her crumpled up on a sofa in the drawing room, her face buried in a cushion, one arm dangling, the letter limp between her fingers, on the point of fluttering to the floor.

He was by her side in seconds. 'My dear, what is it? What is wrong?'

When she made no reply, he bent and retrieved the now fallen letter to quickly scan its contents. She heard his gasp of horror and when he finally spoke his tone was a mixture of anger and astonishment.

'I can't believe your father could do this to you. How could anyone be so callous?'

With that he bent and gathered her up into his arms, she allowing him to do so without any will of her own left to resist.

'I am so terribly sorry, my dear,' he murmured like one crooning to a child. 'I met your poor mother only the once when she came to attend our marriage ceremony but I found her to be an exceptionally nice person. I took a liking to her on the instant of meeting her.' His arms had tightened about her in a new surge of disbelief.

'How could your father withhold her illness from you, much less not informing you of her tragic end, nor of the funeral. It seems to me quite deliberate. Forgive me but how vicious and cruel can the man be?'

Madeleine pulled herself away from his grip to throw herself back on to the sofa, though this time to sit upright, trying to collect herself. There was no need to forgive James his opinions. She was entirely in agreement. It was unbelievable how cruel her father could be. It made her heart ache and she vowed that to the day she died, she'd never forgive him.

Sitting on the sofa beside her, James said quietly, 'You must put it behind you, my dear.' Gently he took her hand. She let it linger there.

'Try to think of nicer things,' he went on. 'Our companionship, the happiness you now have. I *have* made you happy, haven't I, my dear?'

She nodded without speaking as he went on: 'Think back to the lovely time on our honeymoon. I know it was nowhere exotic such as I would have loved to take you were it not for this terrible war. But when it is finally over, I will take you to places you have never seen before. I'll make sure you'll never be sad again, my dear.'

Listening to him, Madeleine's mind went back to that first night at his home before travelling off to Derbyshire. She'd been so on edge, hardly able to concentrate on being introduced to his staff – Merton his manservant, his cook and housekeeper Mrs Cole, the housemaid Beattie, and Lily the scullery maid, and Robert his chauffeur – for thinking of James expecting to exercise his marital rights once upstairs. But he'd done nothing of the kind.

She'd never set foot in any of the upper rooms of his home and with heavily beating heart had allowed herself to be led up there, he preceding her, having not so much as held her hand, allowing her to follow two steps behind. In fact he had been as awkward and embarrassed as she, following him into the large, splendid bedroom with its big double bed which she instantly guessed had once been his and his first wife's, they no doubt far more at ease with each other during their married life than James and she were at that moment, would ever be.

She hardly remembered what he had said, her mind more on the problem of changing into night attire and having to lay beside him. She did remember them both standing in the centre of the room a few inches apart, he leaning forward to kiss her, and apparently sensing her slight, instinctive almost, recoil and had instantly stepped back from her, going to a little table to one side that held a decanter of brandy and two glasses and had said as he poured out a tiny measure for each of them, 'Maybe a small nightcap for us both.'

It was then she'd realized how awkward he too was feeling, and out of compassion for him, had forced herself to relax, taking the glass he'd offered with its tiny measure of spirit.

'To our companionship,' he had said quietly.

The word companionship had come as an overwhelming relief as he'd leaned forward and kissed her cheek – a tender kiss; no embrace, the kiss of an elderly man to a child, not what she had expected. She'd been nineteen, he indeed elderly in comparison, and now her husband. His moustache had felt soft against her skin, his lips even softer; flaccid, and she remembered having instantly recalled the firm demand of another much younger man's lips on hers that had made her insides squirm with desire, and then had come the thought: what had she done, marrying a man thirty-seven years her senior? But she knew – so that one day she'd have her child back.

Since then she had raised the subject time and time again,

yet more than eighteen months later he was still making excuses not to trace the baby – after all this time it might well be impossible; nothing to go on; his stockbroker business demanding all his attention right now; the way the war was going so many other concerns taking precedence.

She'd even suspected a personal reluctance to have a child, any child, especially one not of his blood, around him at his age. She'd begun to ask him less and less these days, slowly seeing the sense behind his reasoning. It had been a long time and that deep longing, that ache she used to feel had begun to diminish a little. Her life had settled down. Other than a reluctance to trace the child, he gave her everything she desired, while continuing to see their marriage as mere companionship for which she was grateful.

He had never attempted to make love to her. The nearest he had ever come to physical affection was a tender kiss on her forehead or taking her arm when out together or to help her in and out his Wolseley limousine before his chauffeur could reach her, even tucking the travelling blanket around her knees which was more the chauffeur's job.

It was always a loving gesture on his part, this care for her comfort and safety and for that she was grateful, in turn vowing to be faithful to him. But every so often came that secret yearning for a younger man's touch and many times she had caught herself thinking of the young man who had run lightly down the steps of the registry office; a lively, loquacious young man of twenty-six in the uniform of an army captain, who had introduced himself as her husband's nephew Anthony. But today there was no such yearning.

The solicitor's letter had loomed back into her mind, smothering those fleeting thoughts that had come from nowhere, unbidden, making her loathe herself for having allowed them in to interfere with her grief, with her intense anger against her father.

Eleven

It was taking forever to pull herself together after hearing about her mother in that way and, despite the solicitor having worded the letter as discreetly and as gently as possible in a bid to cushion the shock, her anger grew each time she thought about it.

'I know how you must feel, my dear,' James said as kindly as he could, aware of her continuing distress. 'It was a dreadful business, I know, but you must try to surmount it or you will make yourself ill.'

'How can you know what I feel?' she shot at him.

'I lost my wife,' he said simply.

She knew instantly exactly what he meant but wasn't prepared to give way. 'How can you compare the two?' she replied with venom. 'No one kept the news from you until it was too late to go to her funeral. You've no idea how that feels. You'll never know! Nor will anyone who's not had it happen to them.'

Rushing from the room she failed to notice the expression of pain those thoughtless words brought.

Her anger and resentment growing rather than diminishing, she knew she could never rest until she faced her father. The following Saturday she told James that she had been invited to spend the day with Margaret Dowling, one of the many friends she'd made from social gatherings she'd begun to arrange since their marriage.

Despite James's preference for discretion, with the war still raging, hardly any ground being lost or gained, lives of thousands of young men still being sacrificed seemingly for nothing, she continued to look for any excuse for a party to liven a life growing ever more dull with the passing of time.

Slowly she was becoming more and more known for them, thus developing a widening circle of friends these past couple of years. Without them life would have become deadly dull for she'd soon discovered that James was no party-giver, much more preferring his privacy. He'd forever be seeking the first chance to leave a social gathering the second it became the least bit noisy, disappearing usually to talk business somewhere else with a few of those who shared his own business interests.

With Margaret's husband, Colonel Dowling, being away in France helping conduct the war from the safe distance of some administrative desk or other, she missed his presence and like Madeleine looked forward to any diversion that might make the void seem more bearable.

She lived well west of London so the pretence of visiting her would give Madeleine ample time to travel on to Buckinghamshire and back home without there being any suspicion of her having gone to seek out her father.

Wisdom kept telling her that she was being foolish but she strove to ignore it as she sat on the train from Marylebone watching West London's skyline change slowly to urban sprawl then to green countryside with small villages trundling by, wartime seeming to give trains every excuse to go slow.

A first-class carriage did afford privacy from the noise and turmoil of second-and third-class ones, but the relative peace only helped to accentuate her thoughts on the possible stupidity of her resolve.

Watching the rain driving across the carriage windows at least helped sweep away that thought but brought instead thoughts of what she'd read in the newspapers of present fearful conditions in Flanders. Reports of men being bogged down in a sea of Flanders mud caused by ceaseless rain and remorseless bombardment around Passchendaele, men being sucked down by the quagmire to their deaths should they slip off the duckboards.

The mounting daily toll of men missing suddenly made her think of James's nephew, Anthony. He too was somewhere in Belgium. She would find herself constantly praying that he still remained safe, though had he been killed or wounded the news would have reached her and James instantly, she was sure.

As his only nephew, he was his favourite relation. In fact on marrying her James had altered his will previously leaving most of his estate to him. It was now only a quarter of that, the rest, James had told her confidentially so as to reassure her, going to herself which amounted to more than she would ever need or want.

'The boy already has enough and more,' he'd told her, 'left to him by his father, my eldest brother Wilfred, Will, when he passed away. So he is already a wealthy young man in his own right and would want for nothing,' adding in fond and glowing terms, 'nor is he at all selfish to begrudge you the major portion of my estate. He is a most likeable young man, I am proud to say. And when this dreadful war is finally over, I sincerely hope to see much more of him. You know, my dear, I do so miss his cheery voice in this house.'

She too found herself hoping to see more of him, suddenly aware of a strange twinge of excitement in her stomach that for a moment managed to smother her feelings of bitterness towards her father.

She should never have come. Alighting from the taxicab that had brought her here from the railway station in Beaconsfield, her first sight of the house she'd once lived in struck her as remote, different to what she remembered, like the momentarily unexpected impression one gets of even a familiar place when returning from long holidaying in distant parts.

Saturday morning, her father would be home. A man of strict habits, he seldom had any engagement on a Saturday until perhaps the afternoon.

In spite of the steady rain, she had the taxi stop well before reaching the house lest in glancing from the sitting-room window he'd see her and bar her way, though he probably wouldn't recognize her all that quickly under the large black umbrella she held well down over her head.

She intended to be inside the house before he knew it, rather than standing on the doorstep in full view of the road for any passer-by to witness the inevitable confrontation she knew would occur. To this end she entered by the servants' entrance, alarming Mrs Plumley in the midst of her cooking as she burst in through the door closed against the steady rain. The woman shot upright like someone scalded, to stand staring at her as if petrified.

'Good God Almighty! Miss Maddie! What in—'

'Shh!' Madeleine hissed. But Mrs Plumley was too flabbergasted to heed her.

'What in God's holy name are you doing here! Your father's home . . .'

'I know,' Madeleine whispered. 'I don't want him to see me until I am standing in front of him. How could he be so wicked as to withhold telling me about my mother, not even how seriously ill she was all that time?'

'I'm sorry, miss . . . Mrs . . . I mean madam . . .' Floundering, she lapsed into silence. Madeleine gave her a stiff smile.

'It's not your fault, Mrs Plumley. Where is he?'

'In the library, miss . . . I mean . . .' Floundering yet again, she gave up but stiffened. 'Please don't go antagonizing him, Miss Madeleine. I shall get in awful trouble for not warning him.'

But Madeleine was already through the door and up the few steps to the hall, making her way to the library, her mind saw-edged.

She found him sitting in his upright leather armchair as she burst in. His startled expression, seeing her there, was almost laughable but instantly changed to one of disbelief. 'What in God's name . . .'

Leaping up, face now livid with rage, his voice sounded strangled. 'How dare you walk into my home? I'll thank you to leave this minute!'

She stood her ground, her own anger dominating her. 'I'm not leaving until—'

'I've nothing to say to you,' he cut in, but she in her turn cut him short.

'But I've plenty to say to you. I can't believe anyone could be so heartless as to prevent their daughter knowing her own mother had passed away. It was evil and you are an evil man and I shall never forgive you. Never!'

'What you choose to do is no concern of mine,' he said slowly. Having regained control of himself, he was speaking now in level terms in the face of her rage, but Madeleine was trembling with anger and hatred.

'I never once imagined it would,' she raged. 'Nor do I care if I never set eyes on you again. I just pray you die as my poor mother did and take a long time doing it. And I'll be happy never to see you again. One thing I want you to know – I don't care about your loathing of me. I'm happily married now and as far as I'm concerned you can rot away and I for one will as they say, dance on your grave.'

Her father remained calm before the torrent, lips curling in a sneer. 'Happily married?' he echoed. 'An elderly, wealthy man, I hear. Turned gold-digger, eh? No more than I would have expected of such as you.'

'I don't care what you expect!' she screamed at him. 'I came here to confront you for not letting me know how ill my mother was. Then not to tell me of her death . . . you disgust me, you and your righteous attitudes!'

Her raised voice filling the house, she could imagine the staff having no need to strain their ears as she raged and she knew that she was losing the battle; had in fact already lost it and had only been in this house a few minutes.

'As far as I'm concerned,' she ended lamely, hating her tone of defeat, 'You're not my father any more and to me you're already dead.'

'I'm not interested in your concern,' he replied, his voice low and controlled. 'Now you have said your piece, I will thank you to leave my home as I have already requested you do. Mrs Plumley will see you out and off the premises.'

With that he turned his back on her and sat back down in his hard leather armchair, taking up a book that lay on the small table beside him, its pages open to where he had been reading before she had burst in, his other hand retrieving the tumbler of whisky that had lain beside that. Ignored now as he bent his head to his book, she found herself dry of words.

All she could do was back out of the room but she managed to slam the library door as loudly as she could, hoping it might make him jump and spill his whisky. Although she would never know, there was some satisfaction in hoping.

Nevertheless she felt diminished, defeated, as she made her way back to the kitchen. How would Mrs Plumley receive her now? Her face turned away from her as she concentrated on her cooking?

Instead the woman was looking at her as she entered. 'Would you like a quick cup of tea before you go as it's a long way back to London, miss?' she asked, apparently having given up on trying to address her as madam, settling on her more familiar 'miss'. 'I'm so sorry things have turned out here for you the way they have, miss.'

She seemed so genuinely sympathetic and on her side that Madeleine felt that here was at least one ally, although what good it would ever do her she couldn't think.

'Why do you still work for him?' she asked.

'He pays me wages,' was the simple reply. 'What about that cup of tea, miss? The master won't be out of his study for ages, not until lunch now.'

'That's kind of you, Mrs Plumley, but no thank you.' Somehow the idea of drinking tea in this house, even hastily, felt abhorrent. 'I need to be on my way. I need to get home well before dinner.'

'Very well, miss. But you take care now. Nice to know you're settled and married . . . I heard it being said. Hope you have a nice life if I don't ever see you again.'

'Thank you,' Madeleine said as she turned towards the outer door.

'You're very welcome, miss, I'm sure.' The kindly words followed her, stayed with her as she made her way to the taxicab whose driver had been paid to await her return, as she knew her stay in that house would be brief. In fact it had been much shorter than she'd anticipated, even less fulfilling.

Rather than her visit being a triumph, the whole escapade, which is what it had turned out to be, had achieved nothing, leaving her wondering why she had even bothered. In the back of the taxi, her disillusionment concealed from the driver by the fashionable broad-brimmed hat she wore, she tried to ignore a heavy sense of defeat deep in her stomach that it hadn't been she who had triumphed but her father, she being made to feel a fool.

It nagged at her the whole journey back to London, though glad to have a first-class carriage to herself affording her privacy to nurse her dejection without being observed.

Arriving home earlier than she had expected to, she prayed not to meet James as Merton opened the door to her. All she wanted was to hurry on upstairs to the privacy of her room and indulge in a few moments of quiet misery. But it wasn't to be.

James came out of his study as she entered the hall, saw her, and called out, 'Ah, there you are! Had a pleasant day with your friend have you, my dear?'

His tone was soft yet to her mind held a note almost of accusation, making her respond far too quickly. 'Yes, very nice thank you.'

There was a pause. Then he said as Merton went discreetly off down the hall, 'Strange, my dear, your friend Mrs Margaret Dowling whom you said you were seeing today telephoned three hours after you left – by which time you should have been with her – to invite you there this Wednesday.'

For a second she froze. Next minute she'd thrown herself into his arms, sobbing fit to burst. 'Oh, James, I'm sorry. I lied to you. I didn't go to see her. I went to confront my father for withholding the death of my mother from me. I needed so much to have it out with him.'

He held her away from him at arm's length to gaze gently into her tear-stained face, his expression sad, stemming her weeping for a moment.

'And did you?' he asked quietly.

Her response was a fresh outburst of tears and again he held her to him. 'There, my dear, you mustn't cry. I know you've been harbouring a great deal of bitterness but it doesn't do. You only destroy yourself.'

'That's why I had to go and face him with it.'

'It doesn't appear to have made you feel any the better, my dear.'

'It hasn't,' she sobbed, glad her lie had been discovered, leaving her free of its burden.

At that moment, with his arms tightly and comfortingly about her, she so wanted to love him, hating herself that she couldn't, not in the way a girl of twenty-one needed to love. He was the kindest man anyone could ever wish for, a tribute completely at odds with his profession as a stockbroker. She couldn't imagine a man in that profession being easy-going in his business, yet with her he was always kind and sweet and thoughtful.

And yet, as he held her to him, murmuring words of comfort to her, sounding so sincere, there came thoughts of his gentle yet stubborn refusal to bow to this longing of hers to trace the baby taken from her. What was it they said – an iron fist in a velvet glove? Maybe that described it. Soft spoken yet hard-headed, biding his time until finally frustrated, she gave up. It was quite possible.

Allowing herself to continue being held close, she saw him for a second or two in a different light, and moments later found herself shaking off these uncomfortable thoughts, almost telling herself that she understood. No man approaching sixty would want to find himself saddled with a baby. There came another thought that hadn't occurred to her before: the baby taken from her all that time ago would now be older. Why hadn't that struck her until now? Yet her mind still saw a tiny scrap wrapped in its shawl, a tiny face gazing up at her, the warm baby smell wafting up to her. She felt the faint impression of tiny limbs against her body, and her senses cried out afresh for the baby they had taken from her.

'I'm so miserable,' she whispered against James's shoulder. 'I'm so terribly unhappy.'

'He is not worth it, my dear,' he murmured into her hair, missing the source of her true unhappiness utterly.

Twelve

There were times when Madeleine wondered if she would ever recover from that traumatic encounter with her father.

Hardly more than a few minutes with him but seven months later those few minutes felt like a lifetime. If only she hadn't lost her temper, screeching at him like a child in a tantrum. He, on the other hand, after his initial shock at seeing her, had remained perfectly composed, until silenced into defeat she had finally fled, still in a rage with nothing achieved, such was her father's ruthless command over others. She should have known the power of his will from past experience.

But she too was strong-willed. She would put the memory behind her, centre her thoughts instead on throwing a splendid party for Christmas Eve, less than six weeks away, as well as for New Year's Eve. It would help her regain her self-esteem, show that she could be the perfect hostess, in full control of whatever situation might pop up. She had already begun to send out invitations and had already received a good few acceptances.

The first-floor rooms, reached by a beautifully carpeted staircase could accommodate fifty people with ease as she had discovered from last year's festive gathering. It had been her first attempt at organizing such a party and she had been nervous then.

James hadn't been at all keen on the idea. 'Do you think it right,' he'd said, 'throwing such a grand function when we're still at war?'

'It's just what we should be doing,' she'd told him, 'keeping up morale. This war has been going on for three years now and everyone said it would be over in a few months. How much longer? We hear so much bad news from the front, people need cheering up. A party would help do that.'

It had all gone splendidly although he had stayed in the

background most of the time. She wondered if he'd do the same this year.

She'd discovered during their first few months of marriage that James preferred to spend the festive season quietly with his widowed sister-in-law Mabel at her home in South Kensington together with her older sister and brother-in-law.

At the time not knowing enough people to organize a party, she hadn't enjoyed spending that first Christmas Day and New Year's Eve with virtual strangers. They'd been nice enough, but like James, rather quiet and withdrawn. Had it not been for his nephew, Anthony, who'd managed to get leave to be with his mother that Christmas, she'd have felt rather like a fish out of water.

His lively chat had been an immensely welcome deliverance from the dull conversation that had promised to endure the entire day. Yet she found he could become serious, even intense at times when discussing politics or the war's progress, still going on more than a year after everyone had said it would be over in a few months.

'I've a feeling it'll be carrying on for several more years yet,' he'd said, his handsome face deadly serious for once, 'certainly far longer than a lot of people expected.'

'What makes you think that?' she'd asked as everyone else adopted half concealed expressions of mild exasperation at his outspoken opinion.

'Stalemate,' he'd continued. 'Dug in as they are which side's going to give way? The whole thing's bogged down in mud and as for this ridiculous business of sending men over the top, mostly at a walking pace, to be mown down in their thousands, like cattle to the slaughterhouse, as far as I can see the big brass are living in the past, trying to conduct a war the way they did back in the last century. It's a wonder they don't stick our lads in scarlet uniforms so they can stand out even more for Jerry to shoot at. It's more like a bloody shooting gallery!'

'Anthony!' his mother had cried out. 'Please, my dear! Please try not to swear in company.'

Madeleine could still remember his response which had

been to give her a cryptic, sideways glance, together with a crooked grin and a brief wink that had had the effect of making her feel as if she was being treated as his confidante. That and the pleasing timbre of his tone had raised her heartbeat so much so that for months afterwards she'd find herself thinking of him, recalling his voice in her head. She would find herself imagining what it might be like to be married to him, be kissed and caressed by him and hear words of love as he lay beside her.

In fact it was what was missing in her own marriage. She and James had slept together only on their honeymoon and for all that had happened there might as well have been a bolster between them down the centre of the bed, he kissing her lightly on the forehead before turning over to sleep, in the morning enquiring if she had slept well – like some fond, elderly father.

Not that she wanted physical love from him. She was fond of James, she told herself, but not that way. Back home, to her relief, it was arranged each to have their own bedrooms, she with her own little sitting room next to hers while he had his library just along the hallway. As he had said, their marriage was purely one of companionship. They ate together, would relax compatibly together in the morning room or of an evening in the drawing room before retiring to their separate rooms for the night, went to the theatre together, met friends, attended meetings together, and this way they got on very well.

But sometimes she would find herself longing to have been married to someone younger; someone like Anthony. At times she was even aware of being glad he was still single. Were he married she might not experience this ridiculous racing of her pulse every time his name cropped up, though why being married should make a difference it was hard to say.

The simple answer came that he would no longer be free for her to daydream about him. Yet were he to marry she'd be devastated. If only she had known him before having met James, she might have ended up with him instead and would have been happy in a normal marriage rather than what she now had. Then common sense would prevail, telling her that had she not met James she would not have known Anthony anyway and she would be angry at herself for these silly dreams of hers.

Even so she found herself jumping each time the post arrived, hoping it might contain a letter from him. Merton would bring it in on a silver tray as they sat at breakfast or at lunch. James would scan each envelope before slitting it open. Now and again they were from friends or his younger brother and he would read them out aloud to her. More often they were business letters or letters from colleagues or his bank or an invitation to a business meeting. But she'd watch hopefully, all the time her heart beating rapidly, only to feel it drop like a dead weight as he lay each to one side.

The few times Anthony had written, hardly more than a couple this year, each letter contained little more than a few scribbled lines to say he was still safe and well while describing life on the Western Front merely as being pretty awful at times. James would read them aloud to her but there was never any mention of her.

The last one had been some time ago, in October. Since then there had been her Christmas Eve party and the one seeing out nineteen seventeen in a fervent hope that nineteen eighteen might eventually see better news. She had finally heeded James's advice to tone down her parties out of respect for a general bleakness at the continuing stalemate along the entire Western Front coupled with news of the Italian army's collapse before a fierce German onslaught. The only news to lighten the heart had been the Canadians recapturing Passchendaele in November and a hope that America having entered the war last April might help even the odds eventually.

Anthony's last letter to his mother had been three months ago and she had become worried sick by it. This morning she arrived out of the blue, to be announced into the morning room and startling Madeleine and James who were taking their ease over a cup of after-breakfast tea.

Her narrow features were drawn and wan. 'I'm so worried. I can't help it,' she mewed yet again in her wavering voice as she gazed into the blazing fire that had been stoked up against the January chill.

The tea Madeleine had poured for her from a fresh pot their maid had brought in over ten minutes ago still lay untouched and was now lukewarm. She looked old. She'd always looked older than her brother-in-law despite being a few years younger, her sallow skin far more lined than his somewhat smooth skin, but this morning she looked positively haggard.

'If anything has happened to him, I would have received a telegram by now wouldn't I?' she asked pitifully.

'My dear Mabel, of course you would,' James told her sternly, looking vaguely uncomfortable as he leaned forward in his armchair. 'You must try not to worry. So long as there's been no telegram, nothing official, no dire news telling you . . . well, you know what . . . you have to believe he is fine, merely not at liberty to write at the moment, far too much going on over there. You must have a little faith, my dear.'

It was obviously no comfort to her nor did it help Madeleine's own fears for his safety. She had to admit that to some extent her own concern for him had taken her mind off that still lingering memory of her traumatic meeting with her father and for that she felt, maybe selfishly, almost grateful.

Even so it was with profound relief two weeks later that Mabel came to say she'd at last received a letter from Anthony saying he was OK but had sustained a shrapnel wound in the soft tissue of the upper part of his right arm; nothing serious, but he had landed up in a field hospital to have the shrapnel removed and had been unable to use the arm for a while. He'd not had the heart to ask any of the overworked nurses dealing with so many terribly injured men to write a letter for him.

His letters were arriving again if infrequently and few and far between. Then around late April they again ceased. News from the Western Front was as depressing as ever, terrifying at times. Madeleine found herself praying almost desperately for his safety, often conscious of tears of premature grief filling her eyes should she let herself imagine something awful happening to him. It felt almost as if she was becoming part of him; far more than was healthy for a woman married to someone else.

She was keeping in as close a contact with his mother as she dared without appearing as if she were harassing her for news of him. She would call on her, usually to take afternoon tea with her hoping she would feel glad to have someone visiting, but she knew that sooner or later she could be in danger of becoming less welcome by visiting too often.

'What do you think must be preventing him writing?' she queried of her as casually as she could while they sat drinking tea, these days without the accompaniment of rich cake.

'I'm sure I don't know!' bleated Mabel, the reply sounding a little testy to Madeleine's ears. 'I daren't think. Maybe it's that he is being troubled by that injured arm of his again.'

'Maybe,' Madeleine agreed, quickly changing the conversation to more trivial matters. But her heart ached with thinking about his safety as Mabel rang the bell for the tea things to be taken away.

In May, with the war well into its fourth year and still grinding on, she had finally yielded to James's requests to curb her extensive social entertaining because there was little to warrant any such indulgence with no promise of peace on the horizon. But she did vow to give the biggest party ever seen the moment the war was over, although that prospect looked as distressingly bleak as ever, kiddies growing up having never known what it was like with this ever deepening food rationing to see a well-laden table. The thought of children inevitably reminded her of her own baby. Where was she? Was she going hungry, those who'd adopted her, uncaring as to how she fared so long as they ate?

As always, she forced herself to shut out that vision knowing it would only start her off condemning James yet again over his obvious reluctance to trace the child for her. She'd tell herself time and time again that she could understand his reluctance – his age, not his child, born out of wedlock – and tried not to think ill of him.

James was not a selfish man. He saw to it that she had everything she wanted except that one thing she had hoped for which was the reason why she had consented to marry him. She would often hate herself for having done so and would find herself thinking, quite irrationally, that had she been married to Anthony, he'd have moved heaven and earth to get the child back.

But it didn't do to think of him too much. It only brought heartache visualizing him somewhere in the trenches facing enemy fire day after day. Other than the wound he'd referred to so lightly, there'd been no notification that he'd been wounded again, or worse – yet for how much longer? A batch of letters from him in June, coming all at once, brought blessed relief, before ceasing yet again. This time Madeleine compelled herself to stop worrying so much, though it was a miracle any man could live through the relentless slaughter going on over there.

A few weeks later that thought seemed to her to have been the parent of a premonition or even an actual courting of disaster as Mabel, assisted by her maid, collapsed weeping into her brother-in-law's arms. All Madeleine could do was look on helplessly, hardly able to breathe, as Mabel's words came tumbling out.

'They've told me my Anthony's missing. They say they've no details. Oh, James, I don't know what to do. What do I do?'

Gently holding her to him, James eased her into an armchair where she promptly sank back as if she were an empty sack and broke out into a fresh smother of tears, her hands covering her face.

He stood up to look bleakly towards Madeleine who could only turn away to hide her own tears. She heard him address Mabel's maid.

'Alice, go down to the kitchen, ask Cook to make some strong tea. And Merton, would you pour us all a stiff whisky for the time being.'

He turned to his sister-in-law, pulling a chair up to sit beside her. 'Did they tell you anything else?'

'Nothing,' was the muffled reply, 'except their deep regrets in having to convey distressing news . . . Distressing! That's all they care! They've no idea how a mother feels to . . . to . . .'

Sobs engulfed the rest of her words and James having moved back from her to listen, now leaned nearer to her again.

'They must have given you more details than that. Surely someone must have witnessed something, seen what happened. He couldn't have been completely alone.'

'They said he was seen going somewhere in the back of a truck but there was a mustard gas attack and no one saw him again. Anything could have happened. I don't know what to do, who to ask.'

Once more James gathered her to him as she broke down again in a limp heap, leaning forward almost on the point of falling out of the armchair.

Madeleine stayed where she was, herself in need of someone's arms about her. She wanted to run to James, have him hold her close, but all she could do was to stand there watching him soothe his sister-in-law as though she was more important to him than his own wife.

If only he would look across to her, call to her, 'come over here, my dear,' and as she came, hold her tightly as well. If she had broken down, wailing like Mabel, he might have noticed her. But all she could do was to stand there, feeling empty and alone and crying silently inside.

Thirteen

Over the next few weeks, news of those over there being pushed back and back; Amiens destroyed, Germans taking Soissons, and Rheims threatened, thousands killed by mustard gas leaving countless families weeping for the loss of loved ones. Madeleine was conscious only of her own heartache.

She had no right to be. Anthony wasn't hers. But even as she prayed for his mother, she prayed for her own relief that somewhere he was alive, even a prisoner of war – anything but dead.

James looked on her sadness as wholesome and purely sympathetic towards his sister-in-law's distress.

'She lost her poor husband, my brother. Were she to lose her only child as well . . .' He let the rest die away, too dreadful to give voice to.

Madeleine said nothing.

Then in September came tremendously heartening news for the whole nation. Under the combined weight of the Canadians, French, American and British, the enemy was at last beginning to be steadily pushed back. The population suddenly perked up, hungrily scanned the newspapers for ever more heartening news as avidly as a sport enthusiast might follow his favourite cricket or football team. Yet still no news of Anthony.

Useless, telling herself not to fret but sometimes she'd break down and weep silently in the privacy of her little sitting room, delaying coming downstairs too soon in case James noticed her bloodshot eyes and asked awkward questions. He was obviously as worried as she, but in a different way of course. He never spoke about it for which she was grateful. They went about their normal routine: he to his brokering business in the City most days, she to visit friends or attend one or two of the women's meetings she'd joined over the years. Madeleine and James still went to the theatre or out to dinner with friends, though with the worsening food shortage some meals were served without meat even in the best of restaurants.

These past few weeks James had taken to occasionally attending a Sunday morning church service, no doubt to pray for his nephew's safe return. Otherwise they seemed to be merely marking time until news – any news – of Anthony came.

On one occasion she persuaded James to take her to a picture palace, a pastime he found no interest in, to see a much lauded, spectacular motion picture, *Intolerance* which everyone here and in America was raving about. She had been overwhelmed by the grandeur of it but he hadn't enjoyed it.

'What pleasure is there,' he'd said testily when they'd left, 'in a story being continually interrupted so the audience can read what the actors are saying? And the noise, people constantly talking all round us.'

But he had enjoyed the antics of Charlie Chaplin on the one other occasion he'd taken her – just to please her – admitting that it had been very entertaining. But she had been upset by the accompanying picture; an actor named Carlyle Blackwell had taken her by surprise, to her mind he had borne such a resemblance to Anthony that her heart seemed to collapse. All she could see was him, the thought of him no longer being in this world. She'd felt tears trickling down her cheeks, frightened James might notice, thankful that the film being a poignant one, she could used it as an excuse.

It took weeks for the feeling of heartache to fade, yet whenever she thought of it, the face of the film actor, not that of Anthony, hovered in her mind, the two becoming confused though the ache in her heart hadn't changed. She realized then that Anthony's features were beginning to blur but all that did was to intensify her personal grief even more.

This morning came a frantic ringing of the doorbell, the sound of a woman's cries as their housemaid answered it. Seconds later Mabel burst in through the door to the morning room where Madeleine and James now stood, having leapt up at the sound of her frantic calling.

Seeing her standing there, face streaked with tears, her driver having followed her in and now trying gently to stop her from collapsing altogether, Madeleine knew the worst had happened, fought to stem her own immediate grief, her knees feeling weak.

James hurried forward, drawing his sister-in-law from the chauffeur's hold, exclaiming, 'My dear Mabel, what is it?' although surely he must have guessed, came the silent, bitter reprimand in Madeleine's head.

'It's Anthony! My dear, dear Anthony!' She was babbling, her words hardly intelligible. 'He was found . . . Oh, my God, James, they found him!'

The words struck Madeleine's half-paralysed mind with a terrifying image. Dead – buried by mud in some shell hole? What sort of state would a body be in after being so long buried in mud?

Mabel was still babbling on, her words disjointed: '. . . wounded they said, taken prisoner . . . not knowing who he was. His identification thing, missing . . . his uniform jacket . . .'

Madeleine's legs began to give way beneath her. Wounded! How bad? Limbs lost? She sank to her knees as if in prayer but no one noticed. James had his attention on helping his sister-in-law to a chair, Mabel's driver trying to assist, the maid standing as if paralysed by the door staring at the trio.

James was saying, 'My dear, wonderful news! I'm so happy for you, so relieved. We all are. Have they told you any more? Are they sending him home? But it's absolutely wonderful news, Madeleine, don't you think?'

Already back on her on her feet as he looked towards her for her response, Madeleine realized he had not even noticed her partial collapse. She smiled, her eyes still filled with tears but that was to be expected.

'Absolutely wonderful,' she managed to echo.

What she wanted was to run to her bedroom, throw herself on her bed and cry her heart out in gratitude. Instead she just gazed at her sister-in-law still weeping with relief. No one must ever guess how deep was her own relief.

Anthony was home 'to convalesce' they were told, pointing to the fact that as soon as he was well enough he'd be sent back; this time maybe never to return. Madeleine wondered which was worse, her earlier fear of his having been killed or that he might yet be. What did they care, so long as even one could be returned to the front line in a bid to defeat the enemy?

He looked thin. He'd always been lean but was now even leaner, withdrawn, remote. She and James went frequently to see him, she for her part needing to see him as often as she could while she could.

'He needs to see as much of his family as he can while he's still at home,' she told him when he expressed the opinion that his nephew might not want them popping in and out so much.

'He needs to spend his time quietly, with his mother,' James said. But she'd had a ready reply.

'Seeing others might help him to stop thinking about what he's been through,' she argued, relieved as James conceded that she might be right.

It was hard to talk to him. His old vivacity had gone. He spoke very little of his experience, saying he hadn't known much about it other than a vague memory of being flung from a truck by an explosion and coming to in a makeshift hospital, his leg in a splint.

Any more than that he wouldn't say and they tactfully didn't push him. He did mention being treated well enough in the German field hospital before finding himself suddenly freed, their front line overrun, the Germans falling back and not prepared to take wounded POWs with them. Dumped along with the rest, the Germans taking only their own wounded, they were left to themselves under a few shreds of canvas in pouring rain. Two days later the Americans came and within days he was being sent home to England.

'So here I am, back safe and sound,' he ended lightly with a faint trace of his old self, though to Madeleine it sounded slightly forced.

She wanted to go and fold her arms around him, hold him close to her, but of course she couldn't. As he sat in his chair, his-half healed leg still in plaster stuck out in front of him, one hand on the stick he still needed to use, he hardly ever seemed to look at her. But his gaze was usually trained on the floor anyway as if to avoid having to look directly at anyone.

She just hoped this evasion of eye contact wouldn't last too long. It wasn't like him, not as she first recalled him. Nor did it last, although she felt the meeting of eyes was being achieved with an enormous effort.

Over the next ten days in his mother's loving care and the healing comfort of home he did in fact begin to perk up faster than she'd anticipated, so that by the end of that second week he was virtually back to his old self. If anything, so it seemed to her, far livelier than before he'd been sent away, yet it made her feel that much of it was being put on. How did he really feel inside?

The next few days, with James at his office, she took to visiting on her own, sitting talking to him and his mother for an hour or two before saying goodbye and returning home. She said nothing of it to James and he was too busy to ask how her day had gone, usually going upstairs to do a little more work in his office at home. By the time he joined her for their evening meal it had slipped his mind to ask. If he had, she would probably have told him the truth, recalling the time she'd lied when she'd gone to seek out her father.

Even so, when she and James went on the Sunday, her insides had clenched up the whole afternoon lest Anthony or his mother happened to refer to her solitary visits. But Anthony seemed to have drawn into himself again, his mother more interested in the progress of the war with its ever more heartening news coming daily from the Western Front, increasing hopes of it being over within months. Her worry of course was her Anthony being sent back when he recovered enough.

'Next time it could be for good,' she said now, tears beginning to flood her eyes as she looked towards him in her misery. 'Next time he may never come back to us.'

It lay heavy on all their hearts even though he chided her in that newly acquired light but cynical, mirthless tone of his.

'For God's sake, mother! We've got Fritz on the run. In a month or two he'll be sneaking back to the fatherland, tail between his legs. So what's the point sending me back out there? Or is that what you want so you can tear your clothes in grief and have another bloody good lament?'

For reply, Mabel leapt up and fled the room, wailing that he was being deliberately cruel to her just to make himself feel better.

Madeleine ran after her, found her in the hall, and put her arms about her. 'He didn't mean it,' she soothed, as Mabel sobbed on her shoulder. 'It isn't only his leg that was wounded. It'll probably take a long time for him to forget what he has been through – a long time for many of them I should imagine – if ever. You must forgive him – try not to take to heart the things he says. He doesn't mean them.'

He must have made quite a few insensitive remarks when they'd not been there and her heart went out more to him than his mother even though she was obliged to stifle the hurt in her breast when he made remarks like that. For in all truth it was the one who found the need to resort to such uncharacteristic remarks who suffered most, deep inside, unable to escape the visions that haunted them.

She said as much as she helped his mother dry her tears and led her gently back into the room – and it seemed to do some good. Even so, she was almost glad to get away, for the first time feeling ill at ease in his company.

'I think we may be outstaying our welcome,' James said as they came away. 'Best to leave him to his mother next weekend, don't you think, my dear.'

She voiced her agreement but resolved to keep visiting on her own during the week. Anthony seemed a different person when she visited alone, almost like his old cheerful self, at least on the surface. It was Thursday, her third visit this week. Today, ignoring the leaden November skies, she found him even more cheery and talkative than she had dared hope.

'You know, Maddie, I look forward so much to your visiting,' he said as his mother left the room to have a word with their cook, his openness taking her by surprise.

'Without you coming here to see me, I honestly don't know what I'd do cooped up all day looking out at that bloody miserable November weather and having to listen to Mother constantly lamenting. Promise me, Maddie, you won't stop coming?'

'Of course I promise,' she said with all her heart.

Having him shorten her name sent a thrill surging through her. But it was the slow, quiet, almost deliberate way he had said it that increased the feeling even more though she merely smiled, lightly adding, 'And I enjoy coming here too. I really do.'

To which he had given a slow smile, one she was at a loss to interpret, leaving her wondering as his mother returned, what else he might have said had they been left alone for any further length of time.

The following afternoon, she wasn't sure why, but after giving Mabel the usual peck on the cheek as she made to leave, she went over to him still seated in the armchair and, bending, planted a swift kiss on his cheek as well.

He looked up at her, a mischievous twinkle in his eyes, something she hadn't seen since his homecoming. 'Now then,' he quipped lightly, 'what's all this sudden flirting?'

But his hand had caught her arm and just for a moment the grip tightened, delaying her from drawing back.

She gave a stupid giggle, instantly annoyed at hearing herself, and pulling her arm away, quickly moved back. But even as she did she saw what seemed to her like a message in his gaze that to her mind betrayed much more than mere banter. Confused she drew away.

'I'd best be off,' she said unnecessarily, gathering up her gloves and following Mabel out of the room. As she looked back she saw his gaze was following her and she knew her own had responded with a lingering look.

In the hall, as Mabel's maid held her coat for her to ease into, her mind still pondered his last look.

Quickly she donned her hat, staring at her reflection in

the hall mirror. It looked strained. Suddenly she drew in a sharp breath. 'My handbag, I forgot it! I left it by the chair where I was sitting.'

Without waiting for the maid to offer to get it for her, she hurried back leaving Mabel and the maid standing in the hall.

'I forgot my handbag,' she said to Anthony who looked startled at her sudden return.

He watched her as she retrieved the bag, then said softly. 'Come here a minute, Maddie.'

Not knowing why, she went over to him. She felt him take her arm; pull her gently down towards him. She let herself slip on to her knees without effort, his arms closing around her, lips closing on hers. Savouring the touch of those warm lips she was lost to the world, but only momentarily as sudden fear gripped her at the thought of his mother coming into the room wondering why she was taking so long and catching the two of them. What if she told James? She pulled away sharply.

'I have to go!' she heard herself gasp.

As she came upright, her face burning, her hand still gripping her handbag in a most ridiculous manner, she expected to see an amused look in his eyes. Instead, there was such a depth to his gaze that she drew in a sharp breath, instantly interpreting its message.

'No, Anthony! We mustn't! I'm married,' she gasped.

'Maddie.' It was all he said, his tone imploring.

She was about to enforce those last words of hers when his mother's voice sounded from the hall, growing louder as she approached.

'Are you all right, Madeleine? Haven't you been able to find your handbag?'

Madeleine sprang away from him as if shot from a cannon. 'I'm . . . Yes . . . it's all right. I've found it.'

Leaping across to where her handbag had previously been found by an armchair, she was just in time to seem to grab it up as Mabel came into the room.

'I was looking in the wrong place,' she said quickly, knowing that she was breathing fast, her face flushed.

She glanced hastily towards Anthony. He was reclining in his chair as if completely at ease, his eyes closed as though wearied by her visit, but she knew instinctively that every muscle was taut.

'I did wonder if you were having trouble finding it,' Mabel was saying in an easy tone as she led her from the room.

'It wasn't by the place where I was sitting,' Madeleine managed to reply by way of explanation as she followed Mabel to the front door which the maid was now holding open for her.

Having kissed Mabel goodbye, she was glad to be outside, her nerves still all a-jangle by what had happened, grateful for a chance to calm herself during the short walk to the end of the road where she could hail a taxicab.

Anthony loved her. He'd not said as much but she knew from the tension she had seen in him as he lay back in his chair. He was in love with her. And she with him, but being in love was now coupled with a craven fear of being so, not daring to look into the future with its lies and hurt and misery. And there was nothing she could do and that in itself was fear enough.

Fourteen

The war was over. Most chose to ignore that it hadn't been so much won as hostilities brought to an end by a signed armistice. It was good enough to know that the fighting and the dying were finally over.

'God knows why celebrations were delayed until today,' Madeleine said as she and James made their way through the prancing crowds to his sister-in-law's house. Though Big Ben had struck one o'clock to announce the official start to the celebrations, flags of all the Allied nations had been flying from every building and crowds thronging the streets all morning.

'They're naming it Victory Day even though the armistice was signed on the eleventh, five days ago on Monday.'

'I suppose they had to be sure, make it official,' James said, his eyes taking in the antics of the crowds beyond the motor car window.

They drove along at a snail's pace to safely negotiate the groups of revellers too happy to pay heed to pavement, kerb or road as they danced and hugged and sang, waving flags and kissing everyone whether they were friends or strangers.

'After all,' he went on, still watching the crowds, 'I suppose it does seem an odd way to end after four years of slaughtering each other, neither side having won outright – just a piece of paper signed by a civilian and a couple of minor army officers with a white flag. It could be that's why it's taken five days to really be sure. Maybe the stock market will start to pick up now,' he finished hopefully. 'It's been a difficult four years.'

She wasn't interested in stock markets. 'I wonder how Anthony is, knowing it's over and that he won't be sent back?' she said, only half her mind on what James had been saying.

'Damned relieved I shouldn't wonder,' James said, continuing to gaze through the window, 'like those out there.'

Madeleine leaned back in her seat. She wasn't interested in those out there. She was thinking more of that last meeting with Anthony eight days ago. She'd not had the courage to go near his home since then. Even now she could still feel his lips on hers.

How she'd got through this week, she didn't know, her mind removed from all else as she relived that previous Friday over and over again. Even on Monday as people began to pour on to the streets at the news of the armistice having been signed that very day, it hadn't touched her other than to breathe a thankful prayer that Anthony would no longer be in danger of a return to the front to fight and probably to die.

James had been in his office at the time. He had telephoned through to her even as she sat at her window watching the growing crowds. She hadn't gone out to join them, mostly thinking of those who must have been sitting behind their own curtained windows mourning their lost ones, some perhaps in the very last days of war.

Her first desire had been to run to Anthony's side, but that had been impossible with James on his way home. Nor indeed could she have brought herself to do it with the memory of that kiss still so strong in her mind.

On the phone James had said, 'I'm coming home, my dear. I do not want you to be on your own on this great day.'

All she had said, her mind miles away, was, 'Thank you, James.'

He was a kind man, thought of her every comfort, did all he could to make her happy, bought her whatever she asked for, totally unaware that the one thing she was most thankful for was that he had never attempted to consummate their marriage. She didn't think she could have taken that.

She was aware that he saw her as a companion who had helped fill a void left by the death of his wife, whom he never referred to or mentioned by name. She knew too that he was deeply grateful to her for – as he'd once put it – '*so generously accepting my offer of marriage as a good friend.*'

Yet despite his kindness and his concern for her happiness he would not agree to her request to search for the baby taken from her. Although after all this time it could prove futile and the memory ceased to bite as much as it once did, it still lay there in the background . . . and she yearned for his consent to at least try.

This had been the main reason why she had married him, that his money might help find her daughter, yet it was the one thing he had never granted, almost wilfully it seemed to her at times. In every other way he was so generous and understanding and kind that she'd become almost reluctant to push him any further on the matter.

Now that lurking wish was raising its head again. Her thoughts returned with a rush to Anthony. It could happen that in the not too distant future she could find herself widowed. James wasn't getting any younger and who knows, maybe sooner rather than later she and Anthony would be together, legally married, he young enough to accept a ready-made family and happy to help trace her baby. But not just that, she loved him. But what if James went on into his seventies? To find out about her and his own nephew would break his heart, his world would crumble; of that she was sure. How could she do that to him?

He must never know. But where did that leave her and Anthony? All these thoughts crowded her mind enough to make her head spin as they drove almost at a snail's pace through the singing, dancing, laughing throng.

Anthony was standing at the window, leaning on his stick as he gazed out at the celebrations; they were, perhaps, somewhat less exuberant here, a little more sedate. He turned from the scene as Madeleine and James came into the room accompanied by his mother.

'Looks like everyone's enjoying themselves out there,' he said without a smile or one word of welcome, almost as if they'd been there for hours.

'Yes, it certainly does,' James returned cheerily, seeming to be quite comfortable with such a reception. 'And how are you?'

'Fine.'

He'd still not smiled and Madeleine realized that he was continuing to gaze at her, his eyes fixed on her face, and immediately she felt her heart turn over. She looked away quickly, fearing her face might betray something she didn't wish James to see. But he probably wouldn't have noticed, utterly innocent of how she felt.

'Well,' cut in his mother. 'That is a fine greeting, I must say, dear, after your uncle has taken the trouble to come and see how you are on such an occasion as this. The least you could say is "hello".'

'Hello,' he repeated, parrot fashion, his tone mocking.

Mabel gave an impatient click of the tongue, saying, 'I'll ring for tea,' and turning to her guests, added, 'I expect you both would like a cup of tea, wouldn't you, dears?'

Madeleine found her voice. 'That would be nice, thank you.'

She could still feel Anthony's eyes trained upon her even though she refused to meet them.

Then suddenly he said, 'Well, sit down, Uncle James, Aunt Madeleine. Make yourselves comfortable. It's so nice of you to come. I very much appreciate it, after you've been pushing through hordes of people.'

Addressed as Aunt, almost deliberately it seemed, made her squirm but she betrayed nothing. Was he being sarcastic or was it for his uncle's sake, or maybe he was trying to convey to her some second thought over what had transpired between them the last time they'd met.

Moving away from the window, he returned to his own seat, Madeleine looking from beneath her brow noticed that he no longer needed to use his stick for support, merely holding it clear of the floor; that beyond a hardly discernible limp he seemed perfectly fine. James had noticed it too.

'I see you've got rid of the plaster,' he remarked.

'Yesterday,' Anthony said. 'Almost back to normal and just in time to savour the peace, long may it last!'

He spoke brightly, yet Madeleine felt she could detect a trace of strain in his tone. She wished he would cease throwing glances at her, too many for comfort. Evading them made it seem all the more obvious that something deeper than family friendship existed between them. She lifted her face to him, her expression hopefully betraying nothing.

'You must be so deeply relieved in not having to be sent away over . . . I mean, well, not finding yourself having to be packed off back to France,' she said, stumbling awkwardly over the words and feeling instantly stupid.

He was looking at her, a faint smile now hovering on his lips. Was he mocking her or embracing her? She couldn't tell.

'Yes, very relieved.' He hesitated, then, 'Hopefully I'll be seeing a lot more of you now. You too, Uncle James,' he added almost as an afterthought which to her ears had a far too significant ring to it for her own peace of mind.

But James hadn't seemed to notice, saying easily, 'Yes, of course, as often as we can.'

Mabel had returned followed by her maid carrying tea on a silver tray together with a plate of dainty biscuits. She placed it on the small round table standing between Mabel's armchair and those of the guests and hurried away on being told, 'Thank you, Susan. That will be all.'

They watched as Mabel poured, helping themselves to milk, sugar and biscuits. Beyond the window the continuing celebrations penetrated the quiet room as little more than a low murmur. James was first to break the silence.

'So . . . Anthony, old chap, I expect we'll soon be seeing you dashing around again, no doubt looking to find yourself a nice girl – unless of course you've already found someone.'

His voice was hearty, overloud, almost forced, and Madeleine shot a glance at him with an instant sense of guilt. What did he mean, *found* someone? Had he detected something in that possibly unguarded look which had passed so briefly between her and his nephew just a few moments ago? But Anthony was already answering him, his own tone easy.

'I'm not intending to look, Uncle. If it happens, that's fine, but I'm not ready to deliberately go seeking anyone, that's for certain.'

To her ears it was a foolish thing to say. She cast a surreptitious glance towards her husband but he appeared to be satisfied and muttering an amiable, 'Of course not,' turned to his sister-in-law.

'I'm so happy for you, my dear, having your son home safe – nothing worse than an injured leg, but it's healing well, and not at all impairing his future.'

'You cannot begin to imagine, James, how happy I am for that,' she returned. Her tone was lighter than Madeleine had ever known. She sounded almost a new woman as she added brightly, 'The Dear Lord has answered all my prayers.'

Leaning forward he patted her hand reassuringly then turned back to Anthony. 'And you, my boy, will soon be returning to normal life, no doubt settling back into banking, hopefully putting these past four years behind you.'

'I don't know about that,' Anthony said a little brusquely and lapsed into silence.

Again that faintly awkward atmosphere settled over the room. Madeleine and James drained their teacups and returned them to the tray together with their plates, biscuits untouched. Mabel continued taking minuscule sips from her own cup. She did not like steaming hot tea, preferring to drink hers lukewarm. Anthony had also drained his, now leaning over the arm of his chair to put the cup on the floor beside him.

As he did so, he looked towards Madeleine. The movement took her attention and as their glances met and held for a second, a meaningful look passed between them, almost tangible, Madeleine hurriedly looking away as she heard James say with a polite sigh, 'Well, I suppose we'd best be going.'

'You've been here barely half an hour,' Mabel protested. 'We shall be having dinner earlier than usual. Why not stay? We had lunch very early, well before one o'clock chimed the commencement of the official Victory celebrations – we didn't want to be eating then, so dinner will be a little earlier. Do stay.'

But James seemed to have made up his mind, leaving Madeleine to ponder if he'd noticed the look that had passed between her and Anthony, reading something into it.

'We merely came to see how you were on this special day, my dear,' he was saying. 'Make sure you're not feeling down you might say. I'm glad to find you both so cheery but I do have some work I need to finish ready for tomorrow.'

'Well, then if you must,' she said somewhat begrudgingly. 'Though how you can think of working on a day such as this . . .'

'Life goes on,' he cut in with a small laugh. 'Perhaps we can take up your offer, my dear, not tomorrow but Sunday, when I have more time. And now we really must be away,' he added as she nodded her acceptance of the arrangement. 'And I am so glad to find you well, my dear, you too, Anthony.'

Madeleine too wanted to be away. She could feel herself trembling inside from the look that had passed between her and Anthony, such a depth of meaning that if James had been looking in their direction, which she fervently hoped he hadn't, he couldn't have helped but notice.

Without daring to look back at Anthony she quickly followed James out to the hall, his sister-in-law accompanying them, cheerfully bidding them goodbye as they donned their hats and coats and left.

'I thought Anthony looked very well,' James said as they drove off, the crowds still clogging the roads. 'You did too, didn't you, my dear?'

Nerves still raw from the way Anthony had looked at her as he placed his cup down beside him, she felt herself reading more into those last few words than maybe she should have and cringed inwardly but managed to answer in a small voice, 'Yes, dear, I did.'

Left wondering just how much he was aware of the feelings between Anthony and her, she found herself reading all sorts of innuendos into almost everything James said when speaking to her. It made her wish they were not going there on Sunday. She wanted so much to see him, the next day seeming to drag, yet there was fear. He would undoubtedly look at her in the way he'd done yesterday. If their eyes met she was sure she would betray herself. If James didn't know now what was going on, he soon would if this continued.

The best solution would be to cry off going there tomorrow altogether but the thought of not seeing him so tore at her that she found herself counting the hours, willing them to pass, at the same time dreading their passing until she wasn't sure what she wanted, her mind in turmoil.

Being driven through the Sunday streets, the November afternoon dull and overcast with daylight seeming already to be fading to an early evening and everywhere strangely deserted after the jubilations on Friday, she remained quiet, hoping James wouldn't notice the turmoil inside her which she was sure must be showing on her face.

It had been suggested they come to dinner but James having a need to work that evening in readiness for Monday morning, it had been arranged they come to Sunday lunch instead. The nearer they got to Mabel's home the more Madeleine's agitation increased, her mind repeatedly asking what if hers and Anthony's glances met the way they had on Friday? Yet to avoid his gaze altogether, would it not leave him wondering what he'd done to upset her? Over and over she wished with all her heart that she'd concocted an excuse not to go – a headache, over-tiredness, feign the onset of a cold perhaps? Yet she knew she couldn't have kept away.

But it wasn't as she'd expected. He hardly looked at her, his greeting when they arrived almost offhanded, avoiding her eyes as they sat across the table from each other. He hardly spoke the whole time, his mother doing all the talking, a totally different woman to the desperate one of six months back. And as they retired to the sitting room to relax after the meal, he seemed preoccupied, hardly joining in the general conversation and to Madeleine's mind, totally ignoring her.

'James,' Mabel said suddenly, breaking through the conversation the two of them were enjoying while Madeleine also sat quiet and withdrawn, 'before it gets totally dark, there's something I'd like to show you in the garden that my gardener pointed out. I'd like your opinion. It won't take long. I didn't tell you, Anthony dear, but you and Madeleine might like to see it. It's quite unusual and very pretty.'

He hardly glanced up, his reply curt. 'No thanks. I need to take it easy, too much on my feet this morning.'

'Yes of course, dear, as you wish,' his mother said easily, glancing questioningly towards her young sister-in-law.

Madeleine knew she ought to go with them, but heard herself saying, 'I think I'd rather stay here in the warm.'

'Yes, it's a little cold, dear. Stay and keep Anthony company.'

The door closed behind the two older people, with Madeleine already at a loss what to talk to him about, as he was behaving so morosely. He rose from his armchair – someone a moment ago too weary to move – and came towards her.

Hardly knowing why, she also got up, something inside her sensing that she needed to. Next moment she was in his arms, his lips pressing almost savagely on hers. Desperately she returned the kiss, her hand reaching up behind his head the better to keep his lips pressed on hers. His hand was on her breast, she felt its warmth through her blouse and silk jumper, even through the thin material of her fashionably loose bodice. Her head reeling, her insides churning, all she wanted was for him not to stop, to go further, go further.

Suddenly he released her, stepping back although his hand had now taken hold of hers in a tight grip. She half expected him to say sorry. Instead he whispered huskily, 'They'll be back any minute. But I will sort something out, darling.'

Fifteen

They were back in their seats, Madeleine desperately striving to compose herself, when Mabel entered the room, chattering away, closely followed by James. He glanced at Madeleine.

'Just as well you remained here in the warm, my dear. It's very cold out there which is why we came back quicker than expected.' Again a veiled remark or so it seemed. Her guilt screamed at her.

She forced a smile, turning her attention to Mabel. 'What was it you had to show James?'

'A most oddly shaped branch now that most of the leaves have fallen. I never noticed it until it was pointed out to me. Seen from a certain angle, it appears exactly like an owl is staring down at one. It could be quite eerie if one were alone out there in the half light. The sky has cleared and what with the twilight glow, it is quite noticeable. But I have to agree with James, it is so very cold out there. We shall no doubt have a frost by morning.'

While she was chatting away, James nodding in agreement to her words, Madeleine stole a furtive glance at Anthony who returned it with a warning one of his own and a hardly perceptible shake of his head. She looked away just as James turned to her.

'I expect you two have been keeping each other company. Not bored?'

There it was again, an oblique hint letting it be known that he knew more that he was saying.

'You weren't gone long enough for us to get bored,' she managed to reply, wishing her heart would stop its rapid thumping, sure that he could hear it.

Life had become bliss, dangerous but bliss. Two weeks before Christmas, Anthony, or Tony as she now called him when they were alone, had indeed found them somewhere to meet – an inauspicious little hotel a relatively safe distance from his home and a short walk from the small private bank his father had owned, where he'd shortly be taking his father's place now the war was over. It was ideal.

It was now well into February. They'd been meeting here once a week for the last six weeks, yet she still felt that rush of excitement in the pit of her stomach as she approached the hotel's modest entrance. So different to the feeling she'd had that first time.

Then she had slowed her steps as she neared the place, doubts so clogging her insides that she had almost turned back the way she'd come. It had been an effort to approach the small reception desk, sure that the young clerk standing behind it would take her for a street walker and turn her away. But he couldn't have been more polite had she been a titled lady. Even so, having to ask for Tony by name was an effort, somehow strangely unsavoury as though the clerk knew what the two of them were about.

But hardly had Tony's name left her lips when someone had leapt up from a nearby armchair, his voice loud and cheery.

'Maddie! Here at last. What sort of journey was it? Pretty delayed by the sound of it. How is you mother, Aunt Beatrice?'

Madeleine had instantly taken her cue from him, making her own voice as cheery and innocuous as his. 'She's very well and sends her love.'

His arm threaded itself through hers as he led her to the lift without a backward glance at the hotel clerk. Yanking aside the gate, he had stepped back to allow her in, then followed, dragging the gate to and pressing the button. The ground floor seemed to sink below them as the lift rose.

When they stopped at the first floor, the corridor beyond had been silent and deserted. He pulled back the gate but instead of helping her out, took hold of her, brought her close, his lips closing on hers. They seemed to stand there forever before finally moving apart. He took her hand, leading her from the lift. Neither spoke as he led her to a door a few yards along the corridor.

In silence he took the key from his pocket and unlocked the door, allowing her to precede him. He followed, closing the door behind them very quietly, not one word having passed between them. Still without speaking, he had kissed her again and, as moments before, with neither of them breaking apart he'd manoeuvred her towards the narrow bed just a few steps away and laid her down, gently lowering himself beside her at the same time. It was almost skilful.

Only then did his lips leave hers for him to lift himself the easier to undo the buttons of her thick coat, her blouse, easing the edges apart, lifting her breasts above the loose top of her bodice, lowering his face to them to take a nipple into his mouth. She had let it happen, joy overflowing with the sensation, the first time he had been so close to her, almost a part of her; so wonderful, she was hardly aware of her top clothing and nether garments being removed, his too, until she felt him enter her, an overwhelming moment of two becoming as one; his breath close to her ear, her own sighing, then gasping, the world whirling about her.

It was over too soon. Lying satiated side by side on the narrow single bed they'd gazed up at the ceiling. It was yellow with old cigarette smoke and slightly uneven in places, the lamp shade not the newest of objects, but the room itself clean and nicely furnished. Strange now to remember that.

As normality moved slowly back into place, he had turned his face to her. 'Are you OK?' he'd asked and she had nodded.

Then had come the memory of an old barn, she lying utterly fulfilled beside the man who'd taken his fill of her, believing him as much in love with her as she with him. The recollection had dragged an involuntary tremulous sigh from her, making Anthony look at her, filled with concern.

'My darling, I didn't hurt you, did I? If I did . . .'

It was then that she'd broken down, all the years of pent up yearning for that foolish time never to have happened, had wrenched itself painfully out of her

Burying her face against his shoulder she heard herself sobbing, the words pouring from her, erratic. 'It was a long time ago . . . I was so young, no idea what it was about . . . there was a baby – taken from me . . . I don't know

where she is. I was never told. My parents disowned me
– settled her elsewhere – I never found out where or who
with. I'm not . . . not a virgin.'

She remembered how quiet he'd become, lost in thought.
Despair had washed over her – she'd lost him, knew then
just how much she loved him. Silence seemed to draw itself
out while she remained with her face hidden, convinced it
was over. Then slowly he said in a low voice, 'It was a long
time ago,' and as if uncertain of her response, added huskily,
'I shall see you next week, shan't I?' as if he dared not hope.

She had turned her face in surprise to his. 'You still want
me?'

'With all my heart. I love you, Maddie. And you, do you
still love me?'

'Oh, yes, yes,' she'd breathed, her whole being overwhelmed by relief.

Today she made her way through the few falling flakes of
snow. She and Tony would make love, a little less tense these
days, would lay in each other's arms, then after a while make
love again. But how long would it be allowed to go on?
That was the only thought that troubled her. How much
longer could she keep it from James? One day he would
become suspicious – a word dropped, a look noticed as it
passed between herself and Anthony, alerting him to something very wrong. How she longed to be free of James, yet
how could she wish him ill? Yet it was becoming more
difficult as time went on, even this short time.

For Tony, meeting her once a week was no difficulty. But
for her it was growing more worrying as time went on.
Lies, pretence, creeping out of the house with excuses of
taking the air. Taking the air? February with its cold flurries
of snow and biting winds on her cheeks and she expecting
it to be believed that she was *taking the air*?

Mrs Cole, James's cook for many years, long before he'd
lost his first wife but who'd very quickly taken to her
employer's new wife, had expressed surprise the first time
she had said she was going out for a breath of fresh air.
Today her reaction hadn't diminished one bit.

'Surely, madam, you're not going out *again*! It's bitter out there. More than bitter – it's killing cold! You'll catch your death before long.'

'I'm well wrapped up, Mrs Cole,' she told her with an easy smile. The air's bracing. It will do me good. Every fire lit, the stuffiness indoors is giving me quite a headache.'

'Perhaps you should have Doctor Williamson look at you, madam, if it goes on. There's all this Spanish 'flu about – an epidemic it's becoming, they say. It's frightening if you ask me. A couple of my nephew's friends are down with it and they're really bad. It's seeing off so many in such a short while. The papers are full of it.'

Madeleine ignored the diatribe on the influenza business – half smiled to herself as she recalled the current sally: *You just watch that girl called Enza because when they opened the window, in flew Enza!'* Yes, it was rife, frightening, getting worse by the day. But she didn't have it.

'A short walk in the fresh air will soon clear my head,' she dismissed. 'I'll go to the park. Half an hour or so should do it.'

She hurried out before any further obstacles could be put in the way, albeit well meant. At least it was dry, cold but dry. Soon it would be March, hopefully a little warmer, lessening cook's over-motherly interest in her well-being. James's chauffeur too was concerned for her, offering to take her for a drive instead, but she'd evaded his offers saying that with petrol still rationed it shouldn't be wasted driving her about.

So far James was too occupied with stock market dealings to notice most of her comings and goings. Nevertheless, she'd told Mrs Cole not to bother him with her worries for her well-being, he had too many other things to think about and ought not be bothered with trivialities. But one day it was sure to come out. What would she do when he began asking questions? Lie to him? Break off her meetings with Anthony? No, that was unthinkable.

Quickly she turned her thoughts from that aspect as she hurried the few hundred yards to where she would hail a taxi. It took less than a quarter of an hour to reach the hotel. Tony would already be there waiting and for a wonderful ten minutes or so they would make frantic love, to lie exhausted in each other's arms, then make love again, more slowly.

How wonderful it would have been to lie in his arms for the rest of the morning. She would dress, hating having to leave him, and go. He would leave soon after, needing to get back to his bank, having started back there two weeks ago. In his capacity he had no one to answer to although he worried about being away for too long, which was understandable. But she had Mrs Cole, the woman quick to badger her should her return seem more delayed than she thought. What if one day it all came out, a chance remark perhaps, the mind immediately making something out of it?

Alighting from her taxi, she took her time walking that hundred yards home, hoping the cold would set her cheeks glowing as if from a surfeit of fresh air, even pinched her nose hard to make it look red. But her outings were becoming longer, dangerously so. Last week Mrs Cole had taken her to task as if she were the mistress and Madeleine the servant.

'Madam, I thought you'd got yourself lost, you've taken so long getting back. You really oughtn't to have been out so long. You could catch your death.'

'It's good for the constitution,' she told her a little testily.

'But what would the master say if he knew?'

'Please don't tell him.' She'd begged, feeling like a child in danger of having a treasured toy taken from her. 'He would worry. I've taken to popping into a little tea room for a nice pot of hot tea and a cake; that's the reason I was a little longer than usual. I so enjoy it, Mrs Cole. I can't bear being cooped up here day after day.'

'But you're not, madam. You have so many friends, appointments, engagements. You're hardly ever at home, what with one thing and another.'

It was true. Always something going on, always busy organizing this and that party or function, she had become well known for it, her social events now famous. With the war, the Great War as it was becoming known, behind them, people were discovering a new freedom, making sure they were going to enjoy it to the full: dances, charity balls, the joy of loose-fitting garments after the restrictions of only a decade ago. Women had found freedom at last to do as they pleased, at least those with money to do so, and she made sure she was part of it.

'I look forward to enjoying a walk entirely on my own,' she told Mrs Cole, 'and I don't want others to spoil it for me. You do understand.'

'I suppose so,' was the grudging reply, leaving her free to go up to her room to dream over her wonderful moments with Anthony.

But it couldn't continue this way forever, she left brooding on what would come later. How many years could it continue like this? Thoughts of the future frightened and depressed her.

There was of course a lot that helped take her mind off such dreary thoughts: the grand Christmas party she'd given, money no object, everyone in high spirits, enjoying to the full the pleasures the peace had brought. The New Year's Eve Party had been another grand event; a prelude to what by next year would be a new decade utterly different from the previous one, lots of jollity, making up for the years of stalemate, all cares flung to the wind. Yes, there was still the struggling poor, but if you had money, life was sweet.

There were parties still to be arranged: Valentine's Day, April Fool's Day with a great fancy dress party planned, Easter with a big garden party, weather permitting, otherwise it would have to be held inside, not quite the same. Then there was the London season, visiting the country and other people's parties: swimming parties, tennis parties, the list went on and on. Yet always in the background was Anthony. She lived only to see him. All the rest could go hang if only she and he were together, permanently.

Maybe one day. Please God let it be soon. She wished James no ill but if only there was a way, any way, out.

Sixteen

Why was it that in the midst of overwhelming happiness the Devil always seemed to raise his ugly head to spoil it all? It was wicked and selfish to be thinking such things at a time like this but that was how it seemed to her.

She and Anthony had been so happy. It was the end of April. They'd been meeting once a week with only one break, when he'd gone up to the Midlands; some business to do with his bank, he'd said. She'd missed him dreadfully and he must have felt the same for their reunion had been passionate to the point of exhaustion.

'Promise me you'll never go away again,' she'd begged as she lay in his arms. 'Promise me you'll send someone else in your stead.'

'I promise,' he'd said.

But life has a way of tearing down the strongest promise. A week later, the day before they would meet, he phoned while James was away at his office, telling her his mother had gone down with the Spanish 'flu.

'It struck almost overnight,' he said. His voice, thin and distant over the wires, was shaky, tinged with panic, his words practically falling over themselves.

'She didn't seem too bad yesterday morning, just said she felt a bit achy but by the evening she'd developed a raging headache and she became feverish. During the night I had to send for the doctor, she was tossing and turning so much, almost in delirium. I can't see you tomorrow, darling. I can't leave her, I have to be with her, it's happened so fast and I'm worried.'

'Is there anything I can do?' she asked when finally she got a word in.

'Not really. Just tell Uncle James she's gone down with it. He'd want to know. I'm just praying it doesn't get worse. So many are . . .'

His voice trailed off but she'd already finished the words for him in her mind: *so many are dying . . .*

'Your doctor is there with her,' she said instead. 'She will be fine, darling. He's a good man. But I'll telephone James right now and we'll be there as quick as we can, and . . .' But he'd already rung off, her last words addressed to empty air as slowly she replaced the receiver, seeing in her mind his distraught face hovering before her.

She and James had dropped everything to be at Mabel's side, shocked by how she looked; scarcely heeding them she lay there, face flushed, eyes when she chanced to open them, heavy with pain, all the while her head moving slowly from side to side as if to alleviate the misery she was in.

They sat around her bed feeling utterly useless, murmuring words of encouragement that seemed to go unheard. Occasionally she came to herself enough to look at them and mutter, 'I'm sorry . . . I'm being such a nuisance to everyone . . .'

'No, you're not,' James told her each time.

'I don't know . . . I don't . . . mean to be . . .' she would gasp. Then on being told she was not at all a nuisance, she would lapse back into semi-consciousness to sigh and moan and twist her head from side to side.

The doctor was there constantly, a nurse too, who would shoo them out of the bedroom in order to attend the patient. Sadly they would go home after hours spent just gazing down at her when allowed, the next day to return to the same procedure.

All the while, Madeleine found herself looking time and time again at Anthony, feeling helpless at the despair and fear in his eyes when her gaze caught his. It made her cringe with sadness to see the way he'd shake his head in defeat, almost imperceptibly.

During one of their daily visits, unable to stand it any longer she excused herself and hurried away downstairs seeking the silence of the library to regain command of a sudden onslaught of emotion.

To her relief Anthony had followed her. Now he stood by the door, his body taut.

'It doesn't look good, does it?' he questioned from where he stood. 'I don't really know what to do.'

Impulsively she came towards him, needing to comfort. 'Darling . . .' But as she made to kiss him, he drew away.

'No . . . not at the moment!' he exclaimed and turning went out of the room, leaving her standing alone.

It was so abrupt a reaction that it shocked her, leaving her in despair as she stared at the closed door. It was over – their time together, their affair. His mother was dying, he was already grieving, and she had been foolish enough to think he'd respond to her kiss, take her in his arms; maybe go further in their love for each other. She was an utter fool! In one unthinking, selfish move she had terminated their affair.

Gazing at the closed door, unable to bring herself to return upstairs, to face him, she on one side of his mother's bed, he on the other, never again to be as they had been to each other, would be unbearable.

A little while later James came to get her. 'Are you all right, my dear?' he asked. 'You rushed from the room so quickly I was worried for you.'

'I didn't want to cry in front of Mabel and Anthony,' she lied. 'He has enough to worry about without me breaking out in a flood of tears.'

'That was so kind and thoughtful of you, my dear,' he said tenderly.

'No, it's just that I didn't want to make a fool of myself, the only one crying.'

'It was still a tender thought, my dear. Anyway it's time we left. Mabel needs to rest and sleep. And Anthony needs some privacy. Mabel's sister and her husband are coming later and I think he may need some time to himself first.'

She nodded, now wanting only to be away. Leaving James to say their goodbyes she tried not to feel troubled while at the same time feeling relieved that Anthony hadn't come down to see them off; having to face him after what had transpired between them would have destroyed her.

His mother died just a week later. It had happened so quickly. They had not been there when it happened. They were notified not by Anthony but one of his mother's staff arriving to hand them a note from him, the wording almost cold in its content: 'Mother passed away early hours this morning in her sleep. Anthony.'

But James saw nothing wrong in his terseness. His eyes filled with tears as he put the short note to one side after reading it aloud to Madeleine and murmured, 'He must be utterly devastated. Such a wonderful woman – a kind and truly wonderful woman – all alone she brought up her son after my brother died, ever soldiering on. Why her? She didn't deserve . . .'

His voice faltering, he drew himself up, his rounded, somewhat ageing features firming. 'We must go to him straight away. He may have need of us there. I shall telephone my office and tell them.'

He thought for a moment while she watched him, then he said slowly, 'I shall have to set about the funeral arrangements.'

'Anthony will probably do that,' Madeleine said, but he cut her short.

'He will need all the help I can give him, a young man having just lost his mother, his father gone, he is alone in the world. He'll need my help.'

As if he were a child rather than a grown man, she thought. But she said nothing, thinking only of him with sadness in her heart, for herself as well as for him; her emptiness telling her she had lost him. How could they go on as they had, while he grieved so? No, it was over and that was grief enough for her, quietly consuming her. And all the time James was regarding her in the belief that her sadness was purely for his nephew's sense of bereavement as he put what he imagined was a comforting arm about her shoulder and laid a light kiss on her brow. If only he knew . . .

The following week beside his mother's grave, while the vicar's dull voice intoned the prayers for the departed, Anthony hardly looked in Madeleine's direction. When he did it was as if across a gulf, his eyes pleading – for what, she couldn't fathom. Aching love for her or the desolate loss of his mother? She ought to have been weeping for her sister-in-law. Instead she wept for what seemed for her the end of their wonderful times together. How would he want that, his mother so recently dead? It would probably feel to him like blasphemy. No, it was ended.

Eventually he would find comfort in some other young woman, fall in love, marry, and she would have lost him forever, destined to live the rest of her life with James, this old man she had married and maybe it served her right for having thought to use someone like him for her own ends. And even that had backfired on her. She was no nearer to tracing her child than at the beginning. She had been a fool!

She tried time and time again to catch Anthony's eye even as everyone came away from the grave, a sad little group, a few friends, she with James to his car, Anthony to his with his mother's sister and brother-in-law, they all returning to his home to the food laid out for them and to reminisce in respectful tones over memories of the one no longer there.

Anthony was deliberately avoiding her she knew that now without a doubt. At the funeral supper he didn't come near her except once to speak to his uncle, then, with her standing beside James, he didn't even cast a single glance in her direction when she uttered a word of two of sympathy.

He didn't look well himself, his face very slightly flushed. It may have been from standing by his mother's grave in a somewhat chilly wind for May, or perhaps from grief, or was it the beginnings of 'flu?

Madeleine's heart almost stopped at the thought. Known to be highly infectious, it could leap from one victim to a dozen others in a single breath. What if he had caught it, sitting so close beside his ailing mother? Dear God, what would she do if it were to take him? She felt the blood suddenly drain from her cheeks at the thought, leaving them feeling cold, and she drew in an involuntary, tremulous breath.

The sound made both him and James glance at her, James asking, 'Are you all right, my dear?' she compelled to answer that she was fine. It was then that she caught the look on

Anthony's face, instantly reading the thought in his mind. 'Don't fall ill. I couldn't bear it if you left me.'

His love hadn't died. It had all been in her mind. Yet instead of being given reassurance of their love, it seemed to tear her heart to pieces.

'Please dear God,' came the silent answering prayer, as she managed a wan smile, 'don't let him go down with 'flu. He does love me and I couldn't bear to lose him, not now. What would I do if that were to happen?'

He, gone forever . . . She, James's wife until the end of her days . . . It almost made her cringe, wanting only to fall into Tony's arms, declare her love. Instead she merely smiled hearing herself repeat, 'I'm fine – really I am.'

The weeks had gone by and she hadn't seen or heard from him at all. She had tried telephoning him at home, but he never seemed to be there. Contacting his bank, the message was always that he was unavailable. Whether that was true or the staff was told to tell her that, she had no way of finding out. She had written to him but there was never a reply.

'Have you heard from Anthony lately?' she casually asked James over breakfast two weeks after the funeral.

He looked up from slicing off the top of his boiled egg. 'Only to say how grateful he was for all we did during his mother's illness. I read it out to you, remember?'

Yes, she did remember, but it had merely begun with *Dear Aunt and Uncle*. Nothing for her at all much less mentioning her by name.

'And for supporting him at the funeral,' James finished. 'As if we would dream of not attending – my own grieving nephew.'

He smiled faintly at his sad little quip and returned to dealing with his egg.

Wanting so much to take the subject further but fearing to betray her feelings, she let it go at that. But after some two weeks of silence from Tony, her anxiety getting the better of her, she dared to venture that she hoped he was all right.

James took it innocently. 'I expect he doesn't think it right to bother us with his private grief. I expect he is sinking himself in his work. Nothing like work to keep the mind off one's loss.'

'What if he's gone down with the 'flu and won't or can't tell us?'

'If he'd gone down with it, we would have been told immediately.'

'We should go and see him though. It looks so churlish to stay away. After all anyone who's bereaved needs other people.'

'I shall telephone him, my dear. But now I must be off to my office. You mustn't let yourself worry over people.'

He dropped a kiss on the top of her head, adding, 'You worry yourself too much over others, my dear. I shall see you tonight. Have yourself a nice day with your friend, and don't exert yourself too much with this Whitsun party of yours.'

She'd told him she was seeing one of her many friends that day so that they could go over her plans for the party she intended to throw at Whitsun. Since her secret meetings with Anthony she'd rather let her social life slip, Easter's soirée being the last of any importance and that not as exciting as it should have been with her mind more on herself and Anthony.

On her way to see May Caldwell-Bell, who'd become a helpful friend and organizer of parties over the years, she turned off and directed the taxi driver to Anthony's home.

'The master must have mentioned to his uncle that he would be going to Scotland for a while,' she was informed by the butler, who answered her ring of the bell. 'He said he rather needed an old friend to stay with a short while to help him recover from his loss rather than worry his relations.'

Madeleine wanted to blurt out that he hadn't told them a thing, but she merely nodded, said she must have forgotten, and hurried away saying she was late for an engagement.

Why hadn't he told her? Why hadn't he written? She

was hardly able to concentrate on the plans for Whitsun, leaving May to frown and ask if she was feeling well. What excuse she made for her lack of concentration she couldn't recall. When James came home she asked him if Anthony had told him where he would be for the next few weeks. He looked surprised at first then recollection seemed suddenly to dawn.

'Ah, I remember now. He telephoned me at my office – completely slipped my memory. I meant to tell you but we've been so busy – business quite brisk now the war is over, even though the country is feeling the pinch. Still we can only be on the up and up – not like Germany, people starving, the German mark not worth a pfennig these days, people having to buy the smallest item with no less than a basketful of worthless marks.'

So jovial, so much unnecessary detail . . . It allowed the old suspicion to creep into Madeleine's mind that he must have some inkling of her relationship with Anthony, and it led her to believe he was biding his time but in the meantime was unable to resist the odd jab.

It was autumn. The Whitsun soirée had gone off better than expected, as had her party for James's birthday as well as the huge fifth of November firework party, all thanks to May who had done most of the planning, revelling in it, while Madeleine found it hard to concentrate.

She and James had gone away to the South of France for almost two weeks, which included the August Bank Holiday. On the beach and by the pool, she had sat under a sunshade most of the time preferring her skin unblemished by strong sunlight, contrary to the new craze of proving one could afford to holiday abroad by exhibiting as much tanned flesh as was decently acceptable in the newest fashion of sleeveless, calf-length, flat-busted evening dresses with deep neckline back and front.

Summer seemed to her to have lasted forever. Now autumn was creeping by and she had never felt so alone. Every now and again there came a letter from Anthony, saying that he was feeling a lot better but felt it hard to come back to

London yet awhile. He still missed his mother and returning to London just yet would only bring it all back to him; he had put a manager in charge of the bank and was in touch by telephone and telegram should the man need to consult him, and so far all seemed to be going smoothly. Not one letter to her personally, her name hardly included in his letters to James except to hope she was well. It hurt, but more, it worried and distressed her. There was no longer any doubt that he had done with their association, their year of love over. Any minute she expected to hear of his becoming engaged, happy to marry and settle down, herself forgotten – that wonderful love they had shared a mere passing phase, never to be revealed. Anthony, everything having been left to him by his parents in their will, was a wealthy man; whoever married him would want for nothing.

She wanted for nothing, materially, James saw to that. But she ached for love. The memory of it haunted her, kept her awake at night; followed her around in whatever she did. Christmas and New Year found her striving to concentrate on throwing her usual parties. People thought they were as wonderful as ever, commented on her beautiful thin figure, she having lost so much weight that her bust had all but disappeared – such a perfect figure they said enviously as she smiled, smoked endless cigarettes at the end of an ivory cigarette holder and danced until dawn and hardly ate a thing. James, noticing the change in her, had become worried.

'I think you ought to see our doctor,' he told her. 'Such a drastic weight loss cannot be right. You could be suffering from something of which you're not aware, my dear.'

But she'd always been slim and told him so.

At other times, should she happen to give a natural little cough, he would study her gravely with a worried look on his round face. He never said the word, but she knew what he was thinking: 'consumption?'

She would smile confidingly and say, 'If I had anything wrong with me, James, I wouldn't be as energetic as I am.'

But hers was a nervous energy, not stemming from health, for at times she felt all she wanted to do was lie abed and dream of Anthony, of him making love to her so fiercely that she would cry out in ecstasy, finally to lie limp in his arms, utterly fulfilled. And having known such sensations, her life had become unbearable now they were no longer there for her.

Seventeen

Dull weeks, never-ending weeks, counting each day as though it was in itself a week. An effort to find any pleasure in her normal rounds of social visiting, planning social dinners, going to the theatre with James. It was becoming an effort to maintain her reputation for throwing excellent parties for which she had been and still was, surprisingly, seen as the most exciting of hostesses in a long time, with people hanging upon her invitations. Yet it all seemed so superfluous, pointless.

This February morning, James having gone off to his office, she sat at her bureau, writing to Anthony, unable to contain herself any longer. She had written countless letters at first. But he'd never replied, not to her personally, writing only to his uncle, maybe including her, almost as an after-thought it seemed, merely by hoping she was well, as any nephew might enquire of his aunt.

It hurt, worse than if he hadn't included her at all. How could he have put her aside so easily, those wonderful times together, how they'd made love, how they would lay in each others arms afterwards, utterly fulfilled. Now he was behaving as if it had never been. A whole year since she'd last seen him, how could he put aside those times so easily – as if they had never been?

Madeleine finally gave up writing letters he apparently refused to answer, and she struggled through this lonely time, surrounded by her social friends, throwing her soirées; she had tried to put her whole self into her Christmas and New Year celebrations, finding no joy in them even though all declared them a huge success, as always. No one noticed how lacking she was in spirit, for she had become adept at hiding her loneliness from the eyes of her world.

Time should have healed the hurt. Instead, it had built up and up, like a child's building blocks. His silence was having another effect, turning her mind inward to another loss: questions that were keeping her awake at night, more now than ever they had before – where was the baby taken from her all those years ago? How had she fared and what sort of life had she been forced to lead?

In the past she'd had dreams in which she would find her child only to lose sight of her again, would wake up weeping, grateful only that she still slept alone, James in his own bedroom, unable to hear her and tell her in his patient tone that she must try to get over it. As the years passed, the dreams had subsided, but memories of Anthony leaving had begun to return and in full force; almost like nightmares, finding herself running through the streets, people staring at her, and she not heeding them, seeing ahead of her, her baby. Yet no matter how fast she ran, the baby – always a baby – would recede at the same pace even though not seeming to move.

She would wake up to lie, tearful and sleepless, planning all sorts of mad schemes to get her back, imagining a helpless child; unloved, living a life of drudgery, misery, hunger, and, dear God, beatings, maybe locked in dark cupboards by those who'd adopted her? Never could she truly see her as living happily, loving and loved by those who'd adopted her, for how could they truly love a child that was not their own. And surely some faint instinct would make her daughter fret for her true mother, just as she fretted for her?

Common sense told her she would no longer be a baby but a little girl, almost six years old now. Yet all she ever saw was the tiny little face gazing up at her as she had held in her arms for less than what, a minute, before she was snatched away from her?

Anthony gone, the need for James to help her trace the child had been growing to almost an obsession though most times she curbed the need to badger him. This morning after another miserable dream, her determination to confront him was so strong that she even vowed to threaten to leave him if he didn't at least try. Never before had she resorted to such an ultimatum. James had been so kind to her, happy to grant her smallest wish – except this one it seemed. She had tried to make allowances – his age, his never having had children about him, her child not being his – always finding herself losing the argument. But this morning she would fight him if need be.

She needed someone to love, to love her. The man who had given her that wasn't here any more and James was a poor substitute. He had married her purely for companionship, for which she'd been prepared to settle in the belief that with all his money and influence he would trace her baby for her. How wrong she'd been, saddled now with an old man.

In Anthony she had found the passion she'd been missing. Now even that was gone – would not come back, of that she was certain, finding it hard to believe that he'd merely been dallying with her, having a good time at her expense. Left desperately needing love she would find her child, hold her in her arms again, protect her with every ounce of her being.

At breakfast she said suddenly, 'I've been thinking a lot lately of the baby I had before we met.'

He glanced over at her from the little side table where their breakfast had been laid out for them and she noticed at that moment just how old he was beginning to look. Now sixty-three, his age showed in the sagging jowls of a rounded face, the face that had become a little podgier this last year or so, his stomach a trace more portly, while she was twenty-four, a young woman still.

He came to the breakfast table and sat down, placing his plate of kedgeree in front of him, his face expressionless as he poured his coffee, drew the sugar bowl towards him and stirred in a teaspoonful of sugar, sipping the brew, taking his time. It was almost as if she hadn't spoken.

'James, did you hear what I said?'

Replacing the cup on the saucer he remained looking down seemingly busy forking over his kedgeree. Now, he said quietly, as though addressing his plate, 'It was a long time ago, my dear, when you lost your baby.'

Madeleine felt suddenly angry. 'I didn't lose her, James. She was taken from me!'

There was another long pause. She waited, growing angrier by the second until she thought she might burst; hard to keep her voice steady as she said, 'I really thought when you married me that you would help me find her, as you promised to.'

Now he looked up at her. 'I did not promise, my dear. I said I would try were it humanly possible – which has not proved to be the case. But you obviously interpreted it as a definite yes, hearing only what you wanted to hear. I have never deluded myself that an extremely comely young woman as you, my dear, would wish to marry an elderly person such as myself unless it was from a hope of availing herself of my ability to pull strings . . .'

'I never . . .'

'Of course you did,' he interrupted. The hitherto mild voice suddenly became sharp, a tone he had never before adopted with her.

'And I in turn married you purely for companionship as well you know. I made that quite clear to you. I have never lied to you on that subject.'

'But you did lead me to believe you would try to trace my baby.'

'Time appears to have clouded your memory I think. I gave you no reason, Madeleine, to believe any such thing, although I recall you alluding to the fact that you'd had a child given up for adoption and hoped one day to be in a position to trace it. It would have been wrong of me to make such an empty promise to help you, knowing how impossible it would be to fulfil. Even less possible now, after all these years.'

'So you were leading me on,' she cried angrily. 'Seeing me as gullible, so you could marry someone to keep you company in your old age. Why me – why not some elderly, lonely woman your own age, or was it that you merely fancied a younger woman around you so you could show her off?'

'I really think we should stop there, my dear!' He stood up suddenly, making her jump. His tone, though hard, was controlled, though the words, 'my dear', far from their usual gentleness, were brittle.

'I'm sorry, James!' she cried. 'I didn't mean it to sound that way.'

'No?' The query was hard.

Things were getting out of hand. She'd never seen this side of him before. Always he had been ever polite and gentle with her, long-suffering, patient, mild-tempered; she now saw a man revealing the face his business rivals saw – a man who took no prisoners. Even when presenting a likeable face to the world of business in which he lived, she realized that a man of any other calibre would never have survived the cut-throat profession of stocks and shares. She had often wondered how someone so placid when with her could command others in a profession so intense and sometimes ruthless. Now, hearing him address her as he had, she knew she had met her match. There would be no hope of tracing her child through him. She must look elsewhere. But where? There *was* nowhere. She felt defeated. Bursting into tears, she rushed from the room.

But two months later something did present itself – in the form of a letter from Anthony, addressed directly to her.

When Merton handed her the post, she immediately recognized the handwriting and her heart leapt. Leaving the rest of the post she hurried up to her bedroom and sat at her neat little bureau, tearing open the envelope with feverish fingers, grateful James had already left the house before the second mail of the day. The first always came very early in the morning, this second one of three daily posts arriving around eleven.

Reading the two pages of closely scribbled writing, joy soared within her like a bird on the wing, but coupled with great sadness for him, and such deep understanding that she found herself crying as she read:

> *My own true darling,*
>
> *I dare not imagine what you must have been thinking of all this past year. Time and time again I wanted to write but could not bring myself to form the words. After losing mother, I felt I couldn't face the hubbub of London. I felt strangely guilty over her death, almost in a panic. An old friend in Scotland said I had to get away, suggested spending some time with him until I was well enough to face the*

world again. I left the bank in charge of Mr Knowles my capable undermanager with whom I've stayed in contact by phone.

I thought of you so often and have been utterly wretched. Yet I couldn't face coming back. The loss of mother affected me so much more than I could ever have imagined. I'd lost all control, rather like a type of shell-shock delayed from the war, coming quite out of the blue the day after losing her. I began to find myself unable to keep a muscle still, feeling I was losing my balance. Even in the quiet isolation of Scotland it's taken a long time to recover. My friend has been so supportive. But for him I could have gone the way of many a shell-shocked man.

I thought I returned from France merely a bit shaken up with no more than a badly fractured leg, but it's the wounds you don't see. Lots of men like it will maybe never be cured. I did wonder if I would ever be the same again. I know I didn't feel one hundred per cent in my mind when I came home to convalesce but couldn't bring myself to tell anyone, not even James, least of all you, my darling. I am so sorry, but I had no wish to inflict my confusion upon you, my sweetest love.

But I think I am recovered now, one of the lucky ones maybe, but for some time I just couldn't bring myself to come back and face a normal life, much less have you see me in that state. So now I can only hope you still love me and want me but I will understand if you don't.

I will be returning to London some time next week and if I can face it (though I'll not know until I do), go to live in my mother's house which, as you know, has been closed all this while. I've written to Uncle James to say I'm returning home (I've never told him either about my condition) but this is a special letter to you fervently hoping that your love and affection for me hasn't died.

Please, darling, write and tell me how you feel about me and if you still feel anything for me. I wait upon your answer with the fervent hope that you still feel about me as you did.

I love you so very much.

Anthony

The letter ended with a long row of kisses to which she pressed her lips before folding it carefully in order to slip it beneath her jumper next to her heart, tearing the envelope to shreds and dropping them into the waste paper basket, not that she wished to destroy even his envelope, but with an irrational fear of anyone, James say, inspecting the basket and seeing her name in his handwriting.

It was a full two weeks before he came home. Having telegraphed James and his mother's sister and her husband as to when he'd be coming home, Anthony found they were all there waiting to welcome him back, having been admitted by his mother's butler whom he still retained.

He looked pale and weary and to Madeleine's eyes, much thinner even though naturally slim. He appeared disconcerted to see them there waiting for him. Glancing from one to the other almost defensively, his eyes had gone immediately to Madeleine and although he didn't smile, she saw some of that tension fade, his eyes soften with relief. She felt her heart go out to him and vowed that she would bring back that boyish grin, perhaps have his hands again roam with confidence over her naked body, her love helping return him to his earlier confident self.

Yet had she ever known him as he would have been before the trauma of war had got to him? Harking back to the days when he'd made love to her, the almost frantic urgency of his hands roaming her body, had he then been in the throes, albeit hidden, of shell-shock? If they ever made love again, would those hands have the same feverishness or would they be far gentler? In her innocence she had loved that sense of urgency. Would that now be lost – that was if he ever made love to her again? She couldn't tell.

From that first exchange of glances, he hadn't looked her way again, almost as if trying to avoid eye contact. She felt isolated as the conversation passed back and forth despite him seeming little interested in joining in other than answering questions as to his present health and hopes that he'd be able to pick up on his life again. Once as his aunt expressed her deep sadness over the loss of her sister, killing the conversation for a moment, Madeleine saw him wince, his lips tighten, until James tactfully turned to the present troubles in Ireland, Anthony for a while forgotten.

Madeleine too felt disinclined to talk, finding herself virtually ignored, and in a way glad to be so.

Finally, the butler came to enquire if they would be staying for tea. James immediately took the hint, catching an anxious message in the look on Anthony's face and saying he thought his nephew was looking tired and perhaps it would be best to leave and allow him to settle into his home to rest after his long journey from Scotland.

Each visitor went over to Anthony to say farewell, the men shaking his hand, his Aunt Lydia kissing him on the cheek a little tearfully, no doubt thinking, if only his mother were here. Madeleine in turn approached him.

'It's good to see you home, darling,' she whispered.

But he merely nodded, saying, 'Thank you, it's good to be home,' for a moment making her doubt the contents of his letter to her.

His head lowered, not looking at her, nothing there to support the words he'd written, she felt her heart drop within her. Then without raising his head, he lifted his eyes to her and they were filled with a silent message of love, before he looked away to the departing guests, his Aunt Lydia giving him a final wave, and leaned back in his chair. Compelled to follow the well-wishers, Madeleine dared not look back at him.

James was waiting for her at the main door. Was it her imagination or was there a strange look on his face? Had he seen what had passed between her and Anthony? If so, had he correctly interpreted it? There was no way to know but she knew they'd come dangerously close to betraying themselves. Yet, strangely, she didn't care. Her heart was sailing with joy in her breast. One day James would find out or be told, and what he would or could do about it, at this moment she couldn't have cared a jot.

Eighteen

Nigh on eighteen months of silence, of loneliness, with no word from him, then hurt and anger at his unexplained silence other than the odd letter to James, she mentioned almost as an afterthought. That was now all in the past. Now she lay in his arms, her heart going out to him when she thought of all he'd gone through in his struggle to force himself back to sanity. Realizing that in the grip of a mental breakdown, he'd virtually isolated himself from everyone, even her, almost broke her heart each time she'd thought of it.

She wanted to creep inside him, comfort him with her warmth, feed him with her love, but all she could do was to take him into her body and afterwards to just lie in his arms.

Apart from that one letter to her three weeks ago now, he had not spoken of those months at all, and she felt it better not to pry. Although he'd bared his heart in his letter, he seemed unable to give voice to them. Maybe she would never know. Maybe best she didn't. Better just to have his arms about her; be grateful just to have him back.

They no longer met in that seedy hotel but at his home, his mother gone. It was wonderful not having to sense people looking at her, guessing what she was up to, especially the hotel porters who would have seen her arrive there regularly once a week. What Anthony's staff thought, they kept to themselves. If James found out, she would know it could only have come from them and they would soon be dismissed, and in this climate of huge unemployment, who would want that? Thus she felt safe, those miserable eighteen months well behind her, merely hoping James wouldn't perceive the change in her from pensive to buoyant, practically overnight.

She had never dared hope for the kind of happiness that

now possessed her, and the year seemed to speed by. Christmas was almost upon them and she was planning the biggest party ever as well as another to see in the New Year, a celebration to outdo all celebrations. She would be the talk of the town.

James as ever was not of the same mind. 'The house will be disrupted as usual, it would be rather nice to have one quiet Christmas to ourselves, don't you think?'

She felt cross with him. 'You hardly ever show yourself anyway,' she ranted. 'It's a wonder you don't escape altogether, to your club maybe.'

'There'd be no one there,' he said quietly, 'My friends and colleagues will no doubt be at home enjoying the festive season, quietly, and it would be nice if we did the same.'

She ignored that hint. 'In that case, I wouldn't be surprised if you wandered off to some common pub to drink there all on your own, as you were doing when I first met you, of all places to expect a wealthy, respectable businessman to be!'

'I'm sorry you think so little of me, my dear,' he said, and adding that it was time he retired to bed, got up slowly from his armchair by the sitting-room fire, leaving her to fume at his refusal ever to rise to argument.

Despite his objections, she'd thrown her parties, enjoying the praise she received, praise that had continued for several months into 1922.

'He's beginning to look old,' she told Anthony. 'And he's starting to frown at the money I spend on my social events, even though he tops up my allowance without question. But then, he never seems short of money. It's amazing how it just rolls in.'

They were lounging on the settee, his arm around her. He'd wound up the gramophone, the record he'd chosen now softly playing *Wyoming Lullaby* in the background. Soon they would be upstairs, the curtains closed against the slanting afternoon sun, with Anthony tenderly kissing her naked body, his kisses growing more urgent until she wanted to scream for him to take her.

'His business should be doing well,' he said. 'The market's

pretty buoyant at the moment. Anyone who's got it needn't worry overmuch about their investments letting them down. Gambling on the stock exchange keeps him a rich man.'

He sat up suddenly. 'That's something you could do, darling, if he's being awkward about your allowance.'

She sat up too, slowly. 'What do you mean?'

He smiled. 'Dabble in stocks and shares.'

'Me?'

'Not heavily of course, but it would help bolster your allowance. You wouldn't be so dependent on him.'

'I wouldn't know how.'

'I'm certain he'd love to advise you. He wouldn't take you as a client himself, of course, but there are plenty of brokers who will with him behind you.'

It sounded a wonderful idea. As she left after she and Anthony had fulfilled their need of each other, her mind was running ahead of her. James would teach her, advise her. With him behind her she couldn't go wrong. Not only that but with her own money, in a few months maybe she could hire someone herself to trace her baby and not have to rely on him. She could hardly wait.

Over breakfast, James was regarding her as if she were a child. 'My dear, how could you have spent this month's allowance so soon?'

She felt angry, finding herself being looked upon as incapable of controlling the money he gave her. She'd had to look after her money prior to marrying him, yet he gave her no credit for that; the husband forced to guide his wife, responsible for her every action as if they were back in Victorian times. She fought to remain cool.

'We've attended so many functions this month,' she said. They were always being invited somewhere, his profession demanding it. 'You know I needed another couple of new gowns. I can't be seen in the same ones over and over again. People will notice.'

'But those you already have you seldom wear more than twice,' he began gently, but it sounded more like an accusation to her.

Leaping up from the table she cried out, 'I refuse to be questioned every time I ask for a couple of pounds or so. If I had my own money I wouldn't need to . . .'

She broke off, seeing that patient look steal into his blue eyes which, she had lately come to realize, meant something other than patience; an icy gaze more alarming than any outburst of anger or raised voice – a warning stare she imagined he'd give a business opponent.

It wasn't as if she had ever been frightened of him. She could never be that, but the look did unsettle her, hurt her. Instantly she changed her tone.

'If I had my own money, I wouldn't need to bother you so much,' she repeated. 'I've been wondering – if you showed me how one invests in stocks and shares, I might feel less . . . troubled about . . . about troubling you so often.'

She was making a mess of the explanation but the icy expression had vanished and he was smiling indulgently, for a moment making her feel once more like a child being taught its ABC.

'And you could spend it as you wish?' Spoken slowly, it was more a statement than a question. 'And when you've exhausted it all, what then?'

He paused, gazing at her from the other end of the breakfast table, the query in his voice still lingering.

She thought quickly. 'Investing – rather like having to earn it – I will know how to look after it. I had to look after what money I had before I met you. I know I can do that again.'

She waited for his answer while he seemed to be considering his reply. Finally he laid down the knife and fork he'd been using and indicated for her to approach his end of the table, which she did after a moment's hesitation.

'Now listen, my dear,' he said indulgently, 'if this is what you really want to do, then I will help you. But you must be guided by me so that you come to no harm. Speculating on the Stock Exchange is no light matter. One can lose everything in the blink of an eye.'

'But one can also gain,' she reminded him.

'Quite so, but you should realize, if you are going to

embark on such a venture, you will have to apply your mind to studying the market at all times. At all times, do you understand? It cannot be done frivolously.'

'I had to watch carefully enough after I left home,' she reminded him. 'I had no resources. I had to keep my mind on what went out and what I had left to see me through a week. I had no one to help me then.'

As her eyes misted at the memory, he took her hand, patted it gently. 'I know, my dear.' He grew thoughtful for a moment then, letting go of her hand, he stood up and went towards door.

'Where are you going?' she called after him, mystified.

'To fetch yesterday's *Financial Times* from the library. I shall be back in two ticks, my dear.'

His sudden enthusiasm had taken her by surprise and moments later he reappeared with the thick, pink broadsheet, saying, 'We'd best go into my study,' and taking her hand, led her from the breakfast room. Spreading the paper on the desk, he made her sit in his brown leather swivel chair, himself remaining standing, leaning over her.

For the next two hours he explained the intricacies of stock market dealings, his tone low and patient, yet she could detect a faint hint of enjoyment. It felt they were closer than they had ever been in all their married life as he explained a little of the jargon used that would help her understand what she read.

'You must realize that as a novice you are up against those who have been investing for half their lives.'

'But I have you behind me,' she said eagerly.

'But you'll still have much to learn, my dear. There are well over two thousand quoted companies to choose from, so you must identify the shares and judge if they are going to behave as you hope. It can become quite time-consuming, but utterly fascinating should you find you've a natural bent for it.'

As he continued to explain and she to listen attentively, his voice grew solemn and patient; a tutor and his pupil.

'There are many types of shares – blue chips, recovery shares, growth stocks . . . But we will not go into this just yet.'

He was turning the financial pages slowly, pointing out the various options, most of it going over her head as yet.

'You will need a portfolio,' he was saying close to her ear as he bent beside her. 'A collection of different shares and other investments designed to spread your risks. There are risks attached – which shares are good and carry low risk and those which could prove far from good. There's a deal of luck attached. You must use your own judgement carefully. With many successful investors it is instinctive. You are a beginner, but you will have me beside you to guide you. And I will guide you, my dear, so that you do not make any glaringly wrong decisions. I will do all I can to keep you safe.'

Madeleine nodded, biting her lip as she tried to take it all in. In all the time she had known him he'd never spoken of his stockbroker business or his own dealings. Now so much candid information came as a surprise.

'Don't let it worry you, my dear,' he was saying, seeing her look of concern. 'I'll be here to prevent you making any costly mistakes. Companies are more than a mere set of investment figures. The smallest, unexpected turn of events, and everything you've made could be lost. It has happened before and it will happen again. You have to be prepared for the unknown. But I will run you through profit and loss accounts and balance sheets of whatever companies you intend to invest in.'

He paused, smiling indulgently. 'I will explain anything that confuses you – if you still wish to go on after all I have explained and all I still have to explain to you.'

Did she wish to go on? She'd thought it would be so easy, seeing how easily he seemed to make money. Now, listening to him, she realized what a huge venture she was taking on. What did she think she was doing, she a woman, trying to invade a man's world?

Yet seeking any other way to find enough money for an investigator to trace her baby, with James seeming so reluctant to help, was impossible. It was a mystery why he was so ready to grant her wish in this venture when he denied her the opportunity to find her child. Well, now she'd do it on her own.

And so she began to cut her teeth on the mysteries of stocks and shares, listening to James, acting on his advice, slowly learning as the months crept towards Christmas, ever fearful of making a wrong judgement as James had warned could happen to anyone and lose what she'd reaped; her rewards were modest but growing steadily. So far she had been fortunate.

Practically dedicating himself to the task, advising, warning against this or that move, he was at times almost overcautious, behaving as though it was all too much for someone like her to get her head around, causing her to resent the implication that it was because she was a woman. In a way he was right as she fought with the seemingly endless aspects of the money market. But as the months went by she was slowly growing more conversant with it all so that by Christmas she found herself needing James's routine advice less and less, although his expert advice was still worth listening to.

She'd discovered that she had a flare for it, a sixth sense that seldom led her astray. She had begun too to notice that while he'd congratulate her on her cunning he seemed to attribute it more to luck than judgement, as if a woman shouldn't be deemed capable of calm judgement. It nettled, but her purpose was of greater importance than getting riled by his attitude, every small success put by with the purpose of accruing enough to hire herself an investigator to find her baby. She was aware that after all this time it could be a lengthy business but was determined that James's attitude was not going to stand in her way.

Neither had she revealed anything of her plan to Anthony; hadn't even told him she was dabbling on the Stock Exchange. Theirs was another world when they were together. Nothing should spoil that. So long as she didn't fret on how long the search for her baby might take, life was sublime every minute she was with him. She prayed constantly that it would never end.

Then, just after Christmas James fell ill with pneumonia, and knowing her place had to be with James, her time with Anthony had to be curtailed.

'It's only until he recovers,' she told Anthony but he wasn't happy.

'And how long is that going to take,' he returned peevishly. 'I need you.'

'He probably needs me more,' she shot back at him a little sharper than she meant to. 'He *is* my husband and a wife's place is by her husband's side if he's ill. I *want* to be with you, darling, more than anything, but what can I do?'

She was worried for James but at the same time angry that his health was interfering with her and his nephew's time together. There was a small voice inside her head which insisted that if pneumonia should chance to end James's life, she'd be free to marry Anthony. Though she fought hard to push such wicked thoughts away they persisted. But as winter faded and James recovered, she found herself deeply relieved – not because he'd survived, but more that she would have been assailed by such a terrible sense of guilt if he hadn't, almost as if the thought itself would have caused him to die.

Although he had recovered, it wasn't the same any more. Illness had left his chest so weak that even the warmer months of early spring didn't seem to help his improvement. There were frequent bouts of bronchitis, their doctor now a frequent visitor, and with James needing specialized care, a nurse was procured. It all put a stop to most of her social arrangements, especially those parties she was known for, as James needed peace and quiet.

More and more Madeleine felt obliged to be with him, and James, less able to go regularly to his place of business, felt obliged to leave the running of it in the hands of his partner, George Foster. He hardly ever left the house these days, and his expressions of gratitude were no help to Madeleine, leaving her feeling guilty on the rare occasions she managed to steal away to see Anthony.

'We really can't go on like this,' Anthony said as she began to dress herself ready to go back to James. The shock of his words pierced her heart as if he had struck into it with a knife.

'Are you tired of me?' she exclaimed then broke down as

a sudden flood of tears overwhelmed her already miserable being; stood before him still half dressed, head bent, trembling hands covering her face.

Anthony, still naked, was beside her instantly, enfolding her in his arms. 'Good God, Maddie! Of course not, my darling! I didn't mean it to sound that way.'

'It was the way . . . the way you said it,' she sobbed into his bare chest. 'It sounded so . . . matter of fact.'

'I didn't mean it to sound that way. I was only thinking of you, my darling, being torn in two.'

'Then what do we do?' she asked, gulping, just managing to control her sobs.

'Bury this feeling of guilt, sweetheart, and start to come here again on our old regular basis. I can't bear not seeing you. I long for those afternoons we spent together. Now it's just as and when you can tear yourself away from him. I even feel jealous thinking of you there and me here. Sometimes I even catch myself wishing he would die and we could be together, always.'

The last was said in a whisper, almost inaudible, but so passionate that Madeleine felt her heart go cold. She reached up and held his face between her two hands.

'You mustn't say such things, Tony!' she burst out. 'I love you with all my heart. I sometimes feel the same – us . . . unable to be together all the time? I want to be with you, always, but we mustn't ever think such wicked things as that . . .'

She heard her voice trail off, knowing he was aware of her identical feelings, but she was too worn down to try convincing him otherwise, loathing herself for such wicked thoughts – thoughts she couldn't help having.

Seconds later her mind had shut down on this confusion of thoughts as his lips closed over hers with a fierce need, the two of them sinking back on to the already crumpled bedclothes.

Nineteen

Whether James could read her mind or merely harboured a premonition of his demise, he said to her one day, quite out of the blue, 'I feel I am being such a burden to you, my dear.'

They were sitting in the lounge where he'd insisted on being despite yet another attack of bronchitis, Madeleine holding his hand as she often did these days.

'You're not a burden, James, not at all,' she said, her tone sharp with guilt, but his fingers tightened feebly about hers.

'I fear I am,' he said. 'I'm so grateful to have you by my side. Had I not met you . . .' He broke off to another bout of coughing, his chest sounding tight and painful. It was late April and yet still he suffered. There seemed no end to it.

Waving away the nurse sitting nearby as she jumped up to help, he went on, 'I don't know how long this blasted condition will last before it sees me off, but in case it does—'

'James, don't say things like that!' Madeleine burst out, but he let go of her hand and held up his own to still her protest.

'In case it does,' he continued. 'I need to do something for you . . . Something you've wanted for a long time. Just lately I've been giving more thought to it. Of course, if anything happens to me you will be left safe and comfortably off, but I need to know that you will not be left on your own.'

'Please,' she began in alarm, now certain that he knew about her and Anthony, but again he held up his hand to quell her outburst.

'I've decided,' he went on, interrupted by yet another heavy bout of coughing and then recovering, while she sat tense with dread of what he knew. 'I have decided, my dear, to engage a reputable enquiry agency—'

'James!' she could only gasp defensively, but again he cut her short.

'My way of expressing my gratitude for all you have done for me,' he continued, misinterpreting her outburst. 'I have held off for so long but it now seems time I made an effort to grant you your wish.'

He stopped to regain his laboured breath, a sound that would usually have pierced right through her, though not this time as she sat tense with self-recrimination, wondering how long he had known.

'I can't say they will be successful,' he finally continued, slowly now. 'All I can say is that we can but try, my dear.' Was he talking about her and Anthony?

'I don't understand, James,' she said.

His hold on her hand again tightened a little. 'I've decided to try and trace your daughter for you, my dear. The firm I have in mind has a fine reputation of being very successful tracing missing persons. And if they do prove successful, and I pray for your sake that they are, I will rest content knowing you'll not be left entirely alone when I'm no longer here.'

There flooded over her an intense sense of relief together with another of overwhelming joy. Quite overcome by the gratitude he was trying to show, all she could do was half collapse in his arms, weeping stupidly.

'I've done nothing to deserve this,' she whispered almost incoherently as she wept.

'But you have,' he said quietly, patting her shoulder. 'You have filled an elderly man's lonely life, and this is the only way that I can thank you.'

Recovering enough to sit up, Madeleine made no reply, her earlier joy melting away to be replaced by her own weight of guilt and the deceit that she and Anthony had practised so cruelly and for so long.

She realized that he was still speaking, so quietly that it seemed to be from a great distance. 'But for you,' he was saying, 'I might well be sitting here, alone, dwelling on a beloved wife taken from me, wanting only for my illness to take me so I could be joined with her again. But you changed all that and I need to see you happy and not left on your own when my time comes. Helping you find your daughter is the only way I can thank you.'

Madeleine made no reply as his voice died away, but her sense of guilt continued to mount. If only he knew how she really felt about their marriage. She hadn't really wanted him to die; had only wanted a solution to present itself so that she and Anthony could be together without causing him hurt. But that had been impossible, trapped in a marriage to a decent man she liked but couldn't love.

And now he was prepared to do this thing for her, this one thing she wanted above all else, other than to be with Anthony always; she felt weak with guilt and gratitude in equal measures.

'You mustn't think so highly of me,' she said in a small voice.

But he had already closed his eyes like a weary soul looking for the chance to drift away from the heavy weight of living.

She'd not told Anthony what his uncle had offered to do. Somehow she felt, maybe foolishly, that it might affect what the two of them had together. Once, when she'd mentioned there being a baby somewhere, he had gone silent. She learned then that it was better not to mention it ever, lest it caused a rift in their relationship. Bad enough that James's illness during the winter kept them apart more often than they'd have wanted, Anthony terrifying her on one occasion by saying, maybe without thinking, that if James's ill health continued indefinitely, he couldn't see what future there was for them.

She had burst into tears that had deteriorated into sobs, crying that she wouldn't want to live if he left her. He'd immediately cuddled her to him, saying he hadn't meant it, apologizing too for his lack of feeling towards his uncle. But she knew how he felt deep down inside for she felt the same.

'We can't let it come between us,' she cried, sobbing against his shoulder. 'I want to be with you but I can't just walk away from him when he's so ill.'

She would never do that she told herself, yet when James

had gone down with pneumonia, a tiny insidious voice inside her head had posed the same question over and over: what if pneumonia eventually took him, and the answer: she would be free to spend the rest of her life with Anthony.

Hating herself, she had consequently felt such a gush of relief to see him recover, sparing her the anguish of believing that those terrible thoughts in her head might have contributed to his demise. But now came a sense of impatience at the length of time his recovery was taking; disrupting her life almost as much as it had that winter, causing her plans for her Christmas Eve and New Year's Eve parties – said to be *the* ones to be seen at in London – to be cancelled. He'd needed peace and quiet and although recovering to some extent by then, her heart would not have been in it; he needed her and she wanted only to be with Anthony.

So she had seen 1922 in quietly, her days taken up helping to nurse him, seeing the year ahead as the same old water flowing under the same old bridge – a repeat of last year. Now suddenly it had all changed.

The coming of spring had helped aid his recovery to some extent apart from the bouts of bronchitis, his health still threatening to deteriorate. But the coming of warmer weather was helping to some extent, and true to his word, he had promised to have a firm of investigators try to trace her baby.

'It might take some time,' he'd said, 'maybe months, even years. She will already be seven or eight now – no longer a baby. Do you still want me to carry on with it, my dear?'

Yes, she did. But what worried her was that Anthony would look on the child as a disruption to their relationship, a fear that grew in strength as the months passed. She'd even begun to question what she really wanted, her baby returned to her or her relationship with Anthony to continue. Somehow it seemed that she couldn't have the two. Yet she longed to hold her baby – it was always a baby she saw despite James's words, recalling still that warm soft skin against her face, hearing that one tiny whimper before it was snatched out of her arms by an alarmed nurse.

Maybe if she explained, Anthony would understand how

she felt, yet whenever she lay in his arms, happy and fulfilled after having made such glorious and prolonged love, courage always failed her.

It was taking so long. October, and still no trace. Then in November came a letter saying the agent had finally located her. 'Living in Derbyshire,' James said after first reading the letter to himself. 'Jones, the name of those who adopted her named her Caroline but call her Carrie by all account.'

Like a dog, came the thought, tearing at her. *Treated like a dog? 'Here, Carrie!' Yes, like a dog.*

'What does the agent say about her?' she cried, overwhelmed by a fierce onslaught of excitement coupled with an instant need to protect. 'Does she seem well? Is she being well treated?'

The old fear of her having been brought up forced to do harsh manual work, maybe living in squalor, uncared for, maybe even having to endure ill treatment, such thoughts had always torn at her.

'Exceedingly well by all account,' James told her. 'Those who adopted her are reasonably well off and already have her name down for a reputable girls' public school when she is old enough. The report says she appears to have everything she could wish for and is apparently well loved and is, so we are told, a normal, happy, contended child.'

It was no consolation. In truth, although she would not admit it even to herself, it would have helped her case in getting her back had she been in need of love and attention. Not that she'd have intentionally wished that on her baby.

'There is, however, a snag, my dear.' James went on, his eyes on the agent's report. 'The adoptive parents are reluctant to have you see her or she to see you. They also fear that you might have a claim on her as the rightful mother, having not given her up willingly, she being taken from you against your will.'

Of course they'd be reluctant, was Madeleine's first thought, her mind going instantly to some ulterior motive the agent might have missed, though she couldn't imagine what, other than love for their adopted child.

'So I cannot see what else you can do,' James was saying, 'except to content yourself that she is well loved and happy. If you love her, my dear, don't take that away from her. It would be so cruel, torn from the only people she has ever known and loved, to be forced to live with strangers. I don't think you could bring yourself to do that to her, my dear.'

Was he trying to be just, or saying this so that he could wash his hands of the whole business? *You've done your duty and now you can rest, relieved you won't be saddled with a small child in your life. She's nothing to you. But what about me, my feelings, my love, my need of her, my desperate need of her?* These thoughts screamed in her head.

'No!' she burst out. 'How do you know if that's the truth? They could have bribed these enquiry people of yours to say good things about her.'

James was frowning, finding his urgent and dedicated search for the sake of the woman he had married and felt indebted to, being questioned.

'They are a reputable firm.' His voice was sharp. 'As a businessman I made certain they were. Why would you think I wouldn't?'

Because at your age you don't want her under your feet, that's why. But she said nothing. But tears had begun to slip down her cheeks, tears she felt she had not the strength even to lift her hand to wipe away.

'If you are absolutely set on this, my dear,' he went on in a smoother tone, seeing her grief, 'I could offer these people, say two thousand pounds to let you see her, and, let's say twice that if they forgo their right to her. If they refuse, however, there is little we can do except resort to a probably lengthy legal battle, which could take years.'

Madeleine found her voice. 'How could they refuse such a sum?' With two thousand pounds, one could buy several decent sized houses. She tried not to acknowledge that James was being almost overgenerous for her sake.

'It was merely a suggestion,' he was saying. 'They are pretty well off, apparently, and totally unable to have children of their own, so why would they relinquish her now, for any amount of money – a child they love dearly? They have, however, made one gesture. That is, in the guise of, say, a distant friend, they agree to let you see her but not to talk to her.'

'But I want her back!' Madeleine burst into a sudden flood of tears.

Having slowly stood up at her outburst, he now gazed down at her as she sank down on the sofa, now sobbing outright. 'I've done all I can,' he said firmly as if hanging on to patience. 'There's nothing more I can do.'

'There has to be,' she wailed, but his voice remained steely.

'I'm afraid not, my dear. I suggest you content yourself with merely going to see her to reassure yourself that she's happy and well cared for . . .'

'I can't do that!' she broke in.

He'd not moved to comfort her; merely stood looking at her, his voice remaining passive as he spoke again, the words biting into her.

'You cannot be so selfish as to take her from a family who loves her and whom she loves – the only parents she's ever known. To drag her away from all that, have her pine for those she loves and has lost, compelled to live with a stranger in a strange house – that is unthinking and grossly selfish and I have never put you down as being that, my dear.'

How she now hated those words, *my dear*. A term of endearment yet they could hold a sting as much as any reprimand. At that moment she hated him with all her heart. She wanted to rush at him, tear his cheeks with her nails, rake at his eyes, hurt him with every means she had. But all she did was sit crouched in misery as he came and gently patted her bent shoulders.

'You would not wish to inflict such a cruel action upon a defenceless child,' he whispered. She found herself shaking her head in agreement as quiet sobs convulsed her whole body.

Twenty

It was arranged. Under the guise of distant friends of the family briefly stopping off on route to somewhere else while passing through, she and James would arrive late afternoon. The child was to be kept far enough away to be seen but not to be spoken to.

In a fever of nervous tension, Madeleine sat beside James in the car, her eyes riveted on their chauffeur's back, not seeing anything of the towns or countryside they passed through. It was taking hours to get there, James holding her hand most of the way. They had lunch somewhere though she couldn't remember where or what she ate or anything of the tiny country pub in which she sat picking at her food, conscious only of the smell of beer and a gabble of conversation.

The agent had arranged the time of arrival and there being no delays on the way, the weather for November being kind to them, they were a little early although dusk was already closing in.

The house stood well back from the road. It was large and imposing, reached by a curving driveway, and it reminded her somewhat of her father's house from where she had been banished long ago. It wasn't a good start.

They were met by a maid servant and conducted to the rear of the house and into a spacious, well-lit conservatory. There they found themselves met with guarded smiles from the couple and an even more guarded but polite handshake by the husband, his wife having moved out of range of any necessity to partake in the ritual, her face taut and almost hostile.

Bidden to be seated at a small, round, wickerwork table, there was no pretence at social niceties, no offer of tea despite their long journey. The couple also sat; the wife a little apart from them, the husband seemingly stationing himself between them and the interior of the house as if guarding against any attempt to rush into the place when the child was brought into the living room, which they could see into, it too being well lit.

'You had a decent journey here?' he began, a formality to which James replied in equally formal tones.

'Very good, thank you.'

'It was long,' Madeleine began, only to find the two people turn their eyes to her, the wife's veiled and slightly guarded, her husband making an effort at a smile.

'It is quite a way from London. I've been there a few times but found it noisy, people hurrying about as if their lives might come to an end at any moment – which I expect they could, seeing the amount of traffic there is.'

He laughed somewhat hollowly at his own little joke. The woman gave him a sharp look upon which he sobered instantly.

'Well, we'd better get on with the business,' he said abruptly and, getting up, went into the house leaving silence behind him, his wife sitting where she was, very stiff, staring down at her hands, while Madeleine looked desperately at James for something to say. *The business*, those words, as if the baby was no more than an item on some committee agenda.

She stood up, James also rising to stand beside her. She fumbled for his hand and felt it tighten around hers. She tried to draw comfort from the grip but her heart was racing. Her mouth felt dry. Any moment now she would be seeing the baby she'd had taken from her.

A movement within the room beyond interrupted her thoughts. The man had come in holding the child in his arms but the window glass was throwing back her own reflection, making it difficult to see through from where she stood.

As he approached her view became clearer and she could see the child, her small arms clinging about his neck; a child of around seven years old. In that second she felt her stomach go over. Even though the years had passed, she had still half expected to see a baby. It came as a shock, a weird sense of looking at a stranger, not her child at all. All these years filled with pictures of a tiny, screwed up face, half buried in a white shawl. Suddenly this didn't seem real at all, no sudden recognition.

As he brought her closer to the window, still clinging about his neck as though unsure what was happening, the room's bright light revealed a round little face, blue eyes wide and round, the rosebud mouth a little apprehensive as if not sure why she was being been brought there.

Slowly, almost cautiously, as one might on being ordered to, the man moved closer still to the window though not right up to it, making it seem he was worried lest Madeleine made an attempt to leap through the very glass. But she could now see better the short, wavy, fair hair, tied on each side of the little head with bows of light blue ribbons. She wore a pale blue, short-sleeved dress, her soft little arms smooth and pink and healthy.

She was so pretty that it took Madeleine's breath away and unable to stop herself she let go of James's hand and made towards the window. The man immediately drew back a fraction as though fearing she might be contemplating running into the house to pluck the child from him.

The woman too had leapt to her feet, was instantly beside Madeleine. 'You can see she's bonny and well cared for.' The voice was sharply protective. 'She's well loved. She knows where she is here. She knows no other life but this one – no other parents but us. All her little friends are here and at her school. They come to her birthday parties. You can't take her away from all that. You couldn't be so cruel.'

Madeleine found herself weeping. She turned to the woman to beg for some understanding of how she felt, only to find the woman too had tears in her eyes.

'Please . . .' the tone was soft yet beseeching in its strength. 'You mustn't take her from us. You mustn't spoil the life she has here for the sake of your own happiness at the expense of hers? You couldn't be that selfish. You can't give a child up and then claim it back when it suits . . .'

'But I didn't give her up. She was taken from me. I had no say . . .'

'Neither has she – taken away and not understanding why.'

'She is right, Madeleine.' James's voice seemed to come from afar. He had come to stand beside her without her realizing it. She ignored him.

'But I've no children of my own. I never will . . .'

'Nor will we have, if she is taken from us,' the woman said quietly. 'And we can give her everything she needs.

'So can I . . .'

'Except the only life she knows, the friends she's made at school, the family she loves. Don't you see? To her I'm her mother, the only mummy she knows.'

A tiny voice was making itself heard in Madeleine's head as she stared at the strained, tearful face of the woman the little girl knew as Mummy: *You cannot do this to her . . . She is happy here . . . Maybe if you had permission to visit her from time to time . . .*

But that would never be enough, would it, pretending to be an aunt, or a friend of the family and watch her own child grow up not knowing her?

James was standing at her elbow. 'Come, my dear, we've done all we can here,' he was whispering in her ear. 'We're upsetting these good people. If you insist on doing this, it should now be done through solicitors.'

She shrugged away from him, but the fight had gone out of her. Even James was against her. But she'd known that all along despite him having gone out of his way to trace her child. Yes, a child, no longer the baby of her dreams, a child she couldn't recognize; didn't even have her looks; more like those who'd adopted her, or maybe not. Then suddenly as James's limousine bore them away, she knew whom she resembled: the one who'd seduced her, the child's real father who, so she'd heard, had been killed in the war.

Sinking back in her seat, feeling suddenly exhausted, she knew she could never take back the child, his child, without cringing at the way his smooth talk had misled her, only to abandon her the moment she'd found herself pregnant. She was glad he'd died – sorry for his fiancée although she was probably happily married to someone else after all this time, but him, he had got all he'd deserved and that at least was satisfying.

But the child – no, she couldn't take her back, not now. Visions of the baby she had once held had seemed strangely to have faded. She told herself now as she sat back in the car that the child was happy where she was, cared for by parents – yes, they were in a way her parents – who loved her; had given her everything she could wish for. The woman was right.

Besides, having her back, under her feet, even with a nanny, could mar her social life, her world in which a small child had no place; but more, could mar her relationship with Anthony. Madeleine glanced at James and as if on cue he turned his face to her.

'Are you all right, my dear?' he asked gently.

'I'm all right,' she echoed.

'Really it is the best thing all round, to leave her where she is,' he murmured, almost hopefully, patting her hand. 'Don't you think, my dear?'

She nodded.

'So we will let the matter drop, my dear? Leave that little family to get on with their lives?' She nodded again.

'I do think it is for the best, my dear,' he furthered. 'And you're not upset, are you? Perhaps thinking you might change your mind later?'

'No,' she said abruptly, wishing he would cease badgering her.

'I'm glad,' he said, his tone betraying his relief that the matter was done and dusted as far as he was concerned. It was what he had wanted all along but he had been gracious enough to give her a choice. She was grateful yet felt a little rattled that it had been so easy for him. But yes, the decision had been hers in the end, yet in a way she felt a sense of loss and of having been cheated somehow. She knew she would be telling herself all the way home that it had been another man's child, a man she wanted nothing to do with, wanted not to remember and that little face would have always forced her to remember. Best left alone.

He gave her hand a final pat then settled back in his seat, a weight off his mind, Madeleine thought as she closed her eyes and let the limousine carry her towards home to the life she knew, back to Anthony, now with no awkward situations over children. One day she might have a child with him, who knows. One day. The prospect helped disperse the final shreds of that which had been driving her for so long, yet now it was gone, solved, she felt deep inside that she had lost something precious.

She remained with her head reclining on the back of the car seat and felt a tear escape from the far corners of her closed eyelids.

She had said nothing to Anthony about her going to see the child's adoptive parents though she imagined he'd more or less guessed. But as he made no reference to it when they met that Wednesday, she felt it best not to stir things up. Better to say nothing than have things turn awkward. He'd made it plain some time ago, when she'd referred to the baby she'd had and her hopes of one day tracing it, that he wasn't ready to deal with a child much less one by another man.

'We've had no chance of a life together yet,' he'd said. 'When finally we do, I want us to be able to make the most of it, go out and about, abroad maybe, have a great social life, stay out to all hours with no need for you to be forever having to tear yourself away.'

All of which bore more than a hint of his expecting his uncle not to live too long into the future. She could sympathize with him though it made her feel deeply uncomfortable with his sentiments. But it was true. Their time together was becoming ever more brief, James having forced himself to go to his office only to spend less than half a day before requiring George his chauffeur to collect him and take him home again, such was his poor state of health after last winter's bout of pneumonia, his chest left in a pitiful condition, which grew more pronounced as the colder autumn weather wore on.

This Wednesday James's car barely had time to disappear before she'd left for Anthony's home, needing to see him in what little time there was left before James returned home. Hailing a taxi she'd fretted all the way there at the time the vehicle was taking, annoying the driver by repeatedly urging him to hurry.

Anthony was already waiting at the door for her as she got out of the vehicle. He rushed out, paid the driver and hurried her into the house, the door hardly closed before he was pulling her to him as if she had been away for weeks, pressing his lips so hard and urgently against hers that she was forced to pull away slightly to catch her breath.

'I can only stay for an hour, maybe hour and a half, my love,' she gasped as he pulled her to him again. 'If James is home before me I'll have to lie as to where I've been, and I hate lying to him.'

'I'd say just by coming here you're lying to him,' he said abruptly, drawing away from the kiss he would have given her, his lips tightening.

'We're both lying to James,' she reminded him, hurt, as they broke apart, she making a fuss of taking off her hat and coat, but he hardly seeming to hear her.

'I miss you. Every day without you is like a lifetime, and now we're asked to spend one hour a week together. It can't go on like this.'

'Then what do you want me to do?' she shot at him.

'I don't know.'

His handsome face distorted slightly in frustration as he turned away. Quickly she hung her warm outdoor clothing on the hallstand peg and went towards him, lifting her hand and laying it on his shoulder. They were alone in the house. As always on Wednesdays, he'd given his housemaid the morning off, telling his butler he'd not be required for a few hours, his cook that he wouldn't be wanting lunch, so they had the place virtually to themselves. The staff would take up their duties again well after Madeleine left. It had become standard practice and though they knew what went on, they were loyal and discreet.

Madeleine's hand on his shoulder seemed to melt his mood and he took it, leading her into the sitting room with its blazing fire, where he poured them a drink. But their hour or so was passing. Before she'd finished her sherry and he his brandy, he was leading her upstairs to his bedroom, reminding her of her statement, almost caustically, even needlessly, that they didn't have all that much time.

'It's getting silly,' he said as they lay naked together after frantic love-making.

'I know,' she agreed miserably.

Her hunger had been satisfied all too soon, even as he took her and she cried out in ecstasy, her mind screamed that James could already have arrived back home and be wondering where she was.

'I hate having to leave like this,' she mumbled inadequately as they had a final drink together. 'If he starts asking questions I feel myself going hot and cold as I make up a story as to where I'm supposed to have been. I hate it! I simply hate it – hate the way we have to go on!'

She wanted to add, I wish he was dead, but blocked the thought in horror, her eyes filling with tears – whether from the thought or the fact that she was frustrated having to leave so soon, not seeing Anthony for another whole week, she couldn't say – maybe a little of both.

Seeing her tears, he put down his glass to hold her to him. 'I know, my dearest, I know. But it can't last much longer, his going on as he is. Maybe this time next year . . . We will be together – for always.'

She knew his sentiments echoed hers though neither of them dared refer to it in so many words as their lips met and they clung to each other.

'But while we wait,' she said when they finally broke apart, 'the whole thing is almost killing me. His time at his office is getting shorter and shorter. He comes home in such a state that at times he can hardly breathe. If he's ill again this winter, I don't know what I shall do. I won't be able to leave him to come here. It could be weeks before I see you again. If that were to happen I think I would just die.'

Her words made him hug her to him again as he whispered that she must try to be strong, that he needed her, that nothing must happen to part them. His words gave her strength, making her body tingle again, and moments later she sank with him on to the sofa as he took her once more, fully clothed, handbag still gripped in her hand as it dangled over the side of the sofa.

Travelling homeward by taxi she alternately prayed that James would not fall ill this winter, but if he were to succumb to another serious bout of pneumonia, maybe it would be a kindness if it took him; desperately trying to convince herself that it was not her wish but in the lap of the gods, and yet again hoping it wouldn't happen.

But as December dawned and the weather turned foul, he was again ill, the pneumonia of last year having taken its toll with yet another bout of bronchitis, this time really laying him low. And now as she had suspected, she was tied to the house, finding herself forced to be by his side despite Dr Peters' regular visits and a permanent nurse tending him day and night.

Whether it was worry over James or the fretting at the difficulty in visiting Anthony, she too found herself suffering bouts of poor health. She felt tired, listless; prone to weep for no apparent reason. Also she'd not seen a period in a while. It was all this worry.

There had been no social event over the holiday season because of James's condition. Who'd want to enter a house with infection hovering around? Even though Dr Peters had said bronchitis wasn't infectious, people were loath to kick up their heels in a place of sickness. It was now February, James recovering slowly. But she felt dreadful in herself, at odd times feeling slightly sick, especially on waking up. Visiting their doctor for a pick-me-up, he'd insisted on examining her after she'd spoken of a lack of energy.

'Yes, worry might be the cause,' he said, 'I shall give you a tonic but it's best to make sure from the start that it is nothing deeper.' He regarded her closely as he questioned her. Finally, he smiled.

'My dear lady, do you not realize your condition?'

'What condition?' she asked. It was then a spark of memory hit her – all those years ago, those same feelings.

Seconds later her doctor was confirming her realization. 'Well, my dear,' he was saying, using James's own expression. 'I am happy to tell you that you are pregnant, and may I be the first to convey to you my sincere congratulations. Your husband will be so very happy – a man of his age, discovering himself a father – wonderful news for you both.'

Hearing him, all she could do was force as bright a smile as she could muster while in her head it seemed her own voice was screaming at her: *you can't have it – you can't – you're going to have to do something about it – somehow!*

'Please,' she heard herself saying. 'I want to tell him myself, if that's all right. I'd be grateful if you say nothing to him not even to congratulate him until I have told him myself.' It sounded almost like a plea, a guilty plea, but he smiled understandingly.

'I shall not say a word until you have. A mother-to-be should never be robbed of her moment of joy.'

She couldn't recall how she had got out of the doctor's surgery, how she had got herself home, her world seeming to have collapsed around her.

Twenty-One

It was a week of abject despair, not knowing which way to turn. Even James, wrapped up in his own ill health as he was, noticed something wrong.

'You're not going down with a chill, are you, my dear. You must take more care of yourself.'

'I'm fine,' she parried, trying to put on a bright smile – a smile that did not feel as if it were working.

'Because I'd hate to see you fall prey to anything you might have caught from me.'

'I'm quite well, James. I'm merely worried for you, nothing more.'

'Then it may be that you are taxing yourself much too much over me. I'm so sorry, my dear, I try to bear up for your sake. But you must stop worrying on my behalf, sitting up with me for hours on end, that sort of thing. We've a paid nurse to do that. You must try to take things easy.'

'It's just that I can't help worrying about you,' she lied.

'Maybe you need a little holiday,' he said, brightening. 'Get away from the worry of me. I shall be all right. There is our staff and I'm in the good hands of our doctor and the nurse. I could arrange for you to spend a week or two by the sea, before the weather turns too foul – a nice hotel . . .'

'I'll be fine,' she cut in but already her thoughts were pulsing – an entire two weeks by the sea, alone with Anthony. His bank would survive without him for two weeks. Life suddenly seemed wonderful again – until she remembered her condition. How was she going to face Anthony with it? What would his reaction be? And James, the ugly business of having to tell him, the pain it would cause him – he didn't deserve that. Even if she withheld the news from him, all too soon he would notice the change in her shape.

The future loomed like a black cloud, ever descending to obliterate her world. She seethed with uncertainty so that even the thought of spending two weeks alone with Anthony suddenly bore no excitement for her.

She gave James as bright a smile as she could muster and said, 'I'll think about it, love.'

What she would do was tell Anthony what James had suggested, and if he agreed, tell him about herself when they were away together, when she thought the time was right. But after that, what then? That prospect she couldn't bring herself to face, much less name. Not yet.

Things seemed to be going her way. James had almost ordered her to spend a short time away from him. When she told Anthony he immediately leapt at the idea.

'I'm virtually little more than a figurehead at the bank. I've a capable and trustworthy staff and Robert my assistant manager could run the place single-handed if I let him!'

He had laughed and held her to him as they lay together snuggled and satisfied beneath the warm bedclothes.

'It's just a shame it's not high summer and we could lie on the beach together. But beggars can't be choosers, any port in a storm, and we'll just have to make do and mend . . .'

'Oh, do shut up!' she laughed gaily at his playful, almost tortured string of clichés.

The following week they drove off to Brighton, trusting that the February weather might be more clement on the south coast. It wasn't. But despite the cold, the continuous rain, the high winds practically confining them to their hotel most of the day, other than dinner at the best restaurants, dancing at the Pavilion, going to a cinema or attending a theatre, the entertainments up with any London West End could provide – life was wonderful.

Each night and most afternoons they made frantic love as though it was their last time, she pushing him to almost insane lengths, leaving them both gasping; at the back of her mind she thought such rough, almost rape-like handling, making her cry out like one in pain, might shock the – as yet – minuscule thing inside her to abort.

Each time, cleansing herself in the bathroom, she would look for signs, but there was nothing, not one drop of blood that might have set her heart soaring. By the end of their stay, she was at her wits' end. She was going to have to tell him. Better him than James. He would know how to handle his uncle. And who knows, he might be excited to find himself a prospective father, for all his talk about not wanting a child. But even that would raise complications – James having to be told and he so ill at the moment. How would it all be solved? No matter how, it would be James who would suffer. That prospect made her feel sick as she and Anthony lay in each other's arms that last night of freedom.

What made her say it, she didn't know, but suddenly it burst out of her. 'Anthony, I have to tell you, darling. I'm pregnant.'

It seemed to her he had stopped breathing. The moment seemed to go on and on. Then he suddenly shot up as if propelled from his pillow to stare down at her.

'You're what?'

She sat up slowly, feeling a little sick, caught by the tone of his voice. 'It must have been one of those times when we were too carried away to use something. It has happened on a few occasions . . .'

'. . . because you were too eager to wait for me to take the necessary precautions first.'

His voice seemed to grate so that all she could think of to say was. 'I'm sorry, darling.'

For a moment he didn't reply. Then in a husky, flat-toned voice, he said, 'Are you sure you're pregnant? You could be imagining it. You could be mistaken.'

'I am sure,' she whispered. 'It's been nearly three months since I last saw my monthlies and I've always been so regular. So I saw a doctor and he confirmed it.'

'Then you're going to have to get rid of it.' His voice sounded almost matter of fact – the voice of one pronouncing the death sentence upon a criminal in the dock, no inflection, no feeling, completely insensitive.

'What do you mean?' she asked stupidly.

He gave her a look then got slowly out of bed, his strong,

naked body lithe and pale in the thin glow of the hotel's lights – the body she never stopped loving to look at.

'You know what I mean?' he echoed, now staring out of the window. 'You can't have it.'

'How can you say that?' she burst out. 'It's yours! Your baby!'

'And what about James – he'll ask questions when he finally sees you bloating up.' That suddenly sounded so coarse to her ears. 'You've told me you've never had relations with him. And when he realizes that you and I . . . What then? It stands to reason he's going to have to divorce you. The pain that's going to cause him, and him being sick . . .'

He broke off, still gazing from the window, his outline beautiful to her eyes – now so clouded with tears as to make his shape indistinct.

'And what if he refuses to divorce you?'

She remained silent, her mind filled with that dread.

'What if he claims to the world that it is his? What then?'

'But it's *your* baby!' she cried out. She saw him turn abruptly from the window to face her, his silhouette now a dark outline.

'What if I say it isn't mine?'

Madeleine could hardly believe what she'd heard. 'How can you say that, Anthony? This is your baby!'

'But I don't want it.'

'What?'

'I – don't – want – it.'

'But it's yours . . .'

'Don't keep saying that! You know how I feel about us. We certainly can't have a child when we're not married and I'm not prepared to face the world in that situation and neither should you be. And even when the time comes – if it comes – when we are able to marry, I don't want kids the second we're spliced. I told you before, Maddie. I need to enjoy a decent social life first, you and me – together.'

But she could still hear those earlier words of his ringing in her head *if it comes,* almost like a threatened death knell to their relationship. She needed to confirm that she had misinterpreted them. All she could think to ask was, 'What if he did divorce me?'

'Then we'd be married, darling.'

Mellowing, he moved back to the bed and stood gazing tenderly down at her. Her rapidly beating heart slowed a little. In a moment he would take her in his arms. It was going to be all right.

'Though I rather doubt he will,' he continued. 'He dotes on you.'

'I can't see what else he could do,' she whispered.

'All I know is, I couldn't bring myself to cause him such hurt and misery,' he answered in a flat tone. 'And I don't think you'd want to either. So as far as I can see, your only course is for him not to know at all by doing something about your condition, and very soon.'

The rapid heartbeats returned with a heavy thump. 'Tony – I can't! I couldn't bear to do such a wicked thing.'

'You've got to.'

'Please, darling . . . It could be so dangerous.'

'If you don't I can't see any future for us.'

His words stunned her. How could he turn off his love for her so easily, think so little of her feelings? All this time, had he just been making out he was crazy over her only so he could take from her that something he needed as a man rather than having to look for it from street whores? No, she was wrong – he wasn't like that.

'You can't mean that?' she cried, throwing herself against him as he stood there. She felt him sink on the bed beside her, his bare body almost wrapping itself about her, warm and comforting.

'Darling, of course not, but for both our sakes, and for his, you can't have this baby. You must know that.'

She was silent, seeing the sense of it. He was right. She couldn't have it and cause James such pain. In truth she didn't want it; had thought she had, but all sorts of complications, James's hurt, his confusion, disillusionment – he certainly didn't deserve it. And Anthony, wanting no baby hanging around, understandably looking to enjoy a free, exciting social life with her and no strings attached. Maybe later, much later – she needed to settle for that. But thoughts of abortion – a dangerous business, what if she were to die?

Another solution had presented itself. If she went away until the baby was born as she had last time, the child quickly adopted, no one would need to know; James would be none the wiser, saved all that hurt, and she and Anthony could pick up their lives together as if nothing had changed.

She almost suggested it to Anthony but she knew what he would say: 'Six months – far too long to be away and what excuse would you make?' She recalled how long it had seemed to her that last time, there all on her own, at the mercy of inconsiderate nurses. This time, not at her father's unkind will, she'd make sure of a top quality nursing home with good food and superb care, but it would still feel interminable.

'You could visit me,' she said hopefully. 'No one will know.'

'Maddie, you're not thinking straight. Why not just get rid of it and have done with it? Not only that, I can see you fretting in years to come, regretting and wanting me to trace it, like you persuaded James. No, I need you to do as I ask. I shall get the best doctors for you. You'll have nothing to fear if that's what's worrying you. You'll be as safe as houses.'

'You have to give me time,' she begged almost feebly, 'time to think, to steel myself. It's not an easy thing . . .'

'I know. And I understand, my darling. But you mustn't leave it too long until it's too late to do anything. The longer we delay, the more danger—' He caught himself and started again. 'The more difficult it will be. Promise me, Maddie, you're not intending to leave it until it's too late to do anything.'

'I promise,' she said lamely and he became instantly brisk.

'Right then, we'll give it another couple of weeks so you can get used to the idea. Then I set about getting the ball rolling,' he said, as if arranging a soirée. A momentary surge of anger consumed her. *Get used to the idea*! All very well for a man – he wouldn't have to suffer the trauma of what she would, or thought she would, be expected to go through.

But he had clasped her to him, tenderly kissing her. 'I know how hard this must be for you, darling. But the sooner it's done the better for us both. You do understand, don't you, sweetheart? It's for the best.'

She nodded, strangely relieved as he moved away that he'd not tried to cement his loving concern for her further by extending that concern with anything more than a few kisses.

It was the bouts of morning sickness, so violent that dear innocent James had become concerned and spoke of their doctor taking a look at her, that helped her make up her mind that much quicker.

'There's nothing wrong with me,' she protested almost too hastily. The doctor she'd consulted hadn't been their family physician so she was safe there. 'It's only because I'm constantly worrying over you,' she lied.

James had been so unwell throughout January that she was truly worried for him. How he had managed to hold his own against such depleting bronchitis, was amazing. He no longer went to his office, making it increasingly difficult to see Anthony. She would make up people she had to visit, knowing he wouldn't query it, so seeing Anthony had become briefer, mainly because she could not bring herself to submit to his kind of violent love-making. Once she had loved it, but oddly not now.

'I told James I'd only be gone an hour. I can't have him asking questions and me having to lie,' she said after they'd kissed in the hallway, but he seemed hardly to hear her.

'It's all arranged, darling – weekend after next. So you're going to have to lie to him once more. Tell him you've been invited to stay that weekend in the country with some friend or other. It'll be all right because he's not well enough to go with you.'

It was said almost casually, as though he was glad James was ill. But she said nothing, her mind centred on the awfulness of the coming prospect.

'Tony, I don't want to do this,' she said as they moved towards the stairs and his bedroom. 'Say if it all goes wrong? I'm terrified. I don't think I can go through with it.'

'It won't. And you have to.'

He sounded so casual, no soothing word of understanding. As they began to mount the stairs she felt suddenly angry. 'You don't seem to care how I feel,' she cried, coming to an abrupt stop halfway up.

'I'll be with you.' But his tone was impatient.

'With me?' she spat. 'Is that supposed to make me feel better?'

'Look. It'll be over in less than a few minutes then a little wait and it'll all come away. You'll have a nice rest, a good sleep, and next day we'll be back here and you can take it easy for the rest of the day. You might be a bit shaky but you can say you felt ill while you were away – or something like that. Now come on, darling.'

He gave her arm a little tug but she stood resolutely where she was, glaring up at him, for a moment, hating him. 'It's all so easy for you, you unfeeling bastard!'

Pulling her hand free of his, she turned to go back downstairs. The next second, she hardly knew how, her foot had slipped on the next step, her body following, and she found herself sliding helplessly down the remaining six steps on her back to finally land with a heavy thump on the hall floor.

She vaguely heard Anthony cry out, 'My God, Maddie!' then he was there bending over her. 'God, Maddie, are you hurt?'

She was crying. 'Of course I'm hurt! I've hurt my back. And my left leg is doubled under me.'

She felt him gently manipulate the leg until he could straighten it to its normal position. It gave her no pain, her back hurting only a little now.

'Can you try to stand?' he asked and when she nodded, saying she would try, he gently helped her up, she resting one arm about his neck. Her leg seemed fine and the pain in her back had diminished to hardly anything.

'I'm all right,' she said, annoyed with herself now for being so clumsy, and with him for being the cause of it.

'Do you still want to go on upstairs?'

Such a damn stupid question! 'No thank you,' she said

sharply. 'I need to sit down in an armchair.' She now found she was trembling. Even a mere six stairs was quite a way to slide down on one's rump.

Carefully he helped her to an armchair in the sitting room, asking after she'd sunk down if she'd like something to drink, a whisky perhaps. She nodded then immediately shook her head. 'I'd rather have a cup of tea if you don't mind.' She still wasn't feeling happy with him.

'I'll tell Mrs Glover. She'll be in the kitchen.'

His cook, a woman he could trust to keep his business to herself, whatever her private opinions might be, was soon bringing in a tray of tea, enquiring as she poured for her if she felt all right, to which Madeleine nodded, thanking her for her concern. Mrs Glover, trusted servant though she was, had no idea of course of her condition and returned to her kitchen convinced that no harm had been done by the fall.

The moment she finished her tea, Madeleine stood up carefully, testing her back and, finding it only slightly tender, said that she felt she would be better returning home, taking an odd sense of satisfaction on seeing Anthony's face lengthen. Surely he hadn't expected her to roll around in bed with him after what had happened?

He was obviously worried for her, telling her he would get her a taxi, cautioning her to take things easy, only to spoil it by hastily going over the arrangements afresh for the weekend after next.

She understood the need for urgency but couldn't quell the return of her queasy anxiety at what was to come, nor the screwed up anger that it was she who must go through it, not him, and refusing to allow him the benefit of her feeling that he too might be keyed up and worried for her.

One more week and it would be all over she kept telling herself but it didn't help. As requested she told James she planned to visit some old friends in Oxfordshire that weekend, but it reaped no strong response.

'That would be nice for you,' he said as he lay propped up in bed, having suffered another sudden bout of laboured, wheezing breath. 'You need to get away for a day or two. No pleasure spending day after day with a sick old fool.'

'You're not an old fool!' she told him angrily, upset with herself mostly for needing to deceive him as she was doing.

'But I am sick – and that can be no fun for you. And a weekend with friends will do you good. Go and enjoy it. Don't worry about me. I'm being well looked after.' All this between each laboured intake of breath.

'Are you certain?' she couldn't help asking.

'Of course, my dear,' he replied but already he was sinking down on his pillow, closing his eyes, seeking rest. 'Now I need to sleep awhile.'

She watched him for a moment longer until he opened one eye and feebly waved her away, whispering, 'Go on, my dear.'

The next days went by far too quickly. All she wanted now was to see Anthony, talk over the coming weekend with him, feel that he was sharing in her worry about what was to happen. She wished with all her heart it could be as it used to be: James leaving for his office, she hurrying out hailing a taxi, in a little while to be lying in Anthony's arms, knowing they had most of the day together.

This Wednesday, as always these days, it would be hardly an hour before she must return home, in case James felt well enough to get up from his bed. She must wait for him to drift off to sleep before she felt it safe to leave the house with no need to make excuses. Meantime she might as well get down her small weekend case and begin selecting what to take with her for those two days. Soon it would be all behind her. The thought brought a surge of excitement as she bent over the case to flatten a couple of night dresses. As she did so she felt something warm on the tops of her inside legs, something liquid, almost as if she had wet herself as she'd bent forward. She gave a small frown and straightened up.

Putting a hand down to where the tiny trickle had made itself felt, she felt something sticky. Bringing her hand back up slowly she stared at it. It was red, sluggish red.

Twenty-Two

Hastily cleaning herself up, she hurried to a drawer in her wardrobe and took out one of the squares of towelling she usually kept for sanitary use, fumbling as she folded the small square of towelling into an oblong shape before pinning each end to the piece of tape she had tied around her waist. It was what she always did when she had her periods, but today she was shaking all over, her trembling fingers hardly able to fasten the safety pins. It felt as if her breath was strangling her as she redressed and as quietly as possible made her way downstairs to the kitchen area. The last thing she wanted was to hear James's voice calling her name should he hear her moving about.

The kitchen was the first place she thought of. She had a need to tell someone – someone whom she could trust. Their cook, Mrs Cole, had more or less taken her under her wing from the first time she had set foot in this house as James's wife, being some thirty-odd years older than Madeleine and well in charge of herself. She had always been there to give advice should Madeleine need it and Madeleine enjoyed taking full advantage of her kind attentiveness, although of course she'd stopped short of telling the woman about herself and Anthony.

Seeing her obvious distress, Mrs Cole ceased whatever she had been doing and, waving to the scullery maid to make herself scarce, hurried over to her employer's wife. 'Whatever's the matter, dear?' she began.

From the first she'd never called her mistress or madam; always 'dear' or sometimes 'love' when on her own, madam only when formality called for it, usually in James's presence. Madeleine had never complained, so it had remained 'dear' or 'love' ever since. And now to Madeleine's ears it held some comfort. Even so, she stood stiff and unyielding before the approach.

'What is it, love?' Mrs Cole said again, bewildered.

'I'm—' Madeleine heard her voice die away, tried again. 'I'm . . .' She took a shuddering breath. 'I'm scared . . .' her voice again dying away. 'Something's happened. I've had some bleeding and I don't know what to do.'

Quickly the woman took over. 'Come with me, love,' she said, guiding her from the kitchen and across the narrow passage to the housekeeper's sitting room, being housekeeper as well as cook. Leading her to the little sofa, she said gently, 'Sit down, love. Your usuals, is it? Are you flooding?'

Madeleine shook her head, unable to reveal the truth, but it seemed that Mrs Cole had taken her own assumption for granted.

'You should rest more. Probably worry – worrying about the master and all. I'll have young Lily bring you a hot drink, then perhaps you should go back to bed for the morning. Rest is what you need. I'll tell the master to arrange for your lunch to be taken to your room. Maybe your monthlies are a bit heavier than usual. They can be a bit alarming if you've not had one like that for a long while, but as you know it'll dwindle in a day or two.'

'It's not my monthlies!' Madeleine cried before she could stop herself.

A brief silence descended, then slowly, 'Then what, dear?'

Without warning, Madeleine leaned forward. Hands covering her face, she broke into sobs while Mrs Cole sat beside her, quite still for a while, just looking at her. At last she asked, 'What are you trying to say, love?'

Madeleine could no longer hold it in. 'I'm pregnant!'

Her voice choked off into silence, not seeing Mrs Cole's face breaking into smiles or the next moment changing to concern. 'You're definitely sure there's bleeding, dear?'

As Madeleine nodded, her manner became urgent. 'But that could be dangerous. You could lose it. We must call Dr Peters immediately.'

'No! Don't do that! Please – no one else knows.'

'What about your husband?'

'He doesn't know either.'

'But surely he knows of your condition?' She sounded

bewildered and Madeleine could guess what she was thinking, that had he been told, by now he would be letting everyone know, making a great deal of it that he, a man of his late years, was to become a father.

'I daren't tell him,' Madeleine whispered desperately. Mrs Cole was staring at her as if not knowing what to make of this.

At last she sat down beside her, laid an understanding arm about Madeleine's shoulder as she whispered, 'Why ever not?'

Madeleine had no idea how to reply; wished she hadn't rushed down here, so fast, so desperate to have someone help her, advise her.

'Because,' she began, breaking off then tremulously beginning again. 'Because . . . It's not his.'

There, she'd said it, instantly wishing she hadn't as the words, 'Dear God!' like a tiny whispered explosion broke from the woman's lips.

'How d'you mean, it's not his?' she said, her gentle tone taking on a harder note.

The question sounded utterly absurd, but all Madeleine could do was break down afresh in sobs of misery. 'It's not his! What's he going to say?'

She felt the arm lift off her shoulders. 'It's not what he's going to say. It's how he's going to feel. The man's ill. Faced with something like this – how could you ever have done such a thing to him? Who is the father?'

That she was not prepared to tell her. She had said too much already and she shouldn't have. She should have gone straight to Anthony. Though maybe he wouldn't have been home yet, or maybe he would, waiting for her, waiting to talk about the following weekend ready to prepare her for the ordeal facing her. If she could make it to Anthony's they could call a doctor from there and perhaps James would never have to know. What the procedure would be she had no idea. Whether a doctor would take it away, or just stop the bleeding, she had no idea, but it must not happen in this house.

Her thoughts were in turmoil. There was a lurking relief

that there may be no need now to go through the trauma of placing herself into the care of an abortionist. She'd told Anthony she wanted a baby, but not at this moment. All she knew was that she needed to be with him. Certainly not here being attended to by James's doctor, with James having to be informed, having to face him. No need for Mrs Cole to observe and maybe tittle-tattle, no matter how trustworthy. No need for James to be any the wiser.

'I must go!' she burst out. 'Don't say anything to Mr Ingleton, please, Mrs Cole.'

'I should think not!' The tone was no longer kind. 'News like that could kill him, ill like he is. How could you treat the master . . .'

But Madeleine was already out through the kitchen door, up the basement steps and hurrying down the hall towards the main door. She had only gone halfway when a sharp little pain seared her insides low down and made her gasp, stopping her in her tracks. Tense, she waited for it to ease, but then a second pain took over, slower, heavier, a deep, more persistent grinding like a fist being turned inside her.

Doubling up, she heard herself cry out, 'Mrs Cole – come quick!'

Mrs Cole arrived in an instant and helped her into the sitting room, lowered her on to a sofa, and made her lie back, saying, 'I'm calling the doctor. No arguments.' Raising her voice she bellowed, 'Beattie! Beattie, where are you?'

'Up here, Mrs Cole,' came a voice from over the landing above.

'Come down here, Beattie, this minute!'

As the girl appeared at the doorway, Mrs Cole turned to her. 'Phone Mr Ingleton's doctor. The number's in the book hanging at the side of the telephone. Tell him it's extremely urgent. Do you understand? EXTREMELY URGENT! Tell him Mrs Ingleton has been taken seriously ill.'

Faintly, between groans, Madeleine could hear the girl asking for the number, then as if calling back over her shoulder. 'Mrs Cole, he's asking if I mean *Mr* Ingleton.'

'No. Tell him it's *Mrs* Ingleton, Mrs Madeleine Ingleton. Tell him it's terribly urgent and to come straight away.'

A moment's pause, then, 'He's asking, what's the matter with her.'

Mrs Cole gave an irritated tut-tut and raised her voice even louder. 'It's for him to tell us! Tell him it's a woman's trouble and looks serious and to come immediately.' She looked down at Madeleine and smiled. 'After all, Mr Ingleton pays him.'

When Madeleine, holding her breath against another sluggish twinge, barely returned the smile, Mrs Cole stood up, calling to the girl in the hall, 'As soon as you're off the phone go to the laundry room and collect some clean towels and a couple of clean flannels. Tell young Lily to heat some water – a couple of kettlefuls will do – pour it in a basin and bring it to me.'

Seconds later, came Beattie's voice. 'Lily's not there.'

'Then she must be outside in the garden or in the loo out there. I told her to make herself scarce. If you can't find her, do it yourself. But be quick about it!'

This last was said almost in panic as Madeleine felt another pain run through her and let out a cry, not one to endure pain in silence. The sound seemed to echo through the house, bringing Beattie up the few stairs from the kitchen at a run, slopping hot water on her way.

'Put it here,' cried Mrs Cole. 'And go and get a waterproof sheet – two waterproof sheets – one for the floor and one for this sofa. Can't have the Master's good furniture all wet and stained.'

'What's happened to her?' Beattie enquired.

'None of your business!' Mrs Cole snapped at her. 'Now go and wait outside the door for the doctor. Bring him straight in here when he arrives. Bring him in here, then you can go into the kitchen till he's gone. I don't want you moving about the house just now.'

'Why not?'

'Don't ask questions. Just keep Lily company when she comes back from wherever she is until I can say you can go about your duties again.'

'What if the Master wants anything?'

'I doubt he will, he's not at all well and won't be down

until well into the morning. Now be a good girl, and go and sit with Lily when she appears. Don't gossip with her about this. If she asks, say I'll talk to her later. Do you understand?'

'But what if Mr Merton comes back down?'

Fortunately, James's butler had been upstairs with him having awakened him and served him his morning tea as he always did first thing most mornings. Since James's health had deteriorated these last couple of years, he'd have Merton stay and chat while he sat in his armchair by the window where the sun poured in if the day was fine, Merton pottering about the room or sitting on a hard chair nearby if James fancied a chat.

Over the years, long before he'd married Madeleine, they'd become almost like friends, more so now that James's health had grown steadily more chronic.

'If Mr Merton returns downstairs, I shall tell him Mrs Ingleton is a little unwell – that's all he needs to know for now. Now go!'

As the girl went out of the door, Mrs Cole turned her attention back to Madeleine. 'How are you feeling now?'

There was concern but no longer any real gentleness in her tone. The woman was obviously disgusted, for all she was merely staff. Madeleine gave a small, wan smile. 'Not so bad now. The pain seems to have died away. In fact I'm feeling much better.'

'Well that's encouraging. Maybe it was only a passing thing.'

'Maybe we don't need the doctor. I'll go upstairs and rest instead.'

'No, best you stay here. Moving about could start it off again. And you must have your doctor to look at you.'

It sounded as if she wanted him to prove her condition, even hope he would relay the good news to James, congratulate him on becoming a father-to-be, sparing her any temptation to confide in others, ending up with it reaching his ears and she being held responsible for spreading it. Madeleine could feel the fear gripping hold of her. How could she even hope to plead with their doctor to keep the news from James without having to explain why?

Within five minutes of receiving the phone call, Dr
Peters was being conducted into the room by the young
housemaid who, on appearing to be hovering, hurriedly
backed out at a sharp look from Mrs Cole.

Dr Peters came to stand over Madeleine, his expression
gentle and friendly. 'Now what have we been up to, my
dear?'

Before Madeleine could reply, Mrs Cole spoke for her.
'Mrs Ingleton told me she's in the family way, Doctor, but
this morning she had . . . well, you know, a little show and
she got herself in a bit of a state.'

'Quite natural,' Dr Peters said slowly. 'Well then, I need
to have a look at her. And she must go straight to bed and
rest.' He looked down at her, all smiles. 'No need for alarm
at this juncture, my dear. We will get you to bed and you
must stay there until all sign of bleeding ceases. But . . .'

Again he smiled, this time with gentle concern. 'I do
need to add that there is every possibility you could lose
the child despite rest and care. We will have to wait and see
how it goes. Hopefully all will remain well. But you must
rest and not fret overmuch. I know that is hard to do, but
you must try to concentrate on all being well. I will tell Mr
Ingleton—'

'No! Don't!' Madeleine cried. 'I don't want him worried.
It might go away and then there'll be no need for him to
know.'

Dr Peters looked mystified. 'Nonsense, my dear, he must
be told or he will be even more upset that his wife has kept
a thing like this from him.'

Madeleine sat up sharply before he could stop her. 'Dr
Peters,' she began, then seeing Mrs Cole still there behind
him, said as nicely as she could, 'I'm so sorry, Mrs Cole.
Thank you so much for all you've done for me this morning,
but do you mind leaving us please?'

She didn't seem that put out by the request. After all, she
must have already guessed what her employer's wife was
about to tell the doctor.

Once they were alone, Madeleine haltingly and almost in
a whisper mumbled her secret to him, her voice threatening

to break as tears began to course down her cheeks, not daring to look up into his face, knowing the expression she would see written there.

After she'd done, he stood there not speaking. Finally he said in low measured tones, 'You cannot keep a thing like this from him, my dear.'

She wished he wouldn't keep saying, my dear, almost as though he were in league with James.

'Even if the bleeding ceases he will want to know what all this is about.'

'We don't have to tell him.'

'Of course you must. All this activity going on in his own home, he is bound to know, ask questions. He is not a stupid man and to be perfectly honest, my dear Mrs Ingleton, you should have thought of him, his feelings, before you embarked on . . . Well, you understand what I am saying.'

Madeleine didn't answer. His sharp tone went right through her. Dr Peters spoke for her.

'I think it your duty to tell him. Or would you prefer I do it? Less traumatic perhaps than coming from you, worked up as you are.'

But Madeleine hardly heard him, as hands covering her face, she broke into a paroxysm of weeping and found herself nodding to his words without being sure why, hearing him say something about having a bed brought down lest climbing the stairs to her bedroom might cause even more danger of losing the fetus. But that was just what she wanted – to lose the thing and have done with it.

She lay in her own bed, no longer pregnant, all efforts to save the minuscule life having been for nothing. It had been a terrible few hours seeming to go on forever, the uncontrollable straining making her moan, wishing she could die. At least she'd been saved the terror of an enforced abortion but she'd no longer cared, just wanting it to end.

While she lay downstairs on the made-up bed, Anthony had telephoned on the pretext of asking after his uncle's health but really to find out where she was, so she had learned later.

Told only that his uncle was well enough but that his aunt had been taken ill, he had come bounding round on a legitimate errand of asking after her. By that time James, alerted by Merton who had returned downstairs to find chaos ruling, had himself come to investigate. It had fallen to Dr Peters to tell him the disturbing news and though he had no doubt been careful with his words, James had gone back up to his room once Madeleine was pronounced out of danger – that was three days ago. He'd not been near her since; hadn't even wanted to know whose child it was. For that at least she should have felt relieved; no third degree, no accusation, no need for her to lie to him; no adding insult to injury in his having to be told it was his own nephew. But that was no relief as she lay or sat around in her room doing nothing, like a nun in a cell, wanting only to close herself off from the world.

Anthony rang once to ask how she was. That was ten days ago. Since then there had been silence. Between weeping and staring at the four walls, Madeleine felt it would have been a blessing to have died, wished even now that she would.

Twenty-Three

Six days more confined to bed, and still James hadn't come near her.

Surely he must have guessed what she'd gone through; must have heard her crying out during the horrible process of something almost akin to a full-term birth yet with nothing to show for it in the end.

She had asked to know the sex but Dr Peters had said the sex of an aborted fetus would not be recognizable. She hated that word aborted. It sounded so unwholesome as if she'd deliberately got rid of it. It shocked her too, that it was not termed a miscarriage, which would have sounded so much more wholesome.

Afterwards she had lain drained, praying that James would decide to eventually see her. He hadn't come near and now she lay slowly recovering and trying not to feel bitter. Tomorrow she would get up, no matter what Dr Peters said. Tomorrow was Wednesday. She'd make herself feel well enough to visit Anthony. The day after her miscarriage Anthony came to the house to visit her, his aunt, as any fond nephew would, but was told that she needed complete rest, no visitors as yet apart from her husband lest she became too stressed. Everyone thought her constant weeping was related to what was now being generally referred to as her miscarriage, her devastation at losing her and James's baby. Only Mrs Cole knew why she cried.

James too was probably devastated but not for the reason the staff believed. He sat alone in the seclusion of his rooms, not even Merton allowed to come near. Madeleine knew he must be feeling utterly lost and betrayed.

Fortunately, as far as she knew, he had no idea of the identity of the father. She trembled to think how much worse it would be if he knew it to be his own nephew. Eventually he would find out and it terrified her — as if she hadn't wronged him enough already. But if only he could bring himself to see her, maybe she could explain how starved of love she had been – then she scolded herself for such a damned foolish thought, expecting a wronged man to sympathize with such a sad excuse.

In all these six days, James had not come anywhere near her; it was like some slow torture, knowing how he must feel and all the while feeling as wretched herself because of it.

Going to Anthony was the only solution she could think of to alleviate this need for someone to understand and sympathize but not for the wrong reasons. In fact Anthony might be deeply relieved that there was no longer any need to send her away for an abortion. She could hardly wait to be with him, but leaving the house without being seen, to be stopped and asked what she thought she was doing, what reason could she give? She couldn't sleep that night for thinking about it.

Next morning she awoke to an idea that seemed to have formed while she'd slept. Of course, the only one who knew her secret was Mrs Cole. It was still early as she got herself out of bed trying to ignore the weakness in her legs from six days of inertia. She dressed warmly, after a fashion, the late February mornings chill and damp, then crept cautiously down the back stairs, one slow step at a time. Her caution had less to do with meeting any of the staff on the stairs as waves of weakness that almost overwhelmed her halfway down to the kitchen where Mrs Cole would be starting her day.

It was a relief not to meet anyone, have to endure a look of surprise from someone seeing her there. Beattie would be in one of the main rooms clearing out a fire grate, resetting it for the day ahead. Young Lily would be cleaning in the kitchen or whatever she did at this time of morning. Merton, if he wasn't with James, would still be in his butler's pantry downstairs.

Mrs Cole turned around at her entrance, startled at seeing her there, her voice shrill with alarm. 'Madam, what on earth are you doing up?'

Madeleine noted the way she addressed her, no dear or love now. In an odd way, it hurt.

Mrs Cole said, 'You shouldn't be up. You should be in your bed,' and seeing her dressed for outdoors, adding almost unnecessarily, 'you're not thinking of going out, Madam! You're far from well enough.'

Madeleine drew herself up. She couldn't be seen slumping against the door for all she felt weak from having descended the stairs.

'Mrs Cole, I need you to get me a taxi, please.' She hated the way she said 'please'. It sounded almost servile, pleading, humbling.

The woman regarded her slowly then motioned to the scullery maid to absent herself. 'Go and put that rubbish over there into one of the bins outside ready for the dustmen,' she ordered then turned back to Madeleine. At Madeleine's look of pleading, her tone became a little gentler.

'You're going to see *him*?' Madeleine nodded. 'Do you think you should be doing that just now? Mr Ingleton . . .'

Madeleine shook her head but replied, 'I have to. I need to . . .' She broke off feeling herself growing faint and unsteady. With an effort she came upright, held on to the door knob to steady the sensation of swaying. The movement seemed to revive her and she took a deep breath. 'You don't understand, Mrs Cole, I—'

'Oh I understand well enough. I suppose there's little else you can do. The master's in shock as you can imagine. And hurt. Deeply hurt. But I suppose if you've no care for him in the state of shock he must be in, you'll do what you feel you have to. I'll telephone for a taxi for you. What goes on or happens after that is up to you, I suppose. None of my business.'

With that she went from the kitchen to telephone for a taxi, leaving Madeleine to sink down on a chair beside the preparation table and wait. Lily came back from putting the rubbish in the dustbin. She eyed Madeleine curiously but said nothing and knelt down beside her bucket to resume her task of washing the floor by the sink.

By the time Mrs Cole returned, Madeleine was feeling much stronger – edgy, but more in control of herself.

'The taxi will be here in about five minutes,' she stated and went on cutting rind off the bacon she'd been preparing in case the master felt like having breakfast, something he hadn't done since this business started, but she'd prepare it anyway as she had done these last six or seven mornings. The rest of the staff had had theirs at the ungodly hour of six o'clock: porridge, as always, very fortifying for a working day.

The door was opened by Jessop, Anthony's manservant and chauffeur, who managed to master a stare of surprise at seeing her here so early and with a smile stepped back to let her in.

'Mr Anthony is still in his bed, Mrs Ingleton,' he said as he conducted her into the lounge. 'I'll tell him you're here. Meantime, please make yourself comfortable. Is there anything you would like? Some tea? Or coffee?'

'I'd simply adore a cup of tea,' she said gratefully, adopting the easy way she and Anthony spoke together, the way all the young modern society people spoke, full of over-accentuations; the way she and James never spoke at home, he still tending to live as if having never left the last decade behind.

The tea was refreshing and was accompanied by a plate of gorgeous bourbon biscuits, several of which she devoured, feeling suddenly hungry. She felt stronger too. In the taxi she'd collapsed back on the seat, her head reeling, her body feeling limp and lifeless. At one time she'd wondered just what she thought she was about, that she should never have embarked on this mad venture. She'd been sure she could suddenly collapse and die in the vehicle. How she had got herself up the steps to Anthony's house she hardly knew.

Having managed to control herself as Jessop opened the door to her, and having managed to walk steady and upright behind him to the lounge, she'd been overwhelmingly glad to sink into an armchair, be left alone for a few minutes to recover until his cook came in with the tray of tea and the biscuits. She hadn't had breakfast but felt she couldn't have consumed more than one or two of them; enough to make her feel human again.

By the time Anthony came down, still in his dressing gown and silk choker, the tan silk trousers of his pyjamas peeping from underneath, she was feeling more like her old self again, glad that she had taken the risk in coming here. She needed to put this last week behind her and that could only be achieved by being here with him.

He stood looking at her. 'How're you feeling?' There was deep concern and such a depth of tenderness in his eyes that she wanted to leap up and throw herself bodily into his arms but the effort might have been too much. Revived as she felt, she knew she still wasn't right and that subsequent six days confined to bed had only helped to weaken her in her opinion.

She smiled up at him. 'I'm a lot better,' she said but he was staring down at her.

'You look drained.'

The conversation seemed stilted. Fear shot through her that he might have lost some, if not all of his love for her because of what had happened.

'I suppose I am,' she said in the same stilted tone. 'But I'll be better soon. Then we can take up where we left off . . .'

She let her voice die away. He was still staring down at her. He'd not moved from the spot.

'I'm sorry,' she went on. 'I realize you wouldn't have expected me to turn up like this. I suppose you've got to be off to the bank, even though it's Wednesday and we usually meet on Wednesdays . . .'

Again she let her voice die away, at a loss, not knowing what to say to him, her heart sinking as if through the very carpet.

Suddenly he exclaimed, 'Sod the bloody bank! Oh God, Maddie, I've been so worried. I couldn't see you. I couldn't say anything. I couldn't tell anyone . . . about us . . .'

As she stared up at him, he broke off and, bending over her, pulled her up into his arms and she clung to him as though she would die if he let her go now.

'James doesn't know it was you,' she whispered, her face buried in the warm curve of his neck and his shoulder.

She so wanted him to make love to her, but instinct told her it was too early after what had happened and maybe even dangerous.

'He'll have to know sooner or later,' he whispered.

'There's no need. Since I've lost what I was carrying, it's done. It's over – no need for him to know whose it was, so long as we're cautious.'

She knew he would be. He had no wish to go through this fear again. 'In time we can get back to where we were.'

He pulled away from her a little way still holding her. 'I don't know how much longer I can go on like this, darling. Maybe it'd be best if he did know. He would divorce you. He may do that even now. And then we can go away together and be married.' It sounded wonderful, but James wasn't well enough it seemed to think of divorce or any other course.

The weeks were going by and still James had hardly left his room. Maybe he did when she wasn't there. She thought to ask Mrs Cole then thought better of it. These days Mrs Cole was keeping herself at a distance. If they happened to have cause to speak, she now addressed her as Madam, no longer love or dear.

Chronic ill health was now preventing James from going to his office, it being managed without him, not quite so efficiently, she felt, as when he'd been at the helm. She had learned a lot about investment business from him and her own money pursuits seemed to falter very little, swelling her bank balance considerably and she had little need to consult him on anything. Not that she could these days the way his health was going.

He hardly seemed to care what she did; whether she was at home or out. At least it didn't seem to matter any more that she went out each Wednesday. She seldom set eyes on him to know whether he cared or not.

'He's going to have to know the truth about us sooner or later,' she told Anthony as she lay in his arms, after they had made love, with Anthony having taken the utmost care to see her safe. Her fear of causing herself hurt after her miscarriage, as she preferred to call it, had now dissolved.

'Of course he's aware that I've had a relationship but he has never questioned me. But then I never see him. Merton says that he's not at all well but I'm not allowed to even go into his room. In fact when the doctor was called a couple of days ago I tried to go to him to see how he was but his door was locked. It seems only he and Merton have a key. Even our housemaid doesn't go in unless Merton allows her. And he takes all James's meals up to him. I don't know what to make of it. I'm sure he hates me.'

Anthony tightened his arm about her, drew her closer to him. 'Why should you let that worry you, my love? The way things are you should be pleased. You're more or less as free as a bird to do what you like.'

She had to agree. 'But I worry about his health,' she couldn't help saying.

On the Friday at the end of March, Dr Peters was called in the middle of the night. Madeleine heard the sound of people moving about downstairs, then someone coming up the main staircase, voices, Merton's and the doctor's, James's door being opened and, as she came fully awake, being closed gently.

Instantly she was out of bed, throwing her dressing gown around her as she made for his room. The door was closed but it opened easily as she turned the brass handle. She half expected James to explode, 'Get out of this room!' but all she saw was Dr Peters bending over him with Mrs Cole standing by.

'What's wrong with my husband?' she burst out. 'Is he very ill?'

Dr Peters turned and came towards her, his face grave as he spoke in terms a layman could understand.

'As you know, dear lady, your husband has been suffering for some time now from chronic bronchitis since last contracting pneumonia. I am afraid he has now suffered an acute attack of bronco-pneumonia and it is serious, very serious. There is also pleurisy and it is crucial he be taken to hospital immediately. At this moment I am waiting for the ambulance. I cannot understand why I wasn't alerted sooner. I should have been called to him much earlier. Did you not realize how ill he was, Mrs Ingleton?'

'No one told me,' Madeleine could only gasp. She turned towards Mrs Cole for help. 'Why wasn't I told? I had no idea.'

'I wouldn't have thought you were that interested,' was the hissed reply, the sting of the words piercing right through her.

'He's my husband!' she cried out, only to receive a curt, 'Humph!' but she ploughed on in anger. 'Yet I've not been allowed to even go into his room to find out how ill he was.'

Dr Peters, stethoscope to his patient's chest, had resumed listening to James's chest, the man's rasping, laboured breathing filling the room. Now he turned abruptly, a finger to his lips for Madeleine to lower her voice.

'Please, Mrs Ingleton, if you don't mind.'

It was almost a command and instantly Madeleine fell silent while in the distance came the urgent jingling of an ambulance bell.

Twenty-Four

'He shouldn't have died!' Madeleine sobbed, Anthony holding her close as the group of mourners came away from the graveside.

It would of course be seen as quite natural to show grief at losing a husband and her grief was genuine enough but no one knew how much self-recrimination was bound up in it; remembering those little unexpected moments when that tiny demon inside her head whispered to her that only by James's demise would she ever be free to marry Anthony.

She'd tried to close her mind to its evil persistence; told herself time after time that she could never be so callous as to bow to the voice, but she knew she had listened. Now it seemed almost as if she had purposely willed his death and her grief felt almost an insult to the man – the kindest man she had ever known. In a way she had loved him even though she'd been well aware that all he had ever wanted from their marriage was companionship. But had she really given him that? She would never be certain.

'I'm so sorry,' she whispered to him as she wept against Anthony's chest.

Misconstruing, Anthony tightened his arm about her and murmured, 'Nothing you could've done. He was too ill. Nothing anyone could've done.'

It didn't matter that he was holding her so close. She was after all, his aunt, it would not draw the attention of those standing in small groups or making their way to their vehicles, Merton, for instance, taking the staff back in the tiny Morris he owned, James having been generous with his wages for years.

She and James's brother and his wife, along with Anthony, would be chauffeured back by Robert in James's limousine, Anthony having left his vehicle at his uncle's house where food awaited the return of the mourners.

Initially it was a subdued gathering, grateful to be out of the chill breeze of late March at last, exchanges made on how sad it was to see him go and he only in his mid-sixties – this from older members of the gathering, many of whom Madeleine had never seen – and that in their opinion he'd seemed to have merely given up on life.

But soon more cheerful anecdotes were being exchanged: James as a young man, his first wife, how they'd met – much of it new to Madeleine, he had hardly if ever spoken to her of his first wife. She often wondered why, though it had never bothered her. She just assumed he felt awkward about speaking of his first wife to his second. Sometimes it had seemed to her as if his first wife had never existed and she often wondered if he had really loved her, even been incapable of cementing love – as she and Anthony did. Was that why his previous wife hadn't had any children, she wondered, as she listened now to the gabble of voices around her talking about his life.

There was a good sprinkling of colleagues of his; businessmen, rival stockbrokers, people from his firm, each with a tale of their own regarding the deceased. She didn't really want to know; stood receiving everyone's condolences, wishing only that they would all say their goodbyes and depart, leaving her and Anthony alone. Here, after the staff had cleared away and disappeared to go about their separate duties, she and Anthony would finally be alone at last, that thought sending a thrill of excitement running through her.

James's relatives and staff were gathered around the large dining-room table, sitting in silence as his solicitor made ready to read the will. As expected, after certain bequests to his relatives, small token gratuities to his staff, everything else had been left to her, his wife, as it should: all his property and valuables together with his business, his investments, it being added that he'd tutored her well in the intricacies of the stock market for her to be well conversant with such transactions.

With no debts to be settled, she was suddenly a rich woman in her own right. As James's solicitor declared that he would take pleasure in acting for her, advising her, making it his business to protect her from any future blips exactly as he had her late husband, her only thought was that now she and Anthony could be married, after a suitable period of mourning of course.

She would sell the house and live with him. James's business would be left in the capable hands of his partner, George Foster, who'd keep her well informed and act on any new instructions she needed to give him. She intended not to let anything get past her. This last year, her dealing, with very few failures, had become almost an obsession with her.

With Anthony's money too, they had as much money as they could ever need; she would follow the stock market to its fullest extent and together they would live a complete and exciting social life, paint the town red almost every night.

James's solicitor Mr Laurence Ferguson, having concluded the reading of the will, was gathering his papers together, as Madeleine come to thank him for his time.

'Now remember, Mrs Ingleton,' he said in his deep voice, 'I am here whenever you feel you need help or advice on anything that might cause you the least concern – as I've always done for your husband. I have been his family solicitor these many years, I might say for as long as I can remember.' He gave a small polite chuckle then went on, 'Your husband trusted me implicitly and I hope you will be able to do the same, Mrs Ingleton.'

Yes, she was happy enough to keep him on. There was little point in fishing around for anyone else. James had trusted him and so would she. But at this moment the small group of beneficiaries needed to enjoy some refreshments and a brandy or two before leaving.

'Will you join us, Mr Ferguson?' she asked and he beamed, thanking her but saying he needed to get back to his office.

'Just one small glass of brandy,' she coaxed, bidding him to go into the drawing room with the others while she went downstairs to see if Mrs Cole had the plates of dainty sand-wiches and little pastries ready to be taken up to them.

She was halfway down the short slight of steps to the kitchen when Mrs Cole's voice filtered up to her.

'. . . Sobbing fit to burst at the funeral, she was. Anyone hearing her would've believed her stricken by grief. But it was guilty conscience if you ask me. Because I know something no one else knows.'

Then Merton's deep voice. 'What would that be, Mrs Cole?'

Madeleine had froze on the middle step as Mrs Cole's voice continued.

'I ain't saying, Mr Merton, but I know something that'd make your hair curl if you knew. I can bet my last ha'penny on that, especially about that miscarriage of hers, that everyone is being led to believe was her . . .'

Her voice went out of range, Madeleine already hurrying back up the steps, passing the open door to the drawing room from which the babble of voices issued, going into the small lounge, closing the door behind her.

There she collapsed into a soft chair to weep as silently as she could. How could the woman have changed so from the friend and confidante she once thought she'd had into that tittle-tattle with such a grudge against her? Had whatever she'd confided to her in the past been bandied about the house without her being aware of it? The more she thought of it the angrier she became. But moments later she had dried her eyes defiantly, her mind working.

Yes, she'd sell this house at the first opportunity. She'd give Merton and the two young girls a glowing reference but there'd be none for a tittle-tattling cook/housekeeper. If anyone asked for one, she'd tell them she had no trust in the woman, which now was true, having caught her at it, and she wasn't prepared to give her a reference. Being out of work might give the woman food for thought. Feeling more composed she returned to the drawing room finding that the sandwiches and pastries had already been brought up, everyone standing about nibbling, sipping their brandy or sherry, the room filled with their chatter, livelier now with the sombre part of the funeral over.

She had to force herself to appear normal but it was hard

not to lay aside what she had overheard. It wasn't until later, after everyone had departed – young Beattie handing each their hat, coat, muffler, gloves, Merton quickly closing the front door after each guest so as to let in as few blasts of wintry March as possible – that it came to her. Would it really matter if her secret did come out? Once she and Anthony were married, would she really care what they thought? They might gossip for a while but she'd be living with him, her own house sold. As for Mrs Cole, perhaps she might give her a half decent reference after all.

The guests gone, she and Anthony now alone, it didn't matter about the staff. She paid their wages. They'd take care not to gossip outside. Even so, it was as well to keep their secret a little longer.

Informing Merton that her nephew would be staying the night, she needing the company and the support of a near relative to help her deal with her loss, she told him she would need the guest room to be prepared for him.

'Mr Anthony will not want early morning tea. He tells me he likes to sleep late,' she added, pleased with her little lie. 'I doubt I shall sleep very well after today's ordeal so will probably not wish to be disturbed either. I will have my tea downstairs instead when I have breakfast.'

Whatever the upright if somewhat chubby man thought, his face gave nothing away as he murmured politely, 'Very good, madam.'

'Oh, and Merton,' she called as he turned to go. 'As I don't expect to sleep very well tonight, I shall probably stay up until quite late so there's no need to wait up for me to retire. Lock up at your usual time and let everyone know they can go to bed at their normal hour.'

'Very well, madam,' repeated Merton, and politely withdrew.

The moment he'd gone, Anthony, who'd been sitting on the opposite sofa to her, got up and slipped a record on the gramophone. As the soft, smooth strains of her favourite tune 'Avalon' filled the room, he came to sit beside her. She cuddled against him, neither spoke. The music ended. They sat on, reclining together. Madeleine closed her eyes in pure

contentment, he continuing to hold her to him, they just
lying in each other's arms, doing nothing, saying nothing,
something she had never known with him before. Their
time together had always been taken up in a frantic scramble
for their fulfilment of each other. This was new and it was
wonderful and the hours slipped by unnoticed. Then as they
lengthened towards midnight, he roused her and led her up
the stairs, first entering the guest room to rumple the covers
and the pillow to give the impression of the bed having
been slept in, then leading her quietly to her room and
closing the door behind them.

Their first ever night together; heaven, knowing they had
no need to rush things; no need for her to hurry away after
she had calmed herself following a mere hour of frenzied
love-making. They could take their time; sleep soundly and
contentedly in each other's arms for what was left of the
night, wake in the morning to revel in the pleasure of each
other yet again.

Wonderful this morning to lay naked in his arms, slowly
waking up knowing that in a little while they would make
love again with no longer any call for her to leap out of
bed, dress in frantic haste, hurry from the house to a taxi,
fretting all the way back here in case James might be
wondering where she was. She was already back here, and
James would no longer be waiting for her, would never
again be waiting for her.

The thought brought unexpected moisture to her eyes as
she lay in Anthony's arms. Quickly she sniffed them back
but the sounds brought him awake, made him look at her.

'Something wrong, darling?'

'No, nothing, love, I just thought of James, that's all,
and . . .'

She broke off. She hadn't meant to say that. Rather she'd
wanted to refer to her earlier thought of how wonderful
it was lying here with no need to leap up and run off; so
wonderful that she'd suddenly felt overwhelmed. It would
have had him instantly pulling her to him to begin making
love to her. Instead he held his body back from her to gaze
at her from his pillow.

'That's all behind you, darling. You have me now. Remember that.'

'I know. I'm sorry.'

'OK then,' he said, and moving his hand beneath her neck, drew her to him, his other hand already caressing her naked breasts, and as their lips met, the hand moved slowly down to her thighs to nestle between her legs and, as she sighed, tightly grasped her there. She gasped in her need of him.

Suddenly he released her, sat up and slewed his legs over the side of the bed, his back to her as he opened the drawer of the bedside cabinet and she knew instantly what he was about.

Waiting for him was an unbearable chasm just as it had been last night while he took precautions to safeguard her from harm.

He'd put that second sheath in the cabinet drawer ready for this morning, thinking of her protection of course, but all she wanted to do was to grab his shoulder, turn him back to her, tell him that it didn't matter if she did conceive; that it was what she wanted – to have his child, she a mother at last, cementing their union of love. If it happened today, they'd still be married in time to keep tongues from wagging. The child would be legitimate, all she had ever wanted, and it would be Anthony's – hers and Anthony's. All these years of yearning, at last she would be happy instead of having to tell herself she was; genuinely happy in her own right an end to all these years of knowing that happiness had always been only an illusion for her.

'Darling,' she whispered as he turned back to her, 'let's not bother using anything.'

She hated the things: harsh, sturdy rubber seeming to rasp against her tender flesh, no feeling of him except for those couple of times last year when carried away in a few moments of madness they had forgone such precautions. The result had been overriding fear of abortion, only to suffer anyway as the fetus decided to rid itself of her nevertheless, it not even formed enough to be recognizable as a human child.

He paused in moving to kiss her. He drew back. 'Sweetheart, we need to be careful.'

She too drew back. 'Why?'

'Because we don't want to spoil the opportunity we have now for freedom and fun.'

'But a baby would make our marriage just perfect.'

It caught her that he'd ignored her mention of marriage, ploughing on with all thought of making love put aside for the moment.

'Why on God's earth would you want to saddle yourself with a baby just when we're free at last to do exactly as we please – going out and about, parties, theatre, meet people that matter, socialize till the cows come home, travel anywhere we please, abroad, to America if you want?'

How could she explain to him how she felt? The baby that had been taken from her sprang into her mind, as it did occasionally out of the blue, but whenever it did, she would inevitably see that likeness to the man who'd taken advantage of her innocence and her longing for the child would fade instantly. What she wanted was Anthony's child, one who'd resemble him in every way and upon whom she'd pour her affection.

'I want us to have something of a good time together before we start to settle down,' he was saying. 'And I know you do too. You've had so little of it with James around.'

'James was good to me,' she said sharply in his defence.

'Of course he was. But any fun you had, it was you who'd arrange it – those parties of yours, he seldom took part. Even when we were together you always had to rush away. Now you're free and we can live it up a little, our whole life in front of us. The two of us, we'll take London society by storm.'

She didn't want to take London by storm! Or maybe she did. Wasn't this what she had dreamed about for years – the two of them, he tall and suave in evening suit; she on his arm, slim and glamorous, her evening dress the latest fashion, flat silhouette, sleeveless, frilled skirt, low hip line, hem slanting to one side; her hair short, fair and wavy, held by a beaded bandeau. They would dance the night away, kicking up their heels, enjoying cocktails and champagne with friends, the centre of attention.

She knew she was attractive, drew all eyes even when with James at those boring business dinners, and at the grand parties and soirées she'd once thrown before he became ill; even as far back as that girl from that horrible boarding house – she'd forgotten her name – and those friends of hers, she was the one the young men glanced at first, their gaze unwavering even as she stood back, uncertain and aloof.

Now she was poised, self-assured, always beautifully dressed, and on Anthony's arm they *would* take London society by storm. The world was at her feet – at last.

'Let's just live a little first,' he murmured against her ear. 'We have plenty of time to start a family. What d'you say, my sweet?'

His breath moved over her hair, tickled her cheek seductively, his hands gently, persuasively, caressing her skin, began to explore, making her shiver deliciously – such a wonderful, overwhelming sensation.

'Yes,' she breathed, forgetting about babies, and lay back ready for him.

Twenty-Five

Madeleine and Anthony had been together sixteen months and this feeling of freedom was as fresh as ever, doing just as they pleased, going to mad, mad parties, coming home around four in the morning with hardly time to draw breath before another round of excitement engaged their attention.

Christmas had been a wow, New Year's Eve even more so – a fancy dress party at one of the big hotels going on until dawn. He'd gone as Mark Anthony, as near to his namesake as he could get, in lightweight Roman armour; she as Cleopatra, a clinging, low-cut gown of silver lamé revealing every curve of her slender figure and a wonderful silver headdress that, oddly in keeping with the present fad for bandeaux, sat low on her brow, crowned by a silver cobra coiled ready to strike.

Hardly giving winter time to pass, they'd spent a few days in Paris then travelled down to Nice, Anthony confidently leaving the bank in the capable hands of his manager and staff. This summer he planned to take her to New York on the *Mauretania*. Life with him was indeed wonderful. Yet something was missing.

'Darling, when are we going t'get married?'

He didn't answer. It was as if he hadn't heard her. It was late, nearly three o'clock. It had been a fun-filled evening, a party at The Savoy Hotel, some sort of celebrations though she wasn't sure what, a little intoxicated by then; going on to another private party afterwards – someone's birthday – lots of champagne!

It was hardly worth getting ready for bed at this hour but tomorrow being Sunday they'd sleep till midday. Madeleine, in her woozy state, again posed the question she had been asking from time to time for a few months now. She wasn't drunk enough not to feel hurt by his failure to reply, but managed to give him credit for perhaps not having quite heard her. Yet for one reason or another he always managed to evade it whenever she broached the subject.

'Tony, did you hear me, darling?' she said.

He was carefully pulling back the bed covers, his naked back to her. 'Yes. But it's late and you look all in. Talk about it in the morning.'

But usually they didn't talk about it *in the morning.* In the morning something else always cropped up: he needed to eat breakfast quickly and get to his bank; had an important client to see; had an important meeting arranged with his staff; needed to discuss certain matters with his undermanager that couldn't wait; and so on, and so on.

She suddenly felt angry. To show it could mean they might not make love tonight. Anyway, maybe he was too tired and a bit too drunk himself to make love, though that didn't usually deter him no matter what the hour and she was always ready for him. But she knew that if they did he wouldn't be so drunk as to forget to take precautions. She understood the need to, but if they were married it wouldn't matter any more, would it?

She stood glaring at him, swaying a little. 'I don' wan'to talk about it in the morning! I wan'to talk about it now! I wan'us t'get married, darling.'

'For Chrissake, Maddie!'

The epithet was like an explosion, making her sway backwards to hold on to the dressing table behind her for support. He never swore in front of her. He probably swore at others. Men did, but she had never heard him. It wasn't like him; maybe the drink.

'Just come to bed, will you?' he hissed. 'Before you bloody well fall down.'

'Right then!' she hissed back.

She'd never heard him speak so harshly. And it shook her. Enough to make her feel not quite so dizzy as she thought she was. In sudden fury, she grabbed for her nightdress which she usually ignored, as they preferred to lie naked together, and dragged it over her head. Seething, she stomped round to her side of the bed, tore back the covers and all but threw herself into it with her back to him, the exertion making her dizzy.

She felt his arm come round her and jerked away. 'Goo'night!' she rasped, but the hand persisted.

'I'm sorry if I've upset you, love. We'll talk about it if you like.'

'We've had months and months to talk about it.'

'We need to give it time to . . .'

'Time!' she twisted back to glare at him in the low light of their table lamps. She was suddenly feeling less drunk now. Maybe just lying down, maybe her anger. 'How much more time do you need? Or am I just your whore?'

'What are you talking about? I said we'd get married, but . . .'

'But what?' she broke in, her body remaining rigid as he tried to put an arm about her. 'But what?' she repeated.

'Darling,' he soothed. 'We *will* get married, and I want our wedding to be huge and memorable, on everyone's lips for years to come. But it does mean taking up a lot of our time making all the preparations necessary for the wedding I have in mind. It could stop us having the wonderful time we're enjoying now. So, for a while, let's not spoil it, eh?'

He spoke so persuasively that she could just visualize the sort of huge affair it would be. But he'd said all this before, crooning, creating wonderful visions, and each time she would respond by melting into his arms, visions of the marvellous wedding they would have floating in her head. But slowly the visions had begun to be replaced by a vague sense of uneasiness turning slowly to bewilderment and lately this feeling that he had never wanted to get married, and even more recently asking why.

Even now a crafty little voice was whispering: because he knew she wanted a baby and he didn't want babies to ruin the good time they were having. He was a good-time person, didn't want it to ever end. Marrying and settling down with a family, a reduced social life, that that was the last thing on his mind. She too had wanted to enjoy life, have a good time, but hadn't quite realized what that might entail.

So when would she ever have a baby to hold in her arms

and croon over, to replace that one which she had been deprived of? She was twenty-eight – another year, four more years, by then in her thirties, it became ever more dangerous to give birth. Probably not so for women who'd already borne several children, but hers would virtually be her first. She couldn't let herself wait for so long.

'I can't see why we don't have a simple wedding and get it over with,' she grumbled, moving back from his effort to kiss her. 'What does it matter about making a big impression? All I want is for us to be a normal married couple. We've waited long enough.'

There was a long silence. Not knowing what else to say, she snapped, 'Anyway, I'm tired. I need to go to sleep.'

Twisting away from him she reached up and switched off her bedside lamp. He had said nothing, but she could feel he was angry as he in turn clicked off his own lamp.

In the darkness they lay back to back, the first time he had ever not attempted to make love to her. In the darkness she lay miserable, no longer feeling tipsy, wanting only to sleep and forget, yet she was still awake as dawn crept through the curtains. He on the other hand was snoring gently, peacefully, and she hated him.

The following morning her love had recovered itself. She wanted so much to say sorry, yet somehow couldn't, for all the forgiveness she felt. As for him, breakfast was eaten in silence, he seemingly more engaged in his morning newspaper brought to him by Jessop.

After a couple of attempts at conversation had been blocked by a grunt or two, she had given up, frustration growing by the minute so that when he'd kissed her on leaving to go to his bank, it had not been the usual lingering kiss but a mere peck on the cheek which she, by now simmering with hurt from that silent meal, had coldly offered. That brief questioning look he'd given her as he drew away had stayed with her all day, worrying her, flooding her mind with all sorts of questions of her own.

Even as she laughed and chatted with friends she'd met for coffee, the lunch she'd shared with several others, afternoon tea with some whom she often met at one party or another, the questions persisted. Why should he constantly be evading this business of marriage; did he truly love her, utterly and completely as he said he did; what if he had someone else in tow – questions becoming ever more silly and ridiculous. Or were they? After all he'd gone behind the back of her husband, his own uncle, with her.

Those times he said he had to *see a client*? Was that client someone with whom he was now involved with behind *her* back? She thought of those social gatherings, dances, parties, how women looked at him, and he at them. Tall, fair-haired, twinkling blue eyes, he must be aware of how he turned their heads. Nor could she ignore the slow way he would look at them, she once happy to believe it to be just good manners on his part!

By evening she'd shrugged off her suspicions, calling herself a fool for letting her imagination run away with her. Was it his fault if his looks drew other women's eyes, and what man wouldn't enjoy the compliment? It was her he loved. It was just this reluctance of his to be married and settle down.

Tonight she would put aside these foolish suspicions. It was Friday. This evening they were having dinner out before going to the theatre, afterwards on to a nightclub with friends. There'd be jazz music and dancing until the early hours. Back home they'd make love as if last night's quarrel had never happened. She could hardly wait for him to come home. There might even be time to make love before dressing to go out.

She made sure to be seductively dressed as he entered, her insides tingling as she thought of his reaction. He seldom missed a chance to make love – if only he didn't always pause to take the usual precautions for all it never took him long to prepare.

Hearing his key turn in the lock of the front door, she quickly wound the gramophone, slipped a record on and lowered the arm, the quiet strains of 'When Day is Done' filling the sitting room. She waited, hearing Jessop's voice say, 'Good evening, sir,' and his response as Jenny their housemaid took his hat and coat from him to hang on the hall stand.

Moments later he was opening the door of the sitting room, she now standing in the middle of the room, waiting for his eyes to light up at the sight of her. Instead it was as if he hadn't even noticed her as he went to the cocktail cabinet to pour himself a whisky.

She stood bewildered. 'Don't I get a kiss, darling?'

'Did you want one?' he said without turning.

Left not knowing how to respond, she brazened out the question with a small laugh. 'A kiss or a drink, love?'

'Either.' His tone was so abrupt that it startled her.

'A kiss would be nice,' she said quietly.

At that he turned. There was no smile on his face as he came towards her to peck her on the cheek as he passed.

The movement left her shocked, standing where she was in the centre of the room while he went to the sofa and sat, sipping his whisky, again as if she wasn't there.

Sudden fury flooded over her – a sudden seething fury. She made for the gramophone, yanking the arm upwards. The music cut off with a horrid agonized screech as the needle was dragged across its surface. She almost wanted to cry but wasn't about to give him that satisfaction. How could he still be holding a grudge from the previous night?

'What's the matter with you,' she hissed. 'Is it because of last night?'

He continued to sip his whisky, but his eyes, now dull, were gazing up at her from under his brows as she stood over him. 'What do you want me to say?' he asked at last.

That he loved her to distraction; that he wanted her this minute; that if she felt so strongly about their being married, he would begin making the arrangements this very weekend; that he was tired of the high life and wished only to settle down and be with her for the rest of their lives?

'I don't know,' she said instead. Then anger took over again, not quite the same as before but more beseeching, her voice beginning to shake. 'And if you don't know then what's the point of me telling you?'

'I've already told you,' he said, 'If that's what you're getting at, we will get married but not yet. As I said before, we need to see a bit of life first.'

'We?' she cried. 'Don't you mean you?'

'All right – me. *I* need to see a bit of life.'

'And what about us – how much longer do you expect me to wait for you to settle down?'

Slowly he placed his glass on the little oval side table next to him. 'I'd rather not discuss it right now, love. We should be getting ready to go out for dinner before the theatre.'

Madeleine stood her ground. 'I don't want to go out!'

Anthony stood up, his features set. 'Then don't, Maddie! But I still intend to . . .'

'And who with?' She couldn't help herself. 'You expect me to believe you're eager to go out all on your own? There must be someone else.'

'There is,' he said evenly, taking her off guard.

'Who?' The question wrenched itself from her before she could stop herself. 'Who is she?'

But although his brows drew together he remained cool. 'Our friends – the ones who'll no doubt be asking where you are.'

But he had evaded her question. 'Don't lie to me, Tony,' she said slowly and coldly. 'There *is* someone else? What other reason would there be for you not wanting us to get married.'

'Don't be ridiculous, Maddie!' He'd begun to pace. 'Why should I want anyone else but you? I love you. I *do* want to marry you but give me time.'

'How much more damned time do you need?' she blared at him, still unwilling to give up. 'What else should I think when you won't grant the one thing I want.' Her voice rose partly in fury, partly in fear. 'Until you convince me, I'm having no more to do with you!'

Giving him no time to answer she turned and ran from the room in a flood of tears, up to their bedroom and slamming the door behind her. And she didn't care if the whole house heard her.

Alone, she slowly calmed, all he'd said going through her head; about how he loved her, how devastated he had looked despite refusing to lose his temper – not that he'd ever had a temper – as she rushed from the room leaving him standing there.

But her accusations had left their mark on them both, the silly things she'd come out with returning again and again, and though little was being said about them, the silent thoughts were there, casting a cloud over the love they had once known. Nights were when she – still battling with the suspicion that he was lying to her despite their continuing to appear together in a flurry of social life – would refuse to let him make love to her, though sometimes she ached for him, her love for him as strong as ever.

It was getting more and more worrying, hurtful. They might as well have been married for all the old frantic love-making they'd once indulged in had faded. Yet she still loved him so much that her heart ached. But the seed had been sown; a gulf had come between them and there was nothing she could say or do to bring the two edges together again. A fear was always there – what if he tired of her, left her, driven away by her own intransigence, to actually find someone else? Then again, doubts: did he in fact have someone else? Men could deceive so easily. That pig who'd first got her into trouble, hadn't she trusted him, been in love with him with no idea that he had been deceiving her all along? Perhaps she had no idea now about Anthony.

As summer progressed her fears finally began to fade. He was being so attentive. As promised, he'd taken her to New York on the *Mauritania* in August, taking a fortnight off from his bank.

It was the most wonderful holiday she'd ever had, shopping in all the great department stores, money seeming to be no object with him; a theatre almost every night; gloriously warm sunny days spent wandering through, or just sitting in, Battery Park, gazing across the harbour or down the canyon called Lower Broadway; enjoying the excitement of Madison Square Gardens; Coney Island with its seaside amusements, dinner at wonderful restaurants, then back to their hotel after an exhausting day to make love before falling asleep, exhausted.

The only fly in the ointment was that Anthony would still interrupt it to take the usual precautions, frustrating her almost to the limit. But so wonderful was the holiday that she'd bite her tongue from begging him to just let nature take its course. But it was sensible if she thought about it. Why rock the boat when it must have cost him thousands so that she could have a wonderful time.

And she had had a wonderful time; had fallen in love with the place. And as their holiday finally came to an end and they had sailed out of the harbour into the Atlantic, such a feeling of nostalgia overcame her as the Statue of Liberty and the New York skyline sank out of sight in a mist behind the rim of the world, she vowed in her heart as she turned away: 'I shall come back one day.' Maybe even next year, she prayed. Maybe even for our honeymoon.

He'd at least made a half promise during one of their more frantic moments of love-making that he'd start making wedding plans as soon as they got home. A wedding some time in the autumn, joy filled her breast at the thought. But autumn was passing and still nothing done towards it. She thought it best not to badger him too much and upset things. She'd done too much of that on their return to England, and was told not to be so impatient. But impatience was hard to control sometimes. Christmas almost upon them, she tried not to fret; not to badger him. He was now suggesting spring, 'a much nicer time for it, darling.' And she so needed to believe it this time.

New Year's Eve, half an hour to go to 1925, the great room of the hotel crowded, people hardly able to move, the dance floor a solid mass of gyrating bodies, twisting and writhing to the Charleston, everyone pepped up with excitement, music, booze and what was currently being termed happy dust in readiness for a mad welcoming in of the New Year.

The noise was overpowering, getting ever more so as the big hand of the ornate clock on the wall crept towards the twelve. With less than twenty minutes to go, Anthony had hurried off, sidling his way through the crowd to fetch a special bottle of champagne.

Left sitting at her table, Madeleine glanced at her gold and diamond encrusted wristwatch. Ten minutes gone already. He was taking his time. He would be at the bar fighting to get served. If he didn't hurry he would be too late for the last stroke of midnight when they would drain their glasses to the bottom in one gulp and half drunk would leap into each other's arms, lips pressed together, his hand inside her low cut dress, fondling her breasts. Would it matter if anyone saw them? No one would care. They'd be busy with their own fondling.

Coming to a decision, Madeleine got up and began edging her way through the crowd in the direction Tony had taken. Reaching the bar, still crowded, she struggled from one end of it to the other. No sign of him. Where was he? Had he gone round the other way to find her and she had missed him. She fought her way on. They would probably meet at their table in the end. A couple were canoodling in a darkish corner where the blazing lights did not quite reach. The man had the girl in a clinch, hand under her skirt, lips against her bosom, the girl sighing in ecstasy. It didn't matter if anyone saw them. No one was taking any notice anyway. Madeleine made to hurry past, meaning to avert her eyes as if they weren't even there.

A second later she stopped sharp, gasped, let out a cry so audible that the man turned his face towards the noise. Moments later Madeleine was pushing through the throng, sobbing, seeing no one as she made for the cloakroom.

Twenty-Six

Madeleine gazed around her drawing room, the morning sun pouring in at the big windows.

She'd had one of those dreams again, of coming upon Anthony with that girl, the dream going further wherein she'd see them actually engrossed in the act; he looking up to find her there and asking her what she thought she was doing watching them. In the dream she'd run off, as they watched her go, arms about each other. She'd wake up, her mind going over what she had dreamed, her heart feeling as heavy as lead. She lay awake, her thoughts not allowing her to sleep again until, seeing the dawn light, she would fall into a deep sleep until awakened by her daily, Mrs Mann. Then she'd have to drag herself out of bed, forced to face another day alone. It had been like this since May, six months ago now, when she had finally walked out on Anthony.

Of course he'd apologized over and over again for that New Year's Eve business, said he'd consumed so much champagne and hadn't realized what he was doing. For five months she'd tried to accept his excuses, fighting to make allowances for him, to forgive him, but it was hard to forget and every time any little argument flared between them, she'd find herself bringing it up again and again. It would lead to a full-scale shouting match with him often walking out leaving her in tears.

Sometimes it was she who fled, to walk for hours, hurt and miserable, wondering why she was being so stupid. She would return, resolving to put it behind her, but it was always there, like a tiny lurking demon. Finally that last terrible fight. After seeing him talking to a girl on the other side of the tennis court at a garden party last May, the girl lifting her face to his, giving him a kiss and his lapping it up, or so it seemed to her oversensitive mind from that distance, she'd had enough.

After walking out on him, she'd gone to a friend, stayed the night there but ignored her advice to go back – that she was only hurting herself by forever bringing up one single small incident. The following day she had gone to an estate agent who found an unnecessarily spacious house – a small act of defiance on her part – where she still resided.

In all this time there'd not been a word from Anthony. She'd had one or two friends tell him where she was, but nothing – no humble note of apology, no phone call, nothing.

From time to time news would filter through to her. Mr George Foster, James's old partner and now hers, who of course knew him through James being his uncle, would keep her informed. Also news came from various mutual friends, some that he'd not so much as looked at another girl in all this time; others that he had been seen with different girls on odd occasions. Not knowing what to believe she could only hark back to last New Year's Eve and find herself ready to believe the latter.

At first she'd wanted to run back to him, listen to his abject apologies; fall into his arms full of forgiveness; have him hold her tight. But it hadn't happened and anger remained. Why should she forgive, listen to his lies? Now, after all these months it had become almost too late; anger, silent recrimination, mounting all the while. Yet she missed him so, fought with herself not to. And there were the ever-present questions: why hadn't he come seeking her? Had he found another girl? Or picked up with that one she had caught him fondling that night?

She thought about it, especially when she lay alone in her bed at night, unable to sleep, the small hours creeping by, oh so slowly, each laden as the small hours always are when sleep eludes: unresolved solutions pinging away inside her head; and while her heart lying like a lump of concrete within her breast, feeling as if it was breaking all over again. Daytime when she could make herself busy, planning and holding numerous social gatherings wasn't so bad – she still had plenty of friends who sympathized with her, knowing her story. She was still the exciting hostess, finding any excuse to throw a party, filling her new home with guests, everyone drinking too much, she included.

There were weekends in Paris, with some of them the occasional jaunt to the south of France, the endless buying of clothes, so many clothes, sending hardly worn ones to the poor – joining a charity committee to help take up the day when she was at a loose end – that or constantly on the phone to friends. At the motor show in Paris she'd bought herself a car, a Citroën, and learned how to drive. There was dinner most evenings, and the theatre with a hired escort though it went no further than that. Days when lost for something to do she'd spend hours endlessly scrutinizing the *Financial Times* studying the stock markets, telephoning her instructions to George Foster who'd become her good adviser and friend, though she saw herself more as a sleeping partner in the firm.

It would be Christmas soon. She intended to throw a social event to dim all social events, even after all these months still needing to push away these persistent bouts of loneliness and thoughts of Anthony. She thought of him now as she gazed through her drawing-room window, Mayfair was a good address, from here a partial view of Green Park – an exorbitant rent but she could afford it. She could have had a country house but she loved the London scene and living in the country would have brought memories of her parents' home, which she'd rather forget. Here she could hold her own dinner parties, her evening parties, weekend parties by invitation at other people's country houses. She and Anthony used to attend weekend parties. Was he at this moment doing the social rounds with some girl or other, she wondered, the thought bringing a momentary stab of depression, making her draw a deep breath to dispel it.

She'd transferred all her money from his bank into one George Foster had recommended, the rest in stocks and shares, as James had taught her. She'd grown quite adept at it or extremely lucky and all was looking solid enough. She still saw herself as something of a novice, but trusted James's old partner – and now hers – with his good knowledge of the market. More especially he'd often invest some of his own money in that which he'd advised her to buy, proving confidence in his own advice – not exactly stooping to illegal insider dealing that, if discovered, might lead to dark frowns though he knew where to draw the line.

She would invite him and his wife Millicent to her Christmas event. She had never done it before and she hoped they would accept. There was a lot to think about: ordering the catering, the music, making sure invitations went out before any others arrived at the homes of her chosen guests. It all helped to occupy her mind to some extent and hardly had she sent them out than replies came flooding back almost by the following post: *'So enormously happy to accept, my dear.'*

Tonight she was giving a small dinner party, a few exclusive friends: Lilian and Howard Greenwood, Elizabeth and Burgess Jennings, Barbara and Stephen Pickford. The Greenwoods and the Jennings knew Anthony and she hoped they wouldn't bring his name up at the table. She'd had several carefully penned notes of sympathy from some who knew of the break-up. Of course she had never explained the cause and assured them that it had been a mutual decision. On a whim she had telephoned George Foster to ask if he and his wife might care to come and he'd said they would be delighted.

A few minutes later the phone had rung again and it was Foster's wife, Millicent whom she'd met once or twice. The woman had phoned to ask if they could be so bold as to bring a young man along with them.

'He lives on his own nearby. He strikes us as being rather lonely,' Millicent said. 'His name is Ronald Thurston Jameson – says his parents live mostly abroad, India, but he never sees them – they even missed his recent twenty-first birthday last week – quite unbelievable how thoughtless people can be – says he and his parents don't get along that well and he'll be somewhat at a loose end at Christmas.'

Listening to the gabble, Madeleine told her she'd be happy to welcome him; knowing personally just what loneliness felt like.

He proved to be a lively, immensely handsome young

man, polite, well spoken, though she wondered why she'd half expected a graceless twenty-one-year-old as she watched him during the evening, talking easily to those he had obviously never met before, drawing them to him, making them laugh with his light and witty conversation. In fact she felt quite proud of him.

As the evening wore on, she found herself watching him, fascinated by the way he'd wave a hand to his almost every word, the wide smile revealing very even, white teeth; amused by the way his dark hair persisted in falling over his brow, without the Brilliantine most men used; the way his brown eyes would flick in her direction, he tilting his head as their eyes met, and she found herself wanting to invite him again. As her dinner guests began to leave, she said she hoped he'd enjoyed the evening. 'Thank you very much. I most certainly did,' he said, his manner more mature than she had expected.

'I'm planning a sizeable Christmas Eve party here,' she said while the Fosters waited to leave. 'May I invite you and your . . .?'

'That would be really wizard,' he broke in with sudden enthusiasm that betrayed his youth but which sent a tingle through her.

'And your parents?' she continued, 'If they would care to come?'

His smile vanished. 'My parents have their own interests.' His tone had grown dark, surprising her. 'Our paths have never really crossed. They lived in India, me at boarding school here. We've nothing in common.'

There was an awkward silence, the Fosters hovering. She was aware of her voice rising higher than it should. 'Then if you're not going to be with them or with friends, then do come!'

'I will,' he said, and his brown eyes seemed to penetrate hers so that she tingled anew.

The Christmas Eve celebration had gone down well.

'Thank you so much for a wonderful time' was the general parting remark as her guests left wearily, around two thirty, with some departing nearer three. 'We so enjoyed the divine buffet, darling, can hardly wait for your next invite. You will invite us, won't you?' Of course she would, she told them.

'And the music, my dear, was quite perfect – exhilarating. I do believe we're quite worn out!'

She had engaged a jazz pianist and a saxophone for the evening. Most of the time she'd danced with young Ronald, as he, without a partner, had arrived alone, the Fosters busy with their own family party.

Chatting throughout each dance, though what about she could not recall, she'd been most conscious of Ronald's hand holding hers so lightly, his other hand warm on her bare flesh, her dress having been cut extremely low at the back, almost to her waist. It was easy to pretend it was Tony's hand on her back, so long as she didn't look into his face. Not as tall as Anthony, his lithe body still retained the slimness of youth, his features she suspected would last him well into his later years.

As her guests began to take their leave, he had lingered. He was still lingering when the last one departed, and what could she do but ask if he would care for a quick nightcap before he too left.

'That's very kind of you,' he said graciously. 'That would be nice.'

Now they sat together sipping brandy, he at one end of the sofa, she at the other, neither of them saying much. When it was that he moved to sit closer to her, very much closer to her, she wasn't sure but somehow the sleeve of his jacket was brushing her bare arm. She should have got up but she didn't – merely stayed where she was, aware of the warmth of his upper arm through his sleeve. 'It's very quiet now, isn't it,' he whispered.

'Yes, it is,' she whispered back.

She was about to say that it must be time he went, but somehow couldn't. Strange sensations were beginning to ripple through her body, sensations of expectancy, like little waves, or tiny needles, exquisite, penetrating, running along her spine, through her muscles and playing inside her stomach. She sat without moving and knew he'd picked up the message her body was conveying to him of its own accord. Anthony wasn't here and she so needed to be made to feel alive again.

It seemed to happen so quickly. As he turned his face to hers, looking for her lips, she found herself offering them and in the silence of the room they sank down on the settee, as he fondled her breast, the low cut décolletage of her flimsy evening dress offering no resistance to his manipulating hand; feeling it urgently travel down over her body to find her eager and willing, moments later having her gasping with the joy of being taken by him, being loved once more.

It wasn't until it was over that she felt the guilt; visions of Anthony racing through her brain like little attacking demons, making her suddenly leap up from the sofa and flee from the room, leaving him staring after her.

What his expression was she had no idea for she hadn't been able to bring herself to look back at him. All she heard was his voice trailing after her: 'What is it Madeleine? What have I done?'

And her reply, high-pitched, sharp, fragmented like shards of glass as she came to a halt the other side of the door: 'You'd – best – go! I'm sorry – it was a mistake!'

Reaching her bedroom, closing the door behind her, she didn't hear him leave; he must have let himself out so quietly with no maid to open the door for him. She had no staff, just a woman who came in daily to cook and generally clean and tidy the apartment before going home. For parties she hired temporary staff.

Why was she thinking this when the more important concern was that he would never set foot here again? Not after the way she'd run from the room, crying like someone who'd been raped, making him wonder what on earth had upset her.

How could she have been so damned foolish, allowing a mere twenty-one-year-old to make love to her and her almost eight years older? Yet it had been so wonderful for those brief moments, so overwhelming, making her forget all about Anthony for a short while, and she had been so starved of love all these months.

Questions had begun to plague her: how could she have treated the poor devil like that? He must have been so embarrassed, bewildered, feeling so awful. She'd have to phone him tomorrow morning, apologize. But it may be better if she didn't – let sleeping dogs lie. Yes, that was best.

Thinking all these things, she ran herself a bath and lay there soaking in the hot water, trying to push away the voices in her brain: Ronald; Anthony – poor Anthony, leaving him like you did, you needed him. But Ronald . . .

He'd made her feel wonderful, for a moment or two she had forgotten the pain of no longer having Anthony to hold her. How could she have treated him like that? Yes, she would phone him tomorrow. She had his telephone number. She would say how sorry she was to do what she did. It would make him feel better. He would understand, might even want to see her again. There came a tinkling excitement in her stomach as that thought touched her.

She went to bed, falling into a deep, dreamless sleep, next morning waking to her new resolution. But instead of her telephoning him it was he who telephoned her.

Why she had expected to hear Anthony's voice as she unhooked the receiver and put it to her ear, she wasn't sure, but she felt that tingle in her stomach again as the voice, young and light, said: 'I'm really sorry I offended you last night, Madeleine. I honestly didn't mean to. It just happened. I hope you've forgiven me.'

'You didn't do anything for me to forgive,' she burst out hurriedly. 'It was me. I should be the one to apologize. I don't know what came over me. I still don't.' She was gabbling. 'I've been so worried that you'd taken offence. You left before I could say sorry for running off like that.'

'Fine, fine!' he interrupted. 'So I'm not in the dog kennel then?'

'Not at all. I was my—'

'Then can I see you again? Perhaps this afternoon?'

She took a deep breath, trying to keep her voice level. 'I'd like that.'

'Then we can both apologize face to face,' he said brightly, sounding so young, so vital.

'Yes,' she breathed, not quite knowing how else to answer.

'Then shall I see you around five o'clock? I have to be somewhere during most of the day. Maybe we could have dinner out together somewhere?'

'That would be lovely!' she exclaimed, feeling suddenly like some young girl herself.

'The only trouble is, at the moment I haven't got the wherewithal,' he was saying. 'My parents provide me with a monthly allowance but it hasn't arrived yet.'

'No bother,' she cried eagerly. 'I'll stand us dinner somewhere really special.'

'Thanks so much, Madeleine,' came his voice, a little subdued as if he felt a weight of guilt. 'I'll repay you the moment my allowance arrives. See you around five o'clock then.'

The phone clicked off, leaving her gazing at it before putting it back on its hook. Five o'clock was far too early to go out to dinner. What would they do in the meantime? But she already knew. They'd sit together and talk as they had done last night, and then . . . This time she wouldn't suffer the qualms she'd had last night. She recalled now how expert he'd been for one his age. This time she would forget Anthony. Her being in this situation was his fault.

From now on she would lead her own life. From now on she meant to enjoy it to the full. Sod Anthony!

Twenty-Seven

'I can't go in this thing!' Ronald was saying in a peeved tone.

Standing at the door to her bedroom, he was holding out the evening jacket for her to scrutinize. Since last year's Christmas party, he'd worn it several times to different evening events. Now she looked over to him as he hovered, his handsome young face flushed from his hot bath – loving the water to be as near to scalding as skin could bear – but looking ever so slightly peeved, and a pang of love swept over her as Madeleine threw him a smile.

'Why ever not, darling? What's wrong with the jacket?'

'Well . . . look at it!'

Only half dressed herself, still in her slip, she had no qualms about him seeing her like this, not after his living with her these past three years. Tomorrow night was New Year's Eve. They'd be off to a huge party to dance away the hours through to 1929, returning home to make love and sleep in each other's arms until mid-morning. Nineteen twenty-nine in two days' time!

Where had those last three years gone, such fabulous years, she and Ronald now an item. It didn't matter he was almost eight years younger than she. Everyone accepted it or maybe they kept their views to themselves but he had made her feel twenty-one again; not as she'd felt when she'd been twenty-one and married to staid old James, nearly three times her age, feeling guilty every time she threw a party, and his reminding her that England was at war, men dying, women made widows – not an appropriate time to hold parties. She had felt young again when she and Anthony had got together behind James's back and later after James's death. But that was then. Now she was with Ronald – lovely, young and vibrant Ronald.

He moved further into the bedroom, holding out the

jacket for her to see. 'Look, both elbows are becoming so rubbed it won't take long for everyone to notice. Shouldn't my new evening suit be ready by now? We ought to have ordered it earlier. I'll look like a pauper in this.'

'Where's your other one?' she asked, coming over to examine the sleeves. 'The one I bought for you a couple of months ago?'

She didn't mind buying him things. She loved buying him things, seeing his young face light up, to immediately grow solemn as he apologized for not being able to afford whatever it was himself. All he had was that poor apology of an inheritance his parents had so niggardly provided when he had turned twenty-one – not enough for a flea to live on. She bought him things because she loved him. She'd buy him the moon if she could.

'The lapel got stained with that caviar, you remember. And we forgot to have it cleaned. But I can't go in this one.'

'No, you can't.' She thought a while. 'Then we'll go right now and gee them up – tell them we'll cancel it if it's not ready by tomorrow morning.'

It was wonderful to see his glum face brighten as he came towards her, letting the jacket fall to the floor.

'You're so good to me. Honestly I don't deserve you,' he said, like some young kid.

Then far from a young kid, he took her in his arms, holding her to him, pressing his lips to hers as he eased her backwards against the edge of the bed to lower her body on to it, his own holding her there, moments later to have her gasping beneath his expert love-making.

No one, not even Anthony, had ever made her feel like this. Inflamed by his energy, she knew she would give him her last sou to have him take possession of her as he was doing now.

He would never know how he had changed her life. No more attending charity committees, attempting to fill her time, counting the hours when she was alone as she had done after leaving Anthony; no more horrible dreams – they disappeared the moment Ronald moved in permanently on her persuasion just two weeks after that first Christmas; no more trying to plan parties all on her own. She still threw her famous dinner parties and evening parties but more often now she attended other people's, she and he together.

Out almost every evening, afternoons, weekends, it didn't matter that he'd hardly a penny to his name while his parents lived half way across the world, well and comfortably off, not one thought for him. He'd never explained why and she never asked, feeling it was probably too painful for him to recall much less talk about, though sometimes she felt curiosity eating at her.

When on one occasion she had tried to question him, that gentle character of his seemed suddenly to change, his face becoming set, his lips tight and grim and his lovely brown eyes hard until she felt alarmed and said no more. Moments later he was his sweet, gentle self again. She never tried to probe again. It was best to let sleeping dogs lie as it were.

What did hurt was seeing him so grateful for everything she did for him, for the things she bought him. She continually found herself assuring him that she enjoyed – no, more than that – loved spending money on him and not to worry about it.

'I adore doing it, buying you things,' she told him, 'seeing how happy you look. I get so much pleasure from the pleasure on your face, my darling. So please, my love, don't deny me that.'

'I won't. But it's not fair.'

'Don't be ridiculous, darling, you deserve it for the joy you've given me, the happiness I get out of it, knowing how you were treated in your life.'

He would nod soberly and say no more, sometimes falling quiet which would worry her a little.

But he'd soon perk up and become his old self once more. That was another thing. He never sulked for long, seldom stayed in the doldrums for long. And he made her feel young again. She loved it when his youth showed through. Yet it was his very youthful moments that changed her. He made her feel like a girl in her teens, the two of them going here, there and everywhere, running about like kids playing chase, getting up to silly antics, laughing, always laughing.

It was only when they were alone in bed that maturity took over – in the way he made love; in the way he never allowed himself to be so carried away as to overlook taking care of the precautions needed. Though he usually made it light-hearted, getting her to help him with what was needed; it became a procedure which usually ended in the senses of both being heightened almost to breaking point in their need for each other. Life was so wonderful. He was so good for her. With him nothing would ever go wrong. She was a wealthy woman, lucky with her investments and making money enough for them both.

There'd been a time when she had thought her life was over, that she'd never be happy again. That was now a thing of the past. If she ever thought of Anthony, she'd immediately shrug the thought off, thrust aside that brief second of anger and think of her life now. She was happy. Anthony could do whatever he liked, be wherever he liked, go with whoever he liked; it was no longer any of her business.

Then out of the blue . . . 'I ran into your Anthony the other day.'

It was February. She and Ronnie, as she often called him, had been together over three years and Anthony was no longer *her* Anthony, despite the woman's remark. So how could his name suddenly turn her mind back, right out of the blue, to prompt this sudden sharp pang of emotion?

She'd been on the way to her hairdresser's, wondering why she was bothering in such weather, her head bent against a high wind, not so bad as that reported in the newspapers this time last year, when she'd been stopped by a female voice calling her name.

It belonged to a woman she'd not seen since she and Ronnie had taken up with each other. Gertrude Peel and herself together with several other friends would meet a couple of times a week for morning coffee. They'd all known Anthony and had sympathized with her over the break-up, she feeling entirely alone, grateful for a little company to get her through those long hours. These days she no longer had need of company and coffee mornings.

'I thought it was you, my dear,' chirped Gertrude as she

came up to her through the thin crowd who'd braved the weather to shop. One hand was holding on to her fashionable domed suede cloche hat lest the wind take it, the brim like a downturned sail, the whole thing almost covering her eyes, not a strand of hair visible. The other held a couple of wide paper bags that threatened to break free from her grasp and sail away on the wind.

Though in her early forties she was dressed like a young flapper: her loose-fitting, wrap-over coat unnecessarily short, its fur collar and cuffs almost drowning her spare frame, its pockets way below the hips. Madeleine also dressed in the height of fashion but she was some ten years younger and still looked well in young clothes. She still did look young and just as well with Ronnie by her side.

'Delightful to bump into you, my dear,' Gertrude was saying, 'and so unexpected. Simply ages since I saw you last! But what terrible weather,' she twittered on, seeming ready to start a lengthy conversation. 'This awful wind – almost as bad as last year after that awful winter we had – all that snow. And that flooding they had then, all those poor people washed out of their homes. Still that was last year. But you, my dear – you look so well, so wonderful. I heard about you and that new young man of yours. I must say, from looking at you, he seems to be doing you a power of good.'

Madeleine nodded, but Gertrude was still rattling on. 'We must have coffee again some time. I still see several of the old faces – we still meet. But perhaps you're too busy these days. You would appear so low spirited when we used to meet. But you had reason to be didn't you, poor thing?'

Hardly pausing for breath, she went on, 'By the way, I ran into your Anthony the other day. He seems to be getting on well too – with a lovely girl. We had a brief chat. They looked very happy and settled, and so it seems are you, my dear, from what I hear and—'

'Sorry, but I have to go, Gertrude,' Madeleine cut in. 'I'm late for my hairdressers.' She saw Gertrude beam widely.

'Hardly worth it this weather. But do let us catch up with each other again, have coffee and a chat. I'll tell the others

I met you. I am still at the same address, dear, so you can always get in touch. See you soon then.'

'Yes, bye then,' Madeleine said, hurrying off, Gertrude having leaned towards her to bestow an air kiss just short of her ear.

Pushing through the indifferent shoppers, hardly aware of them or the noise of traffic or the buffeting wind, the hair-dresser's forgotten, she was aware only of this weight on her heart, Anthony's face, and such a longing to see him again that she was almost on the verge of tears. How could she have walked out on him as she had, let all this time go by until it was too late to ask him to have her back – he was now with someone else; herself forgotten.

By the time she found a taxi to take her home, she'd sternly pulled herself together, set her mind to Ronnie. She had been having a wonderful life these past three years and until Gertrude Peel had spoken to her saw only happiness stretching ahead, everything in the past swept away, all her heartaches behind her, so why was she fretting now?

Even so it was hard not to think of Anthony – he and that young woman whom Gertrude had seen him with. Was marriage on their agenda? Something he had shied away from with her. Did they have their minds on starting a family? Something else that he had made clear he did not exactly look forward to. True, she too had now given up thoughts of children for the time being, having too good a time at the moment, so she could understand how he had felt, enjoying his life too much at the time.

Now the thought crossed her mind that maybe she and Ronnie might move towards a more permanent arrangement. But it couldn't wait too long. He was twenty-four now but in a couple of months she'd be thirty-three and time was passing. But in broaching the subject, he might back off, saying that he could never afford to get married. To say she'd pay for the wedding would make him feel belittled and what man wouldn't be? Fine when it was small things like clothes and jewellery and such, but something so very important and showy, she couldn't see him accepting that.

There was one way out of it. She could arrange for him

to come into her stock broker business, or maybe if she invested some money for him. She knew what she was doing here. What they reaped would make him feel easier in his mind, able to put his hand in his wallet for his own money rather than she having to put it there for him in the first place.

A few days later she told him of her plan. Immediately he protested as he usually did whenever she offered to do something for him.

'All I seem to do is sponge off you,' he said in that humble tone that always tugged at her heart strings.

'Don't be silly,' she told him. 'You can't go anywhere without money in your pocket. And who else can help you on that score – certainly not your parents.'

It was the wrong thing to say, she knew that immediately. 'I don't want to talk about them!' he said sharply, putting an end to it.

This evening they were going to the Savoy to see *The Gondoliers*, he rather liking Gilbert & Sullivan. She'd already bought tickets, good seats, but there'd be drinks to pay for in the interval and supper afterwards. She handed him thirty pounds which as always he took as though it seared his hand, hastily pushing it into his wallet, stuffing the thing into his breast pocket as if it had been stolen.

'I hate it, having you always giving me money for whatever we do together.'

It was then she made up her mind – she would invest in a few shares for him, just enough so that he wouldn't have to feel so dependent on her, embarrassed every time she sought to finance him. So long as it didn't suddenly yield an unexpectedly huge profit as sometimes happens – not often, but possible – suddenly providing him with enough money in his pocket to go off and leave her, maybe for someone else? It could happen. Being left on her own again – she didn't think she could stand it a second time. . .

She pulled her thoughts up sharp. He wouldn't do that. Not after all she'd done for him. That night, they made love and she knew her fears were totally unfounded.

Even so, she'd go for small-yielding stock. She knew what

she was doing – her eye on one particular small company, its shares modestly on the rise. She had already studied the company, weighed the degree of risk attached very carefully. There was always a certain degree of risk in everything but she herself would stand that, her own portfolio healthy and sound. She'd developed a sort of sixth sense about these things – when to take risks and when not to – and so far she'd always done well, give or take a few minor hiccups.

But where Ronnie was concerned she would be cautious about taking risks, judging carefully when the time was right for him to sell. He must not benefit so much that he'd begin to feel independent of her, start to feel his feet, decide to go off into the blue without her.

She was being silly, of course. He loved her, yet always that fear of once again being left all alone sat on her shoulders. But she was judging him before the act. Her fears were completely unfounded. She only had to see the look in his dark eyes when he gazed at her to know that.

The following day she told him what she aimed to do. His protests allayed her fears even more. 'I can't let you do that, Madeleine. Your money . . .'

'To do with as I like,' she interrupted. 'And what I'd like is to see you with a bit of money of your own. Everyone should have money of their own.'

The look of gratitude on his handsome young face made her heart go out to him with all the love in her body.

George Foster, when she told him what she had in mind, was not so happy.

'I'm virtually your financial adviser as well as your partner,' he said, 'and my advice is to think before you do anything. From what you tell me, he seems to take you a little too much for granted for my peace of mind.'

She was shocked by his statement. 'I thought you liked him. I still remember all the nice things you said about him when you introduced us.'

'He's a likeable chap,' Foster said, sitting at his desk, seeming very much intent on shuffling through papers lying there while she sat on the opposite side of the desk watching the exercise.

'All I'm saying is that you shouldn't indulge him so, paying for every little thing,' he said as he looked up at her.

'And even after all this time you . . . we . . . don't know all that much about him. We still don't know who his parents are or why they never come to see him, though that's none of my business.'

'No, it's not,' she countered testily.

'All I wish to do,' he went on in his quiet voice, 'is see you OK. I promised James, your late husband and my old partner, that I'd keep an eye on you, make certain you were safe. And it has worked well so far. But this idea of using your own money – not his – to invest in shares in his name and his letting you do it – his reaping the benefit, well, it's—'

'This was my idea, not his,' she cut in.

'Maybe, my dear, but he'd be better being out there and finding work for himself. Most young men want to stand on their own two feet rather than be beholden to someone else. It does make me wonder.'

'That's probably my fault,' she said huffily.

Having him refer to her as 'my dear', the way James used to made her cringe as it had often done when she was with James. But he was still speaking.

'Millicent and I haven't seen him since that Christmas we introduced him to you. Then we'd felt sorry for him. We'd befriended him and wanted to help him, a young man little more than a boy, all alone in the world, whose parents appeared to have forsaken him. I expect you felt the same. But now you two seem to be all over each other, you practically keeping him – or so it would look to the world. And now this – it's too much, my dear.'

He seemed to be totally against him and she couldn't understand why. Even now she couldn't believe how a person's opinion could change so drastically, as if Ronald was his worst enemy and yet the Fosters hadn't lain eyes on him for three years other than on a couple of occasions attending one of her parties.

'What have you got against him?' she challenged now. For answer, he lifted his shoulders in a small shrug.

'I haven't seen enough of him recently to have *anything* against him. I'm just saying you should be cautious about using your own money buying shares for others. It's different taking risks on our own behalf, but with others . . .'

He let his voice die away, leaving her feeling uneasy. In the end she decided that in this particular case she would use another financial adviser – far less embarrassing – less hassle.

Twenty-Eight

Ronnie was becoming impatient. 'Why are we waiting so long? They're making a nice profit. Shouldn't we be cashing in on them? I hate it, still having to rely on you to buy me everything.'

'You have to learn to be patient,' she told him. 'You've only had them for three months. Give it time.'

They were lying in each other's arms this morning, having made love with no need to get up until midday after a late night at a party.

It was September. By her estimation another couple of months would see his investment rise at least another quarter of its worth. George Foster had said so.

'If I were you I should sell then. By what you tell me, you don't want that young man to get too carried away,' he'd advised darkly, going on to say, 'I have it on good authority that they could drop a little round about autumn. If you want to, and feel sure of him, you can buy in again.'

But he was chafing at the bit, anxious she imagined to have his own money in his pocket. It was that which worried her. Until now he'd relied on her but what if he were to make a killing; no longer needing her? He could walk out of her life, leaving her alone again. If that happened, what would she do? But surely he'd never do that. He was so lovely, so grateful to her, at every turn showing his gratitude. And he loved her.

'According to you, I only had to wait a few weeks,' he said, his tone somewhat sharper than she'd have liked, or was it just her imagination?

'Sometimes, yes,' she told him as evenly as she could. 'But you have to learn to bide your time. It will come.'

She was biding hers too, closely watching a buoyant market that had risen at a fine pace throughout the summer, instinct telling her to wait – that next month, as they began to reach their threshold, would be the time to sell.

'When it does,' she told Ronald, 'we can talk about whether or not you want to sell. Just bide your time. Patience – you need to be patient.'

'And if they drop, suddenly, before I can do that?'

'Trust me, darling. Give it one more month. 'You'll see.'

'What if the company suddenly goes bust and the price suddenly drops without warning?'

'The company's doing well. Why should it suddenly drop?'

But his words seemed to hold a prophetic ring to them, causing the tiniest of shivers to run through her veins, a feeling which she hurriedly shook off.

'You have to trust me,' she said again emphatically. 'You wait, my love, things will start moving around autumn. It often does and you'll be pleased that you bided your time. We'll both be pleased.'

Now it was October and he was again beginning to fret.

'It'll be Christmas soon,' he remarked this Thursday as they sat at home over a welcome cup of tea and slice of cake after having been out shopping all afternoon. She loved having him with her when she bought things. He had a good eye for fashion and it was so nice having a second opinion from someone she trusted.

Most women were either tight-lipped, perhaps trying to hide their jealousy at the money she spent on the latest fashions, or they would be all over her, saying: 'Oh, my dear, that looks simply wonderful on you!' no matter how dubious she felt about the garment. Ronnie she could trust. But time was passing. Christmas was rushing towards them and she needed to find something really beautiful and special for the festive season. As always, her Christmas Eve party would be the biggest and best in London if she had any say in it.

'Investors all need money for Christmas,' he was saying. 'Won't there be a rush to cash in? The market could drop and I won't make as much as I'd hoped. Maybe we should do something about it now before it's too late.'

She was about to remind him of patience, that she had

her eye on the market and to give it just a couple more weeks and then they'd be laughing, when the phone rang. Casually she got up to answer it. It was Foster. His voice was high and panicky.

'Madeleine – have you got the wireless on?'

'No. Why?'

'The New York stock market – it's chaos over there!'

Her mind went immediately to some spectacular bull market, prices escalating like some wildfire, and her heart soared. Some of her shares were connected with the market there. She had been drawn to that market when James had taken her to New York and they'd both spent a little time off from sightseeing to dabble. Now George Foster sounded beside himself and her thoughts instantly flew to what marvellous luck she seemed to have with her dealings – or was it skill? Those that didn't make money were trivial to her mind, easily recovered by other triumphs.

'Did you say chaos?' she queried excitedly down the phone. It was nearly six o'clock and George Foster was still at his desk.

His voice came in staccato spasms: 'Complete madness! Going crazy over there, selling . . . every last man jack – selling – for whatever they can get . . . The market there has crashed! Everyone's going berserk – shares are tumbling, falling like rocks!'

She was having problems trying to catch his words, he was gabbling so – a man who always had control over himself no matter what, a soothing influence always.

'I don't understand,' she stammered.

'Then bloody well try to, Madeleine!'

Immediately controlling the outburst he began to voice his next words as if with an effort – slowly, deliberately, painfully even. 'The American Stock Market in New York has crashed. It's panic over there. People are selling – everything they have for anything they can get. Still going down as I speak. Do you understand what I am saying?'

Her earlier elation had plummeted and she found herself incapable of responding immediately, already seeing the implications, a disaster that could echo across the world. But what of her own investments, surely they wouldn't be affected, not here in this country? She asked this question of him now.

'We'll have to wait and see.'

'Should I consider selling?' There was a long pause. 'What are you thinking about your own portfolio?' she pushed.

The pause lengthened then he said as if talking to himself. 'Selling might be adding to the panic. It could be just a hiccup. Shares might easily recover by this evening. The only fear is that if they rise again after one's got rid of them, one would look a fool – a broke fool. I don't know.'

She'd never known him to be so uncertain. Fear caught hold of her. 'What should I do?' she said, her voice high and tiny.

There was another moment of silence before he said, 'I can't advise you, my dear, not in this instance.'

'Then what do you intend doing?'

More silence. Then he said, slowly: 'I think I'll wait, see what happens. Trading may pick up later. You can never tell. It's still around midday over there – still quite a few hours to go until the market closes. A lot can happen between now and then.'

His voice faded away leaving her wondering if she should trust in his superior judgement. She always had and had always profited by it, with very few exceptions, but this . . .

Perhaps tomorrow would see the market straightened out again and, come Monday, it would all be back to normal trading.

She relayed his words to Ronald. 'Wait a while – see what happens over the next few hours.'

But he was being stubborn. 'I feel I should sell now. I don't care what he says,' he said bullishly in the face of all her efforts to convince him, until she was near to losing her temper with him, something she had never done before.

'All right, if that's what you want,' she snapped. 'I'm done with trying to help and guide you. If you refuse to listen, I can't make you.'

She was prepared to wait. If she made the wrong decision, it wouldn't be the end of the world. Her money was of course with her bank and more than healthy, able to deal with small setbacks. In the investment world one had to take into account the likelihood of a setback at any time; taking chances was all part of the game. But if Ronnie wanted to be silly it was up to him.

In her annoyance she vowed to wash her hands of helping him any more, moments later to ditch that decision. He would come to her, no doubt full of apologies and she, of course, would renew his losses, continue to fund him, as she'd always done. But he would have learned to take more note of what she said in future. In a way it gave a feeling of control.

But it was worrying, she and George Foster standing in the office reading the newspapers, all of them reporting what was happening on the other side of the Atlantic:

'. . . *an unprecedented wave of fear, confusion and panic – nearly thirteen million shares changed hands on the New York Stock Exchange today – dazed brokers waded through a sea of paper clutching frightened investors' orders to "sell at any price".'*

Another paper reporting: '*The market has ceased to function as such,*' and another: '*mad clamour of salesmen looking for non-existent buyers. Stocks being dumped overboard for whatever they can bring.*'

Yet another saying: '*The spree of easy money and overconfidence is now ended, crushing the dreams of an army of small investors who have lost everything. Eleven said to have committed suicide.*'

'I think you should sell while you can,' Foster said suddenly, his tone instantly alarming her even more.

The London market having opened, their tape machine was already showing a small drop in share prices. Yet something kept telling her not to yield to panic. Come tomorrow she would kick herself for yielding to a knee jerk reaction. What if she rushed out and sold huge parcels of shares at lower prices only to find that by Monday they would have gone up. To lose all that much over a moment of panic was stupid; to have to buy back at their higher price would be unthinkable. No, it was best to wait.

He didn't argue. But she knew she was right and wondered at him for panicking. It wasn't like him. Stubbornly she resisted the thought that he knew more than she and she'd be wise to take his advice as she had always done. He'd already dealt with Ronnie's request, Ronnie all chirpy when she came back home, seeing a nice bank balance. So was she being a fool?

On Saturday she felt that she had made the right decision. Yes, her shares had dropped a little, but not drastically, not enough for her to have sold them. In fact trading was slow on the Stock Exchange. Neither had George Foster, after thinking about it, sold any of his.

'I think I'll hang on for a while,' he said to her over the phone which made her feel better about her own decision. Ronnie, however, was looking downcast. She let him stew. Later she would sort him out to his delight.

Sunday's newspapers showed earlier pictures of crowds and crowds of anxious speculators thronging downtown New York – a sea of trilby hats – car owners desperately trying to sell their vehicles to people who didn't want them, could no longer afford to buy a bit of furniture much less a car.

Monday brought a rude awakening. The moment the stock market opened, the fears of investors here were realized as the first shock wave from Wall Street really hit them. Along with every other punter, Madeleine saw her shares fall so sharply as to take her breath away. She should have sold. She should have followed those wise ones who'd got rid of most of their stuff at the first glimpse of disaster and now be buying back at lowered prices.

Yet what if they continued to fall, so far as to be worthless? The bank taking fright would call in their loans, contact her to honour her debts as soon as possible, as she had always used them to finance her dealings.

Hitherto it had never seemed a problem that her money was tied up in her account; that she had bought and sold without a care; that they held the purse strings and if anything went wrong they would call the tune.

She'd taken heart when Friday morning's papers had reported a rally on the New York Exchange the previous afternoon: thanks to an emergency meeting of several big banks and their reassuring statements to prop up the market, there was an actual improvement on the day. The crash was blamed on the inadequacy of the ticker-tape system to cope with a sudden massive volume of trading. But like everyone else, her relief was short-lived. Reports were saying that the spree of easy money and overconfidence was over. The bear market had returned with a vengeance, crushing everyone's dreams of wealth everlasting; and Madeleine one of them.

Ronnie, who'd refused to rely on patience, didn't look so stupid now with money in his pocket. But she had no time to think what that might mean as she found herself at her wits' end on how to deal with her bank's demands for her to settle up, her bank manager no longer her smiling friend.

But there was more to come. She had always been confident that funds would be there; a steadily flowing river supplying her needs whenever she dipped her toes in its waters. Now, suddenly, out of the blue, the stream had dried up. Even her home was in jeopardy, would have to be sold if she couldn't find the wherewithal to settle the bank's demands.

And there would be other creditors too, demanding settlement of debts they had once been content to let ride for a while: milliners, dressmakers, Ronnie's tailor, wine merchants, those who supplied everything she'd needed for her dinner parties and evening parties, those high-class, exclusive establishments of New Bond Street, Kensington and Knightsbridge; all now clamouring for their bills to be settled, bills that would normally have been confidently left for months before she needed to pay them.

Today her brain was spinning with worry as Ronald came into the sitting room where she was lying full length on the chaise longue, not far from tears at the frustration of it all. She twisted her head to look up at him.

'Ronnie darling, I hate to ask, but could you settle with your tailor yourself this time?' She sighed. 'After all, you've some money of your own. I'm so sorry, love. Would you?'

He didn't reply for a moment but stood frowning at her. Then without warning, he burst out, 'Why should I?'

Taken by surprise by the challenge, she was momentarily

bewildered. 'Darling, what do you mean? You're the one with money now. I'm broke. You know that.'

'Then you should've cashed in, like me, when you had the chance. But no, you thought you knew better! Now I'm left paying the bills.'

'I've only asked you to settle your own bills, not mine.' She was beginning to grow angry. 'How can you say that when I've always made sure you were OK?'

It was perhaps the first time she had ever felt truly angry with him, taken aback by this sudden attitude. But she wasn't prepared to let him get away with it. It sounded in her tone.

'You've lived off me for long enough, Ronnie. Now it's time for—'

'You to live off me?' he interrupted. 'Is that it?'

'No, of course not.'

'Well that's how it sounds to me.'

Anger suddenly got the better of her. 'Well, if that's how you feel, Ronnie, you can always go!' she flared. 'Clear off!'

For a moment he stared at her, then turned on his heel and went out of the room leaving her gazing after him, still angry. She heard him mount the stairs, two at a time. He would sit up in their bedroom, sulking for a while then finally creep back into the lounge, say he was sorry. She couldn't help thinking, still angry, that he knew where his bread was buttered. Soon the market would begin looking up again and she would eventually be back on track, making money. Slowly at first, but luck had always been kind to her where money was concerned.

There was no sound from the bedroom and she was damned if she would go up there to try and mollify him. Let him sulk. It might do him good.

Now she could hear him moving about, footsteps above her, the faint sound of drawers being violently opened and shut. She could imagine him giving full vent to his fury. In a while he would come down and tell her he was sorry. She waited. Then after half an hour he reappeared at the door.

'I have to pop out for a moment,' he said in a strained tone.

'What for?' she asked, but he shook his head.

'Nothing – it doesn't matter.' No apology. He still looked tight-faced.

Madeleine half smiled to herself. He was going to settle his tailor's bill. When he returned he might continue to sulk for a while, but soon he would come round, understand her point of view. She smiled at him. From now on she'd have no need to indulge him. Instead he might indulge her. That would be nice.

'Well don't be too long, darling,' she crooned lovingly, glancing down at her hands, but when she looked up he had already disappeared.

She heard the front door close, a little hesitantly as if he was having some trouble closing it. Sighing she got up from the chaise longue and went to glance out of the window, just in time to see him getting into a taxi. It was then she saw the baggage space in the front beside the driver was stacked with two suitcases and a large holdall.

For a moment she stared unable to comprehend what she was seeing as the taxi drew away. Then in a sudden panic of realization, she ran from the window into the hall and upstairs to their bedroom. The place was a mess. His dressing table drawers and the doors of his wardrobe were open and empty, the hangers angling; his shoe rack bare; in the bathroom his toiletry and shaving gear also gone. Gone too was her jewellery, their boxes lying open.

Without knowing what she was doing, Madeleine opened her mouth and let forth a piercing scream, one that went on and on and which she seemed powerless to stop.

Then as her breath gave out, she sank to the floor, sobbing as if her body might dissolve with the effort.

Twenty-Nine

Eight thirty, a weak November sun just starting to peep over the houses on the far side of Holland Park. Unable to sleep this last fortnight since Ronnie had walked out, she realized she had no idea where he was; had prayed he would soon come back saying he was sorry. But there'd been no word.

She had rushed off to his bank to find that he had withdrawn all the money she'd helped him make, using hers to enable him to do so – in other words she was keeping him. He'd closed his account and his bank had no idea – or refused to say – where he was.

Every time the telephone rang she would rush to it and yank it off its cradle, hoping to hear his exuberant young voice apologizing for his actions. But it was always someone else; a friend or close acquaintance looking for a half hour or so of chat.

She would tell them she was on her way out to somewhere urgent, promising to ring them back later. Not once had she done so. To use the phone could cause her to miss that one important call she hoped and prayed would come. But it hadn't.

Each time the letter box rattled to alert her of a postal delivery, she'd run to the door, sift frantically through bills and demands and replies to her earlier invitation to the huge Christmas Eve party she'd planned to throw when Ronnie had been here and all had been well. But there was never anything from him.

She'd no interest now in giving a party; had no heart for a great crowd of people laughing and chatting and her without him at her side. She would of course have to contact people to say it was cancelled, but even that she'd not been able to bring herself to do, though it must be done soon.

Soon! What did it matter? Christmas was six weeks away – six weeks – two weeks – a hundred weeks! It didn't matter any more, nor any future thing without Ronnie – her life pointless without him, the coming year empty – and all the years for the rest of her life . . .

Madeleine gulped – refusing to succumb to fresh tears. She'd done too much crying these last two weeks and they'd done no good except to make her feel ill, look hideous, unable to bring herself to venture out and face the world. She'd have to face the world eventually but it was hard.

Now she stood in the centre of this fine reception room of hers where she'd given so many huge parties, dinner parties held in the large dining room across the hall. Her mind wandered back to happier times when she and Anthony had been together and life had been so wonderful. How could she have let all that slip away?

Four days ago, four days closeted between these walls, she'd come to a decision, summoning up the courage to write to Anthony telling him she was broke, her lovely house to be sold to pay her debts and she had nowhere to go – such a humble, demeaning letter, it made her cringe.

Her daily woman who did the cooking and cleaning, Mrs Crossfield, had posted it for her. He hadn't replied, but what had she expected? She'd not seen him for over three years, her life taken up by new and exciting things with Ronnie; her previous life put behind her. Yet often in the headiness of that lovely life she had thought of him from time to time, wondered vaguely how he was, if he was still with that someone else whom the Peel woman had seen him with, and she'd experience a small pang of regret, soon put aside in her new and wonderful life with Ronnie.

Now he was gone too. All the things she had lavished on him: clothes, money, her love – all her love – and he'd simply walked out without a care for her the moment he saw her virtually destitute. Nor would he come back, she knew that now. Her heart plummeted again weighed down by despair. She was alone once more and this time there would be no one to comfort her.

But she had told him to go, hadn't she? She only had herself to blame, losing her temper with him like that. Yet he had taken her at her word. How could he have done that?

And there came the answer that had eluded her till now.
Ronnie had been a sponger from the start – a sponger with
a silver tongue, beguiling her, stupid fool that she'd been.

From somewhere came a spark of her old self, the self
that had made its way when she'd first come to London, a
girl alone, knowing nothing but her soft, comfortable
upbringing, the one who had so innocently fallen for another
silver tongue and ended up pregnant, spurned by her family;
the old self that had confronted her father all those years
ago, had angrily told him his fortune and had never laid
eyes on him since, nor ever cared to. She had made her
own way in the world no matter that she'd made mistakes,
felt things had sometimes got on top of her. But looking
back she had fared moderately well, had become stronger if
not as strong as she would have liked. But she had confronted
obstacles, surmounted them and come out somewhere on
top hadn't she? She had made money by her own brain,
maybe with a little help here and there. The fact that she
was broke didn't mean that life was over. And yet . . .

There came a slow awareness of her life stretching ahead
of her as she grew older, her face becoming lined, her body
bowed, no one to grow old with her, no one to care, her
wonderful soirées, marvellous parties not even a memory in
people's minds as they went on with their lives. What had
been the point of it all?

As if in a dream Madeleine crossed the room and began
dragging a chair to the centre of it. There, beneath the
chandelier she stood beside the chair and took off the sash
of her dressing gown. There was no other place in this room
to do what she intended. She was alone in the house. By
the time Mrs Crossland arrived, it would be over.

She would tie one end of the silk sash around her neck,
climb on the chair and fasten the other end of the sash around
one of the gilt arms of the chandelier in the middle of this
room where she had held so many of her lovely parties. One
leap and it would all be ended. No more worry, no more
fretting, no more aching heart, no more loneliness – so
simple, so quick.

If she stood on tiptoe on the chair she would just about

reach up to the chandelier. Hopefully as she kicked the chair aside, the jerk would break her neck, this feeling of emptiness would be over, this aching knowledge of having been betrayed – over.

For a moment she stood poised. *Betrayed?* No, in her need to have someone love her she'd allowed herself to be deceived. Not so much made a fool of but having been a fool. From somewhere came a spark of fury. Why was she bowing to the actions of some worthless little swine who had run out on her after all she'd done for him? She was better off without him. So, she had been hurt, was that reason enough to be doing what had been in her mind?

She suddenly felt so angry that it shot through her as if touched by a fire. If she did what she had been intending to do, who would have been the winner? Certainly not her. So she'd be facing life alone from now on. Maybe something would come along.

There came a sudden thought: any minute now Mrs Crossland would be letting herself into the house to begin her cleaning. If she found her lying here, dead . . .

Slowly she let the silken sash fall to the ground and as if in a dream placed the chair back in its place by the wall. It was then she heard the front door open and close. Mrs Crossland. But there were voices. Ronnie? He'd come back. Relief sweeping over her, she made for the door.

Mabel Crossland took her key from her purse to open the door of her employer's lovely home, her mind miles away thinking of her daughter's birthday, hoping she would be back home in time to greet her coming in from her shift at the switchboard of the big company where she held a job despite all the savage unemployment of late. She already had a lovely birthday spread and a big cake. There would be Dad, her grandparents, who lived with them, her brother Sidney, and her two aunts who lived just down the road.

She was smiling, visualizing the warm fire glowing and her house full of people as she made to put the key in the lock, when a sudden movement from behind startled her.

She turned to see a man about to mount the steps in her wake, a taxi at the kerb on the point of drawing away.

Hardly giving her time to gasp, he exclaimed: 'Is this Mrs Ingleton's home? Mrs Madeleine Ingleton?' His tone sounded urgent.

'And who are you?' she demanded, standing her ground.

'I need to see her.'

Mabel Crossland stood rigid, defensive. 'I don't know you, sir.'

For an answer, still standing on the bottom step, he hastily fished in his inside breast pocket and drew out an envelope, waving it at her. He was tall, good-looking, well dressed. The blue eyes beneath the trilby were filled with an expression of urgency. 'She wrote to me some while ago but I have been away. My name's Ingleton. Maybe she has mentioned me.'

'Not that I know of,' Mabel Crossland said tartly, now in control of herself. He could be lying? Though why?

'I'm a relation,' he was saying. 'You can read the letter if you want.'

He held it out to her but she didn't take it. Instead she drew in a deep breath and, gathering herself together, said as she turned the key in the lock, 'You'd best come in then,' stepping aside to allow him to enter first, even now wary of sudden attack.

'How is she holding up?' he asked as he moved past her.

'Not very happy,' she said, not knowing what else to say and still not prepared to tell this stranger how miserable the poor woman had been, listlessly wandering about the house, never venturing out, pining for the young man who had walked out on her, though it wasn't her business to discuss her employer's private life with some man she had never met.

'If you would care to wait here, I'll get her for you,' she added, even now standing her ground, intending to keep her eye on him just in case.

Having taken off his trilby he stood in the hall as the woman called out, 'Mrs Ingleton, someone here to see you.'

He half expected to hear Madeleine call from somewhere in the house that she didn't wish to see him; never wished to see him again. If only he'd been home when her letter had arrived, but he was in Scotland, having fled there as he'd done once before, years ago when he'd last sought consolation from an old friend. Not that his friend – a man of property, a huge house and land that had been in his family for generations – would know how it felt to have lost one's business almost overnight, his bank gone, swallowed up in the sudden remorseless collapse of the world economy following the Wall Street crash back in October.

His bank wasn't the only one. Most small private banks had gone to the wall. Any still going were struggling, desperately calling in debt from those clients no longer able to settle them, companies were closing down, firms going to the wall, thousands were out of work, the unemployed in dole queues around the block with no other course to take.

Some, like his friend, were still buoyant, they with their property, family silver, land. He himself had very little left after settling such debts as he had accrued, wondering how long that would last. He had thought of contacting Madeleine at one time but had then thought better of it, her attitude towards him all those years ago still echoing. Over those years he'd tried to take up with one girl and another but nothing had lasted. Then he arrived home to find her letter sitting on the doormat – he had previously dismissed his staff before running off to Scotland.

At first he'd almost thrown the letter aside in a renewal of anger against her for having walked out on him – and now she needed him, she virtually wanted him to take her back. No, he'd told himself, he would not go and comfort her. She only had herself to blame. All the way here he had told himself that he no longer loved her. But that wasn't true.

Now he stood in the hall while this woman called out to her employer. What would he to say to Madeleine when she responded, when they came face to face after all this time? Her letter had been so full of need. But face to face would their meeting develop into a full-scale row as it had

done before? He should never have come here. He almost
turned to go when he heard her voice. It sounded weak as
if she were crying. It was coming from the closed door to
the right of the hall.

Madeleine heard Mrs Crossland calling that someone was
here to see her, and her relief almost overwhelmed her,
making her feel suddenly faint, realizing how near she had
come to ending her life. Her strength felt as if it were leaving
her as, in a wave of dizziness, she let herself collapse on to
the chair she'd only just dragged back from the centre of the
room. She leaned forward, closing her eyes in an attempt to
control the threatening weakness.

Someone was opening the door, coming into the room,
moving towards her. Someone was kneeling at her side,
taking her in his arms. She leaned in towards the, oh so
solid form, the name forming in her head but not yet
reaching her lips: 'Ronnie . . .'

A voice whispered urgently against her ear. 'Maddie,
darling, what is it? What's the matter? Are you ill?'

Not Ronnie's voice, but Anthony's. 'I'm so sorry, my
darling, I've only just seen your letter. I was away . . . only
just got back . . . found your letter waiting for me . . .
came as soon as I could. Darling . . .'

She was dreaming, hardly able to think, found herself
clinging to the beloved form that at any minute would
dissolve away into nothing. She didn't want Ronnie. She
wanted Anthony – more than she had ever done in her life.

The voice was still whispering urgently in her ear.
'Maddie, darling, it's Anthony. Forgive me, darling, I've
been a fool. I want to marry you. I want us to have a
family, settle down . . .'

There were other words too: 'Maddie, listen to me. I'm
done looking for a good time. I want to settle down . . .
with you, if you'll have me.'

She *was* dreaming, the voice continuing, 'I've no money
any more. The bank's gone, but I can find a similar situation
in some other bank which is still in business. There are still
openings for people like me despite everything and we can
start again, you and I. We can have that baby you so wanted.

I want it as well. You don't know how much I've missed you. I love you.'

The fainting feeling was receding; strength returning and with it an overwhelming need to cling to him even tighter. Without looking up, she whispered in reply, 'I've missed you too – so much.'

Seconds later she raised her head to feel his lips on hers, no more words needing to be said.

She was broke. So was he. But they were together, she knew that now, and together they would forge ahead, start again. And this time they would be a family. She could hardly believe it and she clung to him as if he might float away. But he was real enough. And he was here, holding her to him, his lips on hers.

In the hallway, Mrs Crossland, having overheard the two people, paused by the open door as she made her way down to the kitchen and smiled to herself.

She felt in her bones that Madeleine had at last found the happiness she had been seeking for so long. She'd once heard her remark almost bitterly that happiness after all was very often no more than mere illusion. Well, perhaps not such an illusion as she had imagined.